SISTER BUTCHER SISTER

KD ALDYN

Cover design by Erin Fitzsimmons/Sourcebooks
Cover image © Magdalena Russocka/Trevillion
Internal design by Tara Jaggers/Sourcebooks

Sourcebooks, Poisoned Pen Press, and the colophon are registered trademarks of Sourcebooks.

Published by Poisoned Pen Press, an imprint of Sourcebooks
P.O. Box 4410, Naperville, Illinois 60567-4410
(630) 961-3900
sourcebooks.com

Cataloging-in-Publication Data is on file with the Library of Congress.

Printed and bound in Canada.
MBP 10 9 8 7 6 5 4 3 2 1

For all the lost souls: the displaced, and the departed

And for Gary, my number one fan

Content Warning

This novel of suspense fiction delves into the darkness within one seemingly normal family. It contains subjects and scenes that some readers may find triggering, including addiction, CSA trauma, sexual abuse, mental health issues, and graphic violence.

Prologue

SHE circled slowly, halting every few steps to listen. Her ear was alert for the snap of twigs warning that she was no longer alone in the woodland, for a rustling in the carpet of crisp leaves signaling some hideous nocturnal animal readying for a strike, most of all, for the crackling sound that would herald the growing strength of the fire.

Clouds skipped in front of the pale sliver of moon, making a patchy confusion of light on the ground.

She imagined herself a hunter.

A flash of light from beyond the leadlight window.

Finally.

She took a few more paces so she could glimpse the bedroom where the fire would be causing irreversible damage. The view was alternately softened by a smoky haze and made bright and urgent by hellish flames.

The man was unconscious, sprawled across the bed half naked, his checked winter-wool pants pooled around his ankles, one arm flung between the bed's railings, his head thrown at an awkward angle.

Dirty old drunk.

The flames expanded quicker than she had imagined. In minutes, the bed was awash with licks of red and orange and blue. The fire caressed the man, urging him awake. He may have stirred, trying to rouse himself, but the iron railings of the bedhead had impacted him severely when he fell, and his brain—if alerted at all—would have been in calamity mode.

She heard distant sirens.

Fuck.

She was just ten years old, but she knew how to swear.

She may have seen his body writhe.

The fire trucks were closing in. Crap. Now she would have to run home, slip back through the window of her bedroom, and miss out on the burning.

Luckily, she had a good imagination.

Later, she joined her family in their immaculately landscaped yards, staring vacantly over the clipped hedge at the charred shell of the man's house.

And then, when she was alone in her bed, she allowed herself to picture the sweeping flames licking and eating and tearing at him, as in a scene from a horror movie. She imagined his skin blackening, curling into itself.

She smiled into the darkness, the slipperiness of evil glossing her lips, and moaned softly with a wicked sense of unchildlike excitement at the hell she had created.

1

KATE stood outside number thirty-six, holding her breath. So often she'd stared at the number and wished for this day.

She had walked past his house—she'd still thought of it as his then—just days after he died. Back then, she had heard the red-bud blossoms whisper to her as they buffeted themselves against a strong breeze. Even the blades of grass may have hissed a soft beckoning. The wind had picked up uncannily, almost violently, forcing its way through the pines, causing them to scream.

Come in, come in, they wailed.

Maybe she had planned to push open the tongue-and-groove gate or, if finding it locked, leap over the fence beside it. She might have thought she'd knock on the door to see if anyone was home.

It was hard to recall the details now, but back then, Kate had been hypnotized by the shrubs and the grass and the shrieking wind, by the pine needles, those mini tentacles, and by the woody wisteria vines reaching for her, conspiring to drag her in. Then she had tripped over a boulder and hurtled helplessly forward until the weight of her upper body brought her tardy knees to the ground. She was up quickly though, and to the best of her knowledge, there'd been no one around to witness the ungainly trip.

It was, of course, merely a rock. Kate's sisters used to call her the Mistress of Overstatement. The depth of blackness of her ex-lover's eyes, or the height of the waves buffeting her around that day when she'd lurched overboard into a not-so-stormy sea. And, yes, rocks and pebbles. But other things—important things—she would never dream of exaggerating.

So often she had passed this way, feeling like an interloper, an impostor.

Like the time she'd come back home when yet another lover had broken her heart and she'd been shattered to find the house sold. She'd driven her rental car frantically up the winding road hoping the new owners wouldn't move in, that they would decide they didn't want the house after all. They'd call her grandfather and ask if they could have their money back. She'd have begged him to write them a check.

"Grandpa, I can buy it," Kate would have said.

She could have bought it too. She'd have found a bank to lend her the money, found some way to meet the payments. It could have been done. If only he hadn't sold it without telling her. If only he'd waited to discuss the situation. If only Kate had not been overseas at the time.

If only.

But she'd been too late. It was a done deal. And when she'd seen the precisely coiffed, jewelry-draped woman standing by the silver Mercedes giving orders to the deliverymen she'd thought what an unsuitable house for such a woman. Kate wanted to rush to her and beg her to sell it immediately. She would tell the beige-linen woman that the house was haunted or that termites were determinedly chewing their way through it like subversive terrorists or that it was built upon deeply buried nuclear waste.

The house was part of Kate's genetic code, her grandfather having built it way back, before Kate's father had been born.

She had wanted to tackle the woman, demand the house be returned to its rightful owner, and if the rightful owner didn't want it, then to Kate, the one who wanted it desperately. Instead, she had ambled by silently. Not even a hello. She hinted at a smile, but when the new homeowner declined to latch on to it, it had died on Kate's disappointed lips and she'd walked on, quickening her step, pretending she had somewhere else to be, somewhere important.

Two years later, after her grandfather's death, she'd walked by the house every day for the two weeks she'd stayed in her home state, daydreaming of a For Sale sign that never materialized. She hid behind the neighbor's dense cherry laurel hedge and watched in excruciatingly silent agony as tradesmen traipsed through the gate and presumably up and down the weatherworn sandstone bricks her grandfather had laid as a loving memento to his new bride all those years ago but that remained invisible—if they still existed—from Kate's vantage point.

When the stylish woman had popped her head up from the hidden garden that fine spring day, scaring Kate half to death with her questions—*Are you right there? Did you want something?*—Kate knew she'd gone too far. She was lucky the woman hadn't called the police and had her arrested for stalking. It was time to give up; the house was forever beyond her reach. It belonged to someone else. And that someone else had probably mutilated it, remodeled it beyond recognition.

Although she'd been unable to stop thinking about the house completely, Kate did move on. Since her grandfather's death, she'd grown up a lot, sculpted a life, changed jobs six times.

Experience had marked her face with surprises and desire and sadness. Now, at thirty-six, she had a face angled by prominent cheekbones and precisely defined eyebrows. Eyes flinted. Her hips were more angular, hair a little shorter, the fabric of her clothes a touch more luxurious.

This time was different.

She laughed now, for having such ludicrous childish thoughts back then.

Flighty, her mother used to call her.

She stood by the gate, amazed the house number was still marked out in tiny pebbles set into the stone pillar: number thirty-six. How thoroughly appropriate. She'd waited to celebrate her thirty-sixth birthday in style, never mentioning to any one of her acquaintances, her half a handful of friends, or even to family members, that she'd purchased the house.

Odd to see the pillar and the number still there when the gate had been replaced, along with the side fence and the garage. Anxiety gripped her. So much was different. What would she find when she opened the contemporary steel-gray security gate?

Please God, she thought, let the steps be intact. Surely, if Mrs. Beige had left the numbers, it was because they were solid and functional. If that was so, then the steps would still be there, just as Kate remembered them.

When she opened the gate, the first thing she did was cry, soft tears at first, as she gazed at the beautifully weathered sandstone steps curving from her vantage point down through a garden packed with pink and purple hydrangeas, roses, and multihued carnations. The foliage was interspersed with patches of natural paving where wrought-iron chairs shared space with terra-cotta pots overflowing with mint and parsley.

She'd been wrong about Mrs. Beige; the woman had obviously cherished the garden. Kate sobbed loudly as she pulled off her sensible Doc Martens and black socks, planted the skin of her size nines firmly onto the cool soft gravel sprinkled over the top step, and let her toes curl over the sandstone edge.

She was finally home.

She briefly considered the garden, astonished to see her grandfather's old work shed still standing, though the chicken run had been demolished. There was no hint of anything as practical as a vegetable garden.

Grateful for the new smooth iron railing snaking its way in tandem with the steps, Kate descended. When the path forked, she didn't look to the right, just kept her eyes down until she reached the bottom. As the balls of her feet hit the firm polished concrete floor of the portico, she swiped the salty rivers from her cheeks and reminded herself to breathe.

The front door with the leadlight glass inset was so perfect that she immediately forgot what the original door had looked like. A searing pain in her hand jolted her. She was gripping the front-door key so hard that three dark purple blood blisters were already appearing on her palm.

Once the door was unlocked, she was a woman possessed, running through the empty house, mentally cataloging the changes. The first one was the biggest. The wall between the kitchen and dining room had been demolished, so the service hatch with its sliding wooden door and beautifully carved knob were gone. In that space, in the newly opened room, she heard voices whispering rumors and secrets, all there for the listening. The voices called to her, welcoming her back, echoing around the room.

The kitchen, once a busy haven of green Formica-topped counters with a wall of well-used and less-than-sparkling cooking utensils hanging from oversize hooks, had been transformed with stainless steel and granite, an arc of terra-cotta tiling marking its territory.

The single cantilevered window above the sink had been replaced with huge sheets of glass that stretched across the kitchen wall, providing an uninterrupted view of the distant deep blue waves building and rolling their way toward the shore, lightening in color and forming frothy tips before breaking against the compacted sand.

When Kate was small, she used to turn over Nan's second-largest stewpot—the one with handles halfway down its sides—so she could stand on its base and make herself tall enough to tuck her toes around the cupboard doorknob and hoist herself up onto the sink. Even now, she could recall the delicious pounding of her heart as she stood on the sink listening for Nan's footsteps in the hallway. When she was convinced she was not about to be caught, she'd turn the tarnished lock to fling the window open.

The crisp smell of the ocean would mingle with the warm, woody odor of composting pine needles to provide an aroma of excitement and adventure.

In her usual daredevil manner, the child Kate could rarely resist the impulse to pitch her upper body through the open window, scaring herself half to death when she looked down at the narrow pathway below, which gripped the house on one side and gave way to a rolling grassy slope on the other.

She suspected what had seemed an enormous distance between window and path as a child would prove to be not so vast now, but when she approached the window, she discovered the glass panes were immovable.

The once-familiar diamond motif that had carpeted most of the house was gone. In its place, shiny polished floorboards were patterned with the Oriental rugs Mrs. Beige had included in the sale.

The bubble-glass French doors leading from the lounge to the front veranda were still there. When Kate was a teenager, those bifold doors had framed many a romantic daydream: Kate swathed in white chiffon, racing through the doors and into the arms of a swarthy Mediterranean sea captain with a patch over one eye; Kate wearing a bejeweled crown and a red velvet cloak, flanked by her suitably tiara'd sisters, emerging through the doors onto the terrace to choose a tall, shy man from the crowd to be her prince.

Now, she couldn't resist flinging the doors open theatrically.

Lightheaded, she continued her tour. The main bedroom was barely altered, remaining intimately familiar, with windows that mercifully opened with ease.

In the second bedroom, two squares of slightly faded paint where pictures had hung were the only evidence that it had been inhabited.

Finally, in a heightened state of awareness and filled with a type of rapture, Kate stood on the threshold of the last room at the end of the hall. The sewing room, it had been called, but it was where she'd always slept on school holidays while her parents traveled overseas.

As she opened the door, her breath lodged in her throat, along with a bundle of memories. Her eyes traced the intricately carved cornices she'd stared at so often at night, cherubic angels dancing their way around heaven. On the far wall was the familiar crossword of a window, fine pieces of wood dividing the view into twelve satisfyingly uniform squares. Even the fireplace remained.

She had stepped back in time.

Dizzy, she grasped the doorframe.

Shivering. Panic.

Fuck.

Couldn't breathe. Couldn't swallow.

What the hell was happening?

Blinding light pierced her eyes, and a high-pitched ringing assaulted her ears. She grabbed at her head in fear.

A moan. A loud roar. The realization that the noise was coming from her, just before she passed out.

2

SHE crouched low beside the clipped hedge. The blood pumped through her veins at a furious adrenaline-fueled pace. Her skin burned and she felt a hunger, a longing deep in her belly she hadn't experienced for years.

She was older and wiser. It had been a long time between kills.

She'd been watching him off and on for weeks, a primordial portion of her brain unable to fight the yearning.

He wasn't an easy target, this gregarious surfy type. He was constantly surrounded by friends, doppelgänger sporty guys with blond hair and sun-kissed torsos, nubile flirtatious girls with too much skin showing. Any number of prey could have provided an easier mark, but she had to go with what appealed, had to follow her heart. You don't show someone a plate of succulent roast lamb with mint sauce, she thought, then expect them to eat haggis instead. Ludicrous.

She knew some things about him. The hedge she used for protection against the moonlight was right outside his bedroom window in his mother's house, a white rendered single-story building surrounded by arched walkways that would have been better suited to blinding sunlight and the colors of frangipani on a tropical island.

He should have been living in his own home, she thought. He was old enough but probably too lazy. Better to stay with his mother so she could wash his clothes and cook for him, cater to his needs.

His name was Henry, and he had a dog called Toots. Until recently anyway. Toots had gone missing, and they hadn't been able to find him yet. She wished she had it in her to kill a dog. It would've broken Henry's heart. It was out of the question, of course; she couldn't deliberately kill an innocent animal. But she did take Toots, lured him with sweet talk and biscuits and kept him hidden in a boat shed. He wagged his tail when she took him food, didn't bark, such a good boy. Before dealing with Henry, she'd take Toots for a walk to someone's yard where he could be easily found.

She knew the color of Henry's eyes perfectly. Not because she'd been that close to him yet but because she'd once let herself into the empty house with the key, always conveniently left in the seed tray of an unused birdcage at the side of the house.

The plethora of concrete arches was like a series of props for dramatic entrances. She had stood in front of a wall in the hallway outside his room examining the school photographs of him. Always pleased with himself, was Henry. Always staring straight into the camera, smiling confidently, sure of his privileged place in the world, aware of his charm, in love with his life.

Yesterday, Henry had risen early and scrambled over the headland rocks to a different spot than the one he normally surfed. When his friends arrived at the usual meeting place, they'd probably assumed he had slept in, distraught as he was, missing his dog.

Henry had surfed alone, and then he'd flopped onto the deserted beach over a mile from where his friends laughed and joked. He'd sat on the cool sand, the top half of his wet suit lying next to him like a discarded skin, and he'd bowed his head. She'd wondered if he was silently praying.

She'd allowed a momentary sorrow for him until she remembered she was the cause of his anguish. She was the one who had taken his beloved Toots.

They say that pets come to look like their owners, and Toots resembled Henry in many ways: the same pale coloring, a sort of a dumb-blond countenance, the youthful, coltish exuberance that comes from being loved and sheltered.

Henry was young—under twenty—which might make him easier to catch. Or harder. She wasn't quite sure. His youth meant half his life was spent thinking about sex, so an easy, uncomplicated fuck was a perfect lure. Then again, his boyish good looks afforded him constant opportunities. She knew she would manage it, though, because once her mind was set, there was no stopping her. If she needed to, she could come up with something inventive to get his attention.

Later, she watched from beside the hedge. He'd been out searching all day, but still no sign of Toots. He drew the drapes just as he had other nights. They were cheap curtains that left a two-inch crack of visibility at the edge of the window. Enough for her to make out his reflection in the full-length mirror. Every night he undressed slowly, touching his skin like a besotted lover. Tonight, notwithstanding his worry about Toots, he turned to the side, appraising his cock, wrapping his hand around it, smiling. She smiled too and touched herself. He moved to the bed, where she could no longer see him, and she had to imagine him masturbating, bringing hot liquid forth in a mini eruption for his mother to clean from pristine sheets.

She stayed behind the hedge pushing her fingers deep inside herself, making short grunting noises of pleasure as she pictured him there behind the curtains and then superimposed him onto a set of her own making. She would give him the ride of his life, and then she'd rip the life right out of him and watch his eyes reflect the horror of his mortality.

3

AURORA was in her favorite place, literally and figuratively, when the phone rang, in the glass-banked music room attached to the rear of the house, immersed in her world of music.

She was working on a harp solo inspired by Tchaikovsky's "Valse des Fleurs" introduction. Not so time-spinning, but elaborate and intricate enough to cause her more than a ripple of excitement.

Writing music came naturally to Aurora, but writing for her own instrument was a complicated business, given the extra time allowances for pitch variations and the need to avoid hasty and clunky pedal changes. She scribbled *laissez vibrer* on the sheet, simultaneously reaching out with her spare hand to answer the phone that had encroached into her world.

Her dreamlike state of creativity was shattered by Kate's urgent, breathy tone.

"You'll never guess where I am."

"Correct, sis." Aurora could never understand how her older sister managed to be such a heavy hitter in the world of law when most of the time she came across as being flaky.

"What's correct? What do you mean?"

Aurora laughed. "Correct," she repeated. "I mean I will never guess where you are."

She'd been trying to call her sister since earlier that morning to let her know she had not forgotten her birthday. The four texts she'd sent had gone unanswered. Now, she extricated herself from her harp like a lover disentangling after sex. "All right. I'll bite. Where are you?"

Kate's voice calmed somewhat. "You remember how you used to fold yourself in between the pillars at the southern end of Nan and Grandpa's veranda?"

Aurora remembered it well. She used to push her back against one pillar and walk her legs up the other, pushing herself into an awkward stretch.

She had loved all those holidays spent with her grandparents, days of an innocent exuberance she rarely saw in her own children's lives. Eleven-year-old Stella read books about vampires or glued herself to her iPhone—sometimes both at the same time—and Grant, at nine, preferred playing war games on the computer with his friends to climbing trees or catching frogs and combing the beach for washed-up treasures.

"That's where I am," Kate said.

"What?"

"I'm between the pillars. You'll be pleased to know my butt just fits."

Aurora wondered if her sister, with her brilliance and her skewed view of the world, had somehow gone over the edge. Kate had a weird fixation with that house, an obsession bordering on insanity.

Aurora sighed. So many years, and still Kate could not let it go. "For God's sake, Kate, please tell me you haven't broken in."

"No, I didn't break in. I opened the door, very sensibly, with a key." Kate started to laugh.

Aurora thought the laughter inappropriate. "You'd better tell me everything. Starting with how you got hold of the key."

"Funny thing, that. The real estate agent handed it over. Apparently, it's quite usual when a house is purchased."

"What on earth do you mean?" As she spoke, the truth dawned.

"It's mine." Kate's voice had softened. "I bought it, Aurora. It's my house."

"Well happy birthday to you indeed."

She'd thought Kate had given up on that house years ago. The two of them had a falling-out when Kate discovered their grandfather had sold the house he'd built and lived in for over half a lifetime—*To a stranger, no less!* Aurora had not only done nothing to stop it but had not even bothered to contact her older sister. No amount of apology had set Kate at ease.

"I didn't know it was important to you," Aurora had said. "How could I have known? It was his house to do with as he wanted. What did you expect me to do?"

To Aurora, the house had been one tiny piece of her childhood. They were carefree times to be sure, but the holidays were just one portion of a much larger childhood: school concerts and birthday parties, music lessons and card games, dolls and toys.

Kate hadn't fussed when their parents had moved out of their home into something smaller, so the furor over their grandfather's move had been disproportionate.

"I can't believe it, Kate. I thought you'd stopped thinking about the house."

"No. I just stopped talking about it. And I stopped stalking the owner."

"So? How did you manage to buy it then?"

"The husband died. At the house, actually. The wife was keen to sell. She couldn't bear to live here."

"He died in the house? Seriously? And you want to live there?"

"He didn't die *in* the house but on the grounds. Lots of houses probably have people die in them. You just wouldn't know."

Aurora couldn't think what to say. "Congratulations?" she offered half-heartedly.

Kate launched into a commentary about the state of the house. "When will you come for a visit? Can you come now?"

Aurora sometimes wished for a life as uncomplicated as Kate's: no husband, no children, no commitments, no house. Well, that had changed at least. Kate certainly had a house now, which begged the question: How did she plan on meeting the mortgage payments if she was going to live in it?

"Don't tell me you are going to live here?"

"Well I didn't wait all this time to buy it simply to rent it out to someone else."

"But what about your job?"

"Gone. I threw in the towel. Don't worry—I won't have trouble finding a new one."

Aurora knew her sister spoke the truth. Kate had quit jobs before, once to go on some rustic re-creation of an ancient voyage in a sailing ship, another time to chase her dark-eyed lover to Sicily, where he'd promptly left her rudderless. And there were others. Each time, though, Kate had found a new job easily enough. She was a great lawyer who somehow convinced prospective employers that her unsteady work history was merely due to her search for experience.

"Don't get me wrong; I'm thrilled you've come back to live. I'm just a bit shocked because of how much you loved that job."

"A job's a job," Kate said. "This house...now, that's a different story altogether."

Aurora mumbled through a range of excuses not to visit, eventually settling on the memories the house held. "I'll come soon," she said. "Just give me time for it all to sink in."

When she eventually put down the phone and quit pacing, she tried to return to her harp, to her sheets of music, but the moment had passed. She was no longer in the mood for birthing a new score, not when shadows lurked at the periphery.

Music had always been the biggest love of her life, inherited from a father with a keen ear and a deep appreciation for the classics and nurtured by an ambitious mother with refined taste.

Abandoning the music room altogether, she stepped through the central glass doorway and wandered into the garden. Not much would grow here on the precipice overlooking the sea. The soil was little more than a grade up from sand, and the strong winds could blast seedlings straight out of the ground. So, when they built their dream home, Aurora and Jason had made do with herringbone-pattern paving and a pond, together with ground-covering plants and mosses, some pampas grass and soft mounds of rich heather.

She thought about her grandfather's garden, tried to imagine Kate there now. But all she could see was Grandpa, clipping roses to take to his wife's funeral.

Here's a special one for you to lay on the casket, he'd said, handing nine-year-old Aurora a pale-pink rose in full bloom that had reminded her of her grandmother's hair the time the apprentice at the salon put too much dye in. Aurora didn't have many memories of her grandmother, and as the years progressed and she immersed herself in music, then in her family, even memories of time spent with her grandfather had receded, despite the fact they'd spent all their school vacations at his house and that she had spent more time with him than her sisters had.

She didn't think of him often, but now she took a moment to picture him as he'd been then: blue-eyed, tall and thin, wide-shouldered with a slightly stiff carriage shared by many ex-servicemen—he'd been a navy sub commander—always snappily dressed. He was an early riser and a hard worker, slow to anger and quick to laugh.

Grandpa had been a clockmaker, not professionally, but a master craftsman nonetheless. Aurora sometimes spent whole days in the shed with him, watching his long, artistic fingers create magical timepieces.

She was dragged from her reverie by the squeak of tires and the hiss of the bus's automatic doors: the sounds of her children coming home from school. She caught her breath as Stella emerged from the side path, spooked, not for the first time, by how much her daughter resembled Peggy.

Maybe that's why she didn't think about Grandpa so much.

Thoughts of her grandfather inevitably led to Peggy—the youngest sister—with her drunken histrionics and soul-destroying accusations.

Sometimes Stella's appearance overwhelmed Aurora. At eleven, her daughter was thin and leggy; her sandy-blond hair, worn straight, was lanky and tending to greasy, just as Peggy's had always been. Aurora would often catch herself averting her gaze from Stella, preferring to stare at her son, who had inherited his father's dark Latin features. Some nights, as she rubbed moisturizer into her neck and cheeks in preparation for sleep, she would gaze into the mirror at her own deep-green eyes and chestnut hair and wonder why, when she was so like her mother, with her cupid's-bow lips and perfectly arched brows, Mother Nature had chosen to give her a Rowling throwback for a daughter, why Stella had to be almost identical to the one family member Aurora despised.

Why don't we ever go to see Auntie Peggy? Stella asked one morning when they'd driven directly past the block where Peggy and Bo lived.

Aurora had gripped the steering wheel tight. *We don't have time, honey.*

Aurora and Stella had been en route south for vacation, Jason and Grant having gone ahead two days before. Aurora had played the harp at a VIP wedding the night before, and it was one of those A-lister, bride-arriving-by-helicopter, beluga-and-fireworks kind of nights that Jason would always run a mile from but that Stella was thrilled to attend with her mother, having made a list of the celebrities she would be likely to see.

"I'm not talking about now," Stella said that day. "But shouldn't we go to visit them sometimes?"

"What a silly thing to say," Aurora had snapped uncharacteristically. "You couldn't possibly remember Peggy. And you've never met Bo."

"But I've seen pictures, and Bo is my cousin. Auntie Kate said..."

"Oh, Stella. Don't listen to your Auntie Kate. She sees the whole world through rose-colored glasses."

Especially when it came to Peggy.

Aurora had some fond memories of the youngest sister, many of them set in their grandfather's garden: Peggy picking bunches of daffodils to stuff into squat jars as bedside ornaments, the sun-bleached gold of Peggy's hair standing out amid the brilliant reds and yellows of the maples in Grandpa's garden, the three of them—Aurora, Peggy and Kate—dressed in fairy wings dancing on a carpet of bluebells and cyclamen.

But all those memories were overshadowed by so many pictures of a drunk or drugged Peggy standing outside Aurora's house yelling abuse; whimpering, smelling of poverty and urine in the local jail; swaying and trembling in the courthouse with pollution pouring from her lips, shaking Aurora's world to its foundations.

Since moving south again, Aurora lived not far from Peggy's house and was on constant alert whenever she was shopping or running errands, lest she accidentally run into her sister. She normally made a point of steering clear of Peggy's suburb altogether.

She'd seen her little sister once or twice in recent years—in a shopping mall and distantly at the beach—but had walked straight past as if she didn't exist. Once, Aurora hid in an office-building entryway to watch Peggy and Bo ambling along the street, awed by what a normal boy he seemed.

Each time she had seen Peggy, she'd cried fresh tears for her dead grandfather.

Let it go, Kate always said. *You have to forgive her.*

But Aurora could not forgive Peggy.

"She's your baby sister," Kate said.

Aurora had stopped thinking of her as a sibling a long time ago.

4

SHE was back behind the hedge at the side of his house early in the morning, having slept little, to find him up and dressed in his board shorts, his curtains pulled back, the bedside lamp switched on, revealing the disheveled bed he would not bother to straighten.

She'd already released Toots into a stranger's backyard. The dog would soon be found and returned home.

She raced to the beach, removed her clothes and jumped into the surf. She had plenty of time. His friends wouldn't have wiped the sleep from their eyes yet.

When Henry walked over the sand toward the water's edge, zipping up the front of his wet suit, she emerged naked from the semidarkness and stood before him. His features in the murky predawn grayness were hazy, but there was no mistaking his sharp intake of breath.

"Well, well, well," he said with youthful confidence. "A naked stranger, and a gorgeous one at that. What a lovely surprise."

"Indeed."

"Synchronicity," he said.

"And serendipity," she replied.

"Let's make the most of it."

She giggled. "Grab the bull by the horn, so to speak."

Oh, so easy.

She scooped up her clothes and led him over the rocks, around the headland, up through a path barely visible through overgrown ferns, and in through the side door of a boat shed.

The shed and the house beyond were owned by a rich judge and his wife, who came to stay only once a month. She knew she had a good couple of hours before the sun would be high enough for anyone to venture to this end of the beach, and the shed was tucked far enough away as to be virtually undetectable. But she needed to be home before the sun heralded daytime, she reminded herself.

It wouldn't take long.

She was pleased about the gloomy half-light, not wanting this handsome young stud scrutinizing her while she fucked him senseless. She threw her rolled-up clothes onto the blanket she'd found in the corner and had placed there the night before. The blanket was red: the color of lust and blood.

He leaned his yellow board against the closed door, pulled his arms from the wet suit, and raked her naked body into his chest. He kissed her, timidly and somewhat awkwardly, before pushing her away to drag his wet suit the rest of the way off, over his slim hips and muscular thighs.

She eased him to the blanket and straddled his nakedness, cooing and moaning, knowing she needed to orgasm quickly or she'd be unable to concentrate on the task ahead. As she rode him, she used her fingers to reach her peak swiftly. Once she'd gotten the first part of her pleasure out of the way, she slid down the length of his body. It wasn't long before he was panting and writhing.

She timed it perfectly. His wanton shock and painful longing when she pulled away were priceless. He was like putty, allowing his wrists to be tied, groaning, urging her back to the task at hand. He didn't even protest when she tied his ankles. Fool.

She gave him a little more head, just to mess with him, and then, with fluid movements, she crouched above him and grabbed the hammer from its hiding place beneath the workbench. She stood tall, sucked in a lungful of air, and swung the hammer down, two-handed—with superhuman strength—toward his baby-soft hair. She heard a crack. He gurgled something. One hand twitched.

She grabbed the knife from beneath the bottom corner of the blanket and prepared to plunge it into his slender neck.

She thought she saw a flicker of fear behind those pale-blue eyes before they went vacant.

Fuck.

How on earth had that happened?

She hadn't meant to kill him so fast. She enjoyed watching them suffer, these miserable representations of humanity. It brought her great joy to play with their fear and watch their confidence evaporate.

But maybe it was for the best. A lucky strike. As his muscles had contracted beneath her writhing body moments before, she'd become aware of how much damage he might be capable of inflicting, how easily he might have been able to fight back.

She'd planned it all to move slower than it had, had imagined he would be semiconscious as she garroted him with the strip of wire she'd stowed beneath the red blanket. She had painstakingly wrapped shiny blue tape around the ends, fashioning strong handles she could grip and press down on. She'd done it before, and it worked quite well. Now here he was, dead as a rock at the bottom of the ocean, at her feet.

By pushing the wire down hard and sawing back and forth, she managed to partially decapitate him. Then she used the wire to cut off the pathetic representation of his manhood. She hummed softly and took her time, attending to the structure of the scene, placing the body just so, turning the half-removed head a touch more toward the door so the staring eyes would greet whoever came through it.

She didn't have much time, but she briefly fiddled with the body and with the blood on her red-carpeted playground before running back down the overgrown path, across the sand and the rocks, into the raging surf to wash the blood and lust and the stench of Henry's sex from her sacred body. At the same time, she disposed of the knife and wire, tied to the hammer and wedged beneath rocks on the sea floor.

As she walked back along the beach, she thought for a moment about the boy's family. She knew the mother would be upset at first, when it became clear her son was dead and his body mutilated, but at least she would have Toots for company. Perhaps, in years to come, the mother would thank her for removing something evil from this world.

She was home in the shower well before the neighborhood came alive fully with its faint glows of bedside lights and morning television.

5

PEGGY walked to her son's school the long way, as she always did. Once, feeling brave in the company of her caregiver, she went via the creek path, over the main bridge, past the gift shops and restaurants and almost to the corner bar. She'd timed the walk then, an easy seven-minute stroll. But it had been tough, and she knew she didn't want to go that way on her own. She wondered if she ever would.

Her normal route—along the railroad tracks, through a quarter mile of national park on lightly cleared paths, over the rocks beside the creek, and down the hill to the back of the school—took twenty-five minutes at a brisk pace. Coming back the same way, she'd lose almost an hour from her day. The alternative, while not untenable, made her deeply uncomfortable.

She met Bo at the back gate and, as was customary, made the trip home an adventure for her eight-year-old son.

"You stepped on the crack, Bo! Move back three paces."

Bo grinned. Peggy could tell he'd stepped on the crack on purpose to make sure she was paying attention.

They played games all the way. There were certain bushes you couldn't touch or you'd have to walk around them three times; cracks in the path that had to be avoided, the penalty being a count to sixty with eyes closed; particular rocks that, if stepped on in a moment of forgetfulness, would incur an extra ten minutes of either homework or housework, depending on whether you were the son or the mother.

Bo would often ask her the names of the plants. Peggy had little idea about most of the native bushes, but when she and Bo wound through the suburban streets, she'd point out the delphiniums, peonies, irises, and daylilies. Sometimes she would regale him with tales of her grandfather's garden. It was the place where she'd spent much of her childhood—climbing trees and smelling flowers and making mud pies for her older sisters.

She could distinctly remember the day her grandfather planted the peppertree near the front gate when she was barely three years old.

One of the world's strongest anti-inflammatories, Grandpa had said.

"You couldn't possibly remember that," Kate said years later. "You were too young."

She did remember it though. Peggy remembered many things her sisters didn't.

"I didn't know what it meant," Peggy said. "I didn't know the significance of it. But I remember it clearly."

Kate said she knew Nan was sick then. All Peggy recalled was the size of the miniature tree and the incomprehensiveness of the twenty-foot height to which it would eventually grow, according to her grandfather. She remembered the feel of the slender young stems, and she remembered her grandfather's tears. At the tender age of three, she hadn't asked why he cried. In the same way she didn't ask why anything happened...things just happened.

Peggy could admit now that letting things just happen had been her biggest downfall. Unlike her sisters, she'd never had a sense of direction when she was young. Kate was adventurous and sporty, always determined to win medals and cups that overfilled the family's trophy cabinet. Aurora used to talk nonstop about interior design, clocks, and music and, once she'd discovered the harp, every spare minute was taken up with it.

Peggy, on the other hand, had never found a passion—not in childhood anyway. From the age of about sixteen, she'd certainly become passionate about alcohol, but before that, nothing stood out.

She had played with dolls, and she enjoyed watching television at Grandpa's house because it was so rarely on at home. Peggy's father once sentenced her to the hard labor of washing dishes every night for a week after he caught her watching cartoons on television after school.

Now, when Peggy walked home with Bo, she was sometimes guilty of allowing her mind to wander. She would think about how maybe tomorrow she would take the short route. She pictured herself ambling off at two forty-five like the other moms, or maybe she would leave earlier and browse in the gift shop for something special to take to Bo, maybe a book or a piggy bank. Perhaps she'd try on a dress in Sassy's Boutique, and the redhead who owned the shop would complement Peggy on her flat belly and pert boobs. On her imaginary walk, she only ever got as far as the post office, from where she could see the front bar of the hotel. Even in fantasyland, her lips would parch with the lust of it all. It was an indescribable pain, this terrible longing for something cool and yeasty, or ice-cold and clear; or warm and fruity. Even in her imagination, she was incapable of walking past the hotel. That one time when she'd gone with the temporary caregiver imposed on her, the woman gripped her arm tightly and they'd turned down the side street before the post office. Peggy still wasn't ready to do it alone.

It wasn't that she couldn't go out. She saw her psychiatrist once a week, she went grocery shopping. She regularly walked to the beach. But everything was regimented; she had a time frame to leave the house, travel a predefined route, and return home. It was the only way she could be sure of keeping on the straight and narrow. No dillydallying. No deviations.

Whenever she wanted to do something different, like take Bo to a movie or try on clothes or shoes, it was necessary to plan.

She knew where most of the bars were and always worked out how to get where she was going without passing one. If it seemed impossible, then she simply would not go. She trusted other people far more than she trusted herself.

Today, she amused Bo with the news that Auntie Kate had come back to live.

His eyes became full-moon orbs. "With us?"

"No. But her house is not far away."

"Will she come to visit?"

Peggy ruffled Bo's hair, light and fine like her own, grateful for his excellent health, his exuberance, his purity. After all she had put him through, she could barely believe his innocence. "Sure. She'll come to visit sometimes. She probably needs time to settle in, though."

"When can we go to see her?"

"That would mean a bus trip, Bo." He suffered terribly from motion sickness. A car was bad enough, but a bus was his worst nightmare. In fact, they'd be able to walk to Kate's using the coastal paths, but she wasn't about to admit that to Bo.

"I can do it, Mom. The bus."

Peggy was stunned into a momentary silence.

Then, she imagined being on that bus. She caught the number six into the city every three months. She knew when to look right, when to look left, but a new trip, with no idea of the route the driver would take, was daunting. She thought any bus between her and Kate's place would take a circuitous route. On her imaginary trip, she saw herself passing any number of bars and not crying out to the driver to stop. But imagining it and doing it were two entirely different scenarios.

Maybe walking the coastal tracks was a better idea, but she didn't think Bo would be too pleased with the steep hill at the end.

There was a bigger reason for not wanting to go: What if she made it there but found she could not cope with seeing Kate in those surroundings? What if false memories overwhelmed her?

What if she imagined, as she had all those years ago, that terrible things had happened to her as a child? She would be unable to deal with all that in the absence of vodka, the sweet elixir of past lives.

"We'll see" was her ineffectual answer to Bo.

She attempted to conjure an image of Kate in the house, but all she could see was her grandfather's crestfallen face across a crowded courtroom.

Peggy swallowed with difficulty, trying to capture happy images and push away the unpleasant ones as her favorite psychiatrist had taught her to do.

Kate in the kitchen. That's what she remembered most. Kate loved to cook.

Aurora and Grandpa in the shed. They spent half their lives in there, making clocks and presents, mending things.

Watching television. That's what Peggy had loved about Grandpa's house: an unlimited diet of old sitcoms, cartoons and movies about princesses, to go with all the delicious food her big sister kept churning out.

Peggy would sit with one or two of Nan's old dolls and immerse herself in whatever world was being played out on the screen in front of her while she waited for Kate to come in with a plate of lemon cookies or a bowl of last night's leftover trifle or a slice of Christmas cake, which was always in abundance until a couple of months before the next Christmas came around.

Bo continued to pester her about visiting his Auntie Kate until Peggy remembered to tell him about the books that had arrived, among them a boxed set of the Shadow Children series Bo's teacher had insisted dealt with issues too complex for an eight-year-old. If

Miss Pellat had any idea of the complexity of Bo's young life, she'd understand that not much in fiction would faze him.

"And *Galax-Arena*, Mom? Did it come?"

She nodded. The award-winning Rubinstein novel had been around for decades, but Bo had only recently read a review on the internet.

"Just don't tell Miss Pellat, okay?"

Bo gave one of his perfect imitations of the teacher, lips pursed, cheeks sucked in. "That book is for teenagers, Bo. For young adults," he said in perfectly clipped Miss Pellat–ese. "I really must speak to your mother about suitable reading material for an eight-year-old."

They laughed easily together, as they so often did these days. Bo was more than her son; he was the thread holding her together.

He grinned with mischievous suspicion. "I bet you've been reading them already."

"Not on your life!"

Books had been Bo's greatest joy since before he could read: picture books he'd received as presents that he'd stare at and trace his fingers over when he was two; bedtime storybooks that he took to his room to examine, despite the words being incomprehensible; a collector's-edition encyclopedia set his Auntie Kate had delivered on Bo's first birthday.

Peggy shuddered, not remembering Bo's first birthday but imagining it. She would have been drunk, no doubt celebrating the event with one or another of her fair-weather friends or incompetent lovers. Thankfully, between the lot of them, someone must have remembered to shove a bottle into the child's mouth.

Sometimes, when Peggy woke shivering with guilt in the early hours of the morning, she fancied she could remember singing softly to her son, rocking him from side to side, coaxing him with his bottle. Had she done that for him? Had she ever been sober enough then to have created such a memory?

She was so stoned in those days, she hadn't named him until he was five days old. Not because she was being picky or because her love for her child blinded her to rational thought; only that after seven months of no hard drugs and, for her, very light drinking followed by two days of forced abstinence in the hospital, she'd gone on a cheap-wine-and-dope bender of extraordinary proportions—partly to celebrate a successful birth and obliterate a disastrous conception but also to squash the fearful images that came to her when her veins were clean. Visions of bulky manly shapes, of musky wanton scents. Surreal scenes that left her howling with imagined pain and brought back the old self-hatred that made her want to slash her wrists. Much safer to smoke out the visions or to drown them with bloodred liquor.

In those post-hospital days of revelry, she vaguely recalled some old wino with a wallet full of cash singing a song from an earlier era: *Baby, I'd love you to want me.*

"Lobo!" she'd yelled, recognizing the song and the man who'd made it popular, from her Auntie Tanya's record collection. She'd picked up the baby then and felt something vague. An abstract maternal feeling.

"I hereby name thee Lobo Rowling," she'd drawled in a drunken parody of a priest at a christening. "The way that it should be."

She never could recall exactly what Kate had said when she

phoned to find out how mother and son were doing, but she did remember Kate calling her son Bo. And after *Bo* was the first word to come out of those boy-cherub lips, Peggy forgot *Lobo* was even on his birth certificate and she let Bo be his name.

By then, she could barely remember the wino with the thick wallet. That would come to her in flashback, like so much of her life.

6

KATE's fainting fit when she'd first arrived at her new home had been a one-off. At the time, it left her disoriented but, after a couple of hours sleep and a soothing cup of Lipton's, she had convinced herself it was caused by nothing more than a bug. Probably something she'd caught on the plane.

She'd never been the sickly type. Practically all her life, she had been active, a study in perpetual motion: sailing, windsurfing, competing in marathons, riding her bicycle. She couldn't sit still when she read or talked on the phone, preferring to pace, ideally outdoors, but corridor lengths would do. During her school years, she'd carted home medals every year: long jump, high jump, gymnastics. In college, she'd captained the basketball and soccer teams and spent early hours in the gym. These days, she was happy with a run and a swim six days out of every seven.

She never had time to be sick. Certainly, she was far too excited now to fall ill for long. There was still so much to explore, so many plans to make.

Despite being only a short drive away, Kate had been unable to talk Aurora into popping in for tea. Busy with events. Kids and school. Excuses, excuses. Eventually, Kate had worn her down and she'd consented to a visit, with conditions.

"I'm leaving the kids at home this first time," she'd said. "They are both busy with school."

Kate was elated. "Great. Will you stay over? Then we can drink wine and get properly tanked."

Aurora had agreed to stay the night only after Kate, begging, had assured her there was absolutely no chance of running into Peggy.

"I know you think we can all be one big happy family," Aurora had said. "But life isn't like that."

"I just think you should find it in your heart to forgive her and move on." It was Kate's standard refrain.

Kate was in her grandfather's old work shed when she heard Aurora's Toyota pull into the driveway. She ran to the front gate, wrapping her sister in a bear hug.

"Let me look at you," she whispered, pulling back. "As beautiful as ever." She noticed Aurora's sparkling eyes. "Don't you go crying on me now."

A neighbor peeking out from their curtains or from behind a lush garden bush would no doubt guess they were sisters, or at least relatives. Kate was taller and more athletic in build, but they both had a soft, vaguely olive complexion and dark green eyes. The sun would occasionally highlight auburn streaks in their chestnut hair, Kate's short and tucked behind her ears, Aurora's falling in thick waves to her shoulders.

Aurora traced her finger over the number thirty-six. "Will you look at that."

"Amazing, isn't it?" Kate opened the gate wide, gesturing expansively with her arm. "And here's the garden."

She heard Aurora's breath catch at the sheer grandeur of it all. "I never expected it to be like it was when Grandpa lived here."

"Isn't it incredible?" Kate steered her sister to the work shed. "You'll notice a few changes inside, but there's something I want you to see first."

"My God, look at that." Aurora stopped in the middle of the walkway as she caught sight of the three weeping willows in the marshy corner of the property.

Kate, who'd been racing ahead excitedly, retraced her steps to stand beside her sister.

"Haven't they grown?"

They stared at the trees: the two more mature willows dwarfing the tinier one in the corner. Grandpa had planted them in honor of his grandchildren. "That way, wherever you are when you are grown-up, I'll know a part of you is here with me."

A lump rose and expanded in Kate's throat. Her eyes stung, a threat of tears. "Come on, Aurora," she whispered. "Let's not get sad."

Aurora moved but only to halt in her tracks a few steps farther on when she saw the pond and again when she caught sight of the path that once led to their secret hideout in the bushes.

Kate was impatient with Aurora's stop-start progress. She grabbed her sister's hand and practically dragged her along the path.

Aurora's reaction to the carcass of a grandfather clock in the corner of the shed was priceless. "How could it still be here after all these years?"

"Strange, isn't it?" From what Kate could make out, Mrs. Beige must have been one of those people who couldn't bear to throw anything away, so whatever she'd found when she moved in had been shoved in the work shed to be forgotten.

Aurora ran her fingers over the dusty old wood. "Why on earth would Grandpa have left the shell of a longcase here anyway?"

Kate had no answer. Their grandfather had spent half his life in this shed building clocks. He enjoyed the precision, the scientific nature of it, the steady vibrations of the crystal quartz or the regularity of the pendulum swings. He also loved the art itself: the graceful curves of the wooden cases, the intricate carvings and shiny brass fittings.

"What did he do with all those clocks anyway?" Kate asked. "He could have opened a shop."

"I think he sold some in the early days. And gave them as gifts of course. Did you know I have one?"

"No." It wasn't something Kate had thought about before, but given the amount of time Aurora had spent with Grandpa and his clockmaking, it stood to reason. "Did he give it to you?"

"No." Aurora was pensive. "I took it from Auntie Tanya's house when she died. I was quite disappointed when I found that Grandpa hadn't kept any. He wouldn't allow me to help with the move, and by the time I came to pick him up, he'd given away or sold the last of them. I certainly didn't know this grandfather case was here, or I'd have taken it."

The old anger bubbled beneath the surface. "Hmm, well, if you couldn't keep him from selling the house, I don't suppose you could have done much about a few clocks."

"Oh, for the love of God, Kate. Don't drag all that up again."

Kate forced a smile through the narrow lips she'd inherited from her grandfather and that provided a startling contrast to Aurora's curvaceous mouth. "I know, I know, you couldn't stop him. It wasn't your fault." She steered her sister to an old wooden case in the opposite corner of the shed. "There's a whole box full of bits and pieces here." She watched the emotions play out over her sister's face. Aurora used to spend so much time helping Grandpa with his craft. "Look at all these books."

Aurora's fascination and joy over the clock parts were akin to Kate's feelings about the house itself. "You should have them," Kate said.

"Oh, I couldn't."

"Don't be a pain in the ass, Aurora. This clock stuff doesn't mean anything to me. If you don't take it all, I'll send it to the dump."

"You would not."

"Try me."

Aurora's mouth curved in appreciation.

Kate took her sister on a tour of the garden before they ventured inside, where she gestured to the area between the dining room and kitchen. "I'm planning to have the wall rebuilt here. Remember the big wooden knob on the hatch door?"

"Good luck getting another one the same."

"I won't have to." Kate moved to the kitchen counter. "Found this in the shed." She held up the wooden knob their grandfather had painstakingly carved after the old brass handle broke off the door. It was as though Mrs. Beige had known exactly what to throw out and what to keep.

Kate knew the hard work their grandfather had put into the huge circular knob. First, he'd had to find the right piece of wood from which to carve his masterpiece. Then he'd measured his wife's hand to make sure the size of the handle would be the perfect fit.

Kate could recall the tenderness with which Grandpa had held Nan's hand as he measured from middle fingertip to the crease at her wrist and then across the width of her palm. The pair of them had been seated at the mahogany dining table, and Kate's vantage point was from the corner balustrade on the front veranda, around which she had wrapped one leg.

Grandpa jotted down his second measurement, placed his pencil gently on top of the pad, and then lifted Nan's hand slowly to his lips. He'd kissed the palm of her hand, and Kate had thought it was the most romantic thing she'd ever seen.

She remembered a passage in one of her mother's contraband Harlequin novels where a man kissed a woman's hand, but she was sure her grandfather had done it much better than the fictional tall dark stranger in the book.

It had taken Grandpa two days to carve that handle, and Kate had watched him constantly. Usually, it was Aurora who spent time in the shed, sharing as she did their grandfather's fascination with clocks. A handle was something quite boring by comparison, but to Kate, who had watched her grandparents' romantic interlude, the creation of the handle was a beautiful thing to witness. By the time Grandpa fitted it to the sliding door, Kate felt she'd helped to create it.

One glass of the Moët Aurora had brought to celebrate the new-old house was enough to bring up the proverbial elephant.

"I have moved on, Kate, but I can't forgive her for what she did."

"But it wasn't her. Can't you see that?" They'd been through it all a million times. "It was the drugs and the booze."

Peggy had been a perfectly normal girl, maybe a tad spoiled by a mother who was older and much less career-focused than she had been with her first two children. On top of that, Peggy had two older sisters who doted on her. All the attention didn't go to her head, though, and she had been thoroughly likable. But when she was sixteen, she'd become involved with the wrong crowd and fell into drugs with fascinating ease, grass at first, but then uppers and Ecstasy, and eventually heroin. Any time she'd managed to leave the drugs alone, alcohol had taken their place.

"And that crappy psychiatrist was the last straw." Kate had said those words so often, they'd become the chorus of Peggy's life.

"I can't get over what she did to Grandpa," Aurora said. "She as good as killed him. You know that."

Kate sighed. "Peggy didn't kill him. You know that very well." Their grandfather had died of a heart attack.

"Of course, she didn't literally kill him. Anyway, it doesn't matter," Aurora said. "Nothing you say can make me forget."

Later, with a tipsy Aurora tucked into bed in the second bedroom, Kate lay awake in the main room—she could see she'd outgrown the sewing room of her youth—reliving the trauma Peggy had ultimately wreaked upon the family.

Soon after the death of their father, Peggy had tried to stay with their mother to help her through her inconsolable grief. What a ridiculous idea. By that time, after years of drug and alcohol misuse, Peggy couldn't even look after herself, let alone support Mother. But Kate had been busy hundreds of miles away, recently admitted to the bar, forging her career in law and falling in and out of love, and Aurora was enthralled with her interior decorating business and her harp and her husband. They were all to blame. They should have seen Peggy was a train wreck. She had managed to get off the drugs, but only with the help of an inexperienced and far too experimental psychiatrist who planted memory seeds in Peggy's fragile brain that were quite simply fabricated.

To Peggy, the "memories" grew with every visit to her shrink and, later, became all the more real when fueled by Smirnoff. Soon, their beloved grandfather had been dragged through the court system, accused of molesting and abusing his youngest granddaughter on a systematic basis over a number of years.

Kate's tears were never far from the surface whenever she remembered the pain in Grandpa's eyes as he'd had to listen to the terrible accusations Peggy's court-appointed guardians and lawyers flung at him from across a crowded courtroom. As if he hadn't suffered enough, losing the love of his life to cancer and then less than a decade later, his eldest son—the girls' father—when a semitrailer had skidded on an icy corner. Grandpa could barely conceive of the accusations, and when he was exonerated by the court, when Peggy's psychiatrist was revealed as a fraud, when Peggy—temporarily off the drugs and the hard liquor—was reevaluated and treated properly and conceded that her "memories" were actually false, their grandfather was unable to recover.

Kate could never forgive herself for being unable to help her grandfather to come back from the terrible shocks he had endured. By the time it was over, their mother was unreachable, languishing in a high-care facility. For Kate's own sanity, she'd left them all alone: left Grandpa to rattle around in the house he had built for the love of his life, the home away from home he'd provided for his grandchildren; left Peggy to fight her own demons and battle against her addictions; left Aurora to try to pick up the threads of her singed life.

Aurora was the one who'd comforted Grandpa and shielded him from the suspicious eyes of the outside world. Aurora was the one who'd visited him constantly, making four-hour round trips from her then home up north, to let him know he was loved and worthy, helping him sell his precious home after he bought a smaller unit.

Kate had run away.

And now, she was stuck in the middle, torn between her love for her little sister, who had been duped by an unscrupulous professional, and her love for the middle girl, Aurora, who had cared for their grandfather unconditionally and had suffered because of it.

As Kate drifted into that neverland between wakefulness and sleep, phantoms came out to play. She had memories of her own she suspected were flights of fancy brought on by Peggy's invented abuse, things that made Kate question her grandfather's innocence, that made her wonder why the sisters were constantly sent to stay with him anyway, that made her question if her mother and father were fit parents. And while, alone at night, she might try to analyze their strange childhood, she was not prepared to bring her misgivings into the light.

7

SHE was not as fulfilled with her kill as she would have liked. It was nothing compared to her last murder, years back. That was one that still excited her when she managed to remember it. Whenever she got the craving, she would immerse herself in the memories of that day and was satisfied enough to keep the hunting urge under control.

Recently though, the hunger had become stronger and more insistent, and thoughts of the victim's pain and fear had only made her crave more. Where once she had held fast to the memories of the warm silkiness of fresh blood and the fascination with her first sight of human entrails, the visions had lost their shine, and she desperately needed to create new pictures.

That was what Henry was supposed to do. She'd had such elaborate plans for Henry, but when the time came, excitement had overcome her. Perhaps it was the sex. She'd perceived a vague sense of his power over her, and it had made her reach for the hammer much quicker than intended. She certainly hadn't thought she was strong enough to kill him with one blow. Must have been a weak little prick. His sudden death was an anticlimax.

But having experienced the surge of power and sexual prowess she'd felt before, it would only be a matter of time before she killed again. This time, she'd plan it better, and she wouldn't allow herself to become overexcited and finish it all too quickly.

Unlike Henry's name, the previous one was easy for her to forget, but his name had never been important anyway. In her mind, she always referred to him as The Man. He could never remember her name when they were together. He always called her Baby.

The Man had been close to forty, quite handsome, his face tanned and ruggedly weathered. He sported a thick head of dark straight hair with a streak of gray swooping backward from his temple; a distinguished embellishment. He was a snappy dresser too, almost always in a suit and tie.

On the day she had chosen to be his last, they'd met in the parking lot as arranged and headed off for a walk and a picnic. He'd been dressed in a pair of jeans—so well-ironed he could have worn them to the casino—teamed with a black T-shirt and two-hundred-dollar hiking boots.

By the time they reached the deserted hut she'd scoped out earlier and she'd made it patently clear he would definitely be getting laid that afternoon, he could barely contain himself.

She had him tied up and eating out of her hand—literally—in the space of less than ten minutes. He'd practically come in his perfectly laundered jeans when she first told him she was partial to a spot of bondage, and when she straddled his spread-eagle body and fed him strawberries from the picnic basket, he'd moaned ecstatically: "Oh, Baby."

"Take it easy," she told him as he bucked against her. "We have plenty of time."

Even when she waited for him to finish the last strawberry and then began to stuff a strip of pillowcase into his mouth, he continued to smile wantonly. It wasn't until his cheeks were bulging with fabric and she produced the roll of heavy-duty tape, tearing off a piece noisily with her teeth, that she saw the expression in his eyes change. Confusion at first: *Jeez, what's she up to now?* Followed by a hint of fear: *Christ, I didn't expect her to get this carried away.* Then it was horror: *Fuck, she's going to tape up my mouth. I can hardly breathe as it is.* Caginess: *Stay calm, old boy; you've got to get out of this.* Stealth: *How tight are these ropes? Don't let her guess you're scared. Holy shit, I can barely move.*

By the time the tape had sealed that lying, seductive mouth closed, The Man had well and truly lost his erection, but it didn't bother her. She didn't need him for that. Oh, she needed far more of him than he could ever give her with his dick...limp or otherwise.

She'd placed a thick piece of rope across his belly and disappeared beneath the bench-like bed to form the rope into a tight knot. Standing upright again, she'd stared at his shriveled scrotum. Her eyes roamed over the soft flesh of his belly, his somewhat skinny thighs and hairy shins. His chest was interesting: funny misshapen nipples with a smattering of dark hair.

She'd been watching men for months, seeing how their mouths

moved when they hawked their petty lies, watching their eyes twinkle as they flirted and dreamed of fucking anything that moved and remotely resembled a female. In the end, she'd started to see them all as disembodied penises, and severed heads, pieces of organs, bits of bone and river flows of blood. They were nothing more than great slabs of meat waiting to be appreciated and carved and rearranged and positioned just so.

It had been such a thrill to have one tied up beneath her. He would have begged for mercy if he could talk. He'd made tiny grunting noises, and his nostrils flared with the effort of trying to communicate in a silent language. His eyebrows had taken on a life of their own: pleading, begging, screaming like sideways exclamation marks.

Dear little tears escaped from the corner of The Man's eyes.

"Oh, poor thing. Are we scared?" She chuckled softly and tweaked her aching nipples. "Is The Man wishing he had stayed home with his wife and children? Does The Man want to go home?"

He'd started breathing so hard through his nostrils that muddy bubbles of snot emerged.

"Now that's just not attractive," she told him. "The least you could have done would have been to keep yourself nice."

She'd smacked him across the face with her open palm and then wiped his nose with the edge of the fabric dangling from the side of the tape.

"If you want to get out of here alive, I suggest you at least make an effort to remain inviting."

She saw his eyebrows form a question, his eyes registered some hope: Just behave, he was telling himself, and everything will be fine.

"Is that hope I see in The Man's eyes?" Her chuckle was soft and sensuous. She took the knife from the picnic basket then and watched the hope turn to panic again. "You shouldn't believe what I say. It's time for you to screw that hope into a tight ball and throw it in the trash can. The only way The Man is getting out of this cabin is in pieces."

The tears had flowed freely then. He'd grunted like a pig and muffled a yowl like a distant cat in heat as the snot ran down over the bright green tape.

Green is for go, she thought.

Let's get the party started.

He blubbered behind the tape again, and then she saw his eyes glaze as something suspiciously like vomit erupted from his nose. She had the presence of mind to rip the tape from his mouth instantly. She turned his head as much as she could and dragged the chuck-soaked pillowcase from his mouth as he tried a poor imitation of a scream and then swung his head from side to side.

"I'm so sorry," she said, and The Man stilled. "I never should have been so cruel."

There was that flicker of hope again, and the power was absolutely intoxicating.

"Wait," she whispered. "I'll clean you up."

She took wipes from her bag and swiped around his mouth and nose, making apologetic cooing noises. "Baby is sorry, so sorry," she whispered.

Even after all he'd been through, there was an immediate resurgence of perceived power. "It's okay, Baby," he groaned, his voice showing not a trace of a tremor. "Just untie me, okay?"

"In a minute." She jumped off the hard wooden makeshift bed.

"What are you doing now?"

"I'm finding something to help take away the pain."

"Never mind that," he said.

Oh so brave, she thought, as she moved close to him again.

"Undo the ropes, Baby."

She couldn't stand his voice. He was distracting her. In one swift movement, she grabbed the roll of tape, pulled out another strip, and jammed it across his whining mouth. She bent to rip the edge with her teeth, and she could smell the acrid stench of his fear and see it reflected in his eyes just inches from hers.

Again, he started snorting and pushing out his bubbles of snot as she retrieved the knife from the floor where it had fallen as he'd bucked. It was a beautiful object, that knife, perfect for filleting fish, she'd been told. She imagined it would be suited to many things.

Despite the fear and the horror, all hope did not disappear from The Man. She could see it in the whites of his eyes, in the slight raise of the eyebrows.

Amazing how the human spirit can still manufacture this ridiculous emotion when it should be as plain as the nose on your face—and the snot erupting from it—that there was no hope left for The Man.

She didn't remember much after that. It was a blur of emotions and hunger and sensuous experiences.

She'd read something of it in the paper at the time and was stunned by how calm she had remained. There was not one fingerprint; there was no one to connect her to The Man or the cabin.

She had never been seen in public with him, had never been in his car or to his apartment.

The whole beauty of the kill returned in dribs and drabs and with such clarity that she could see how the horror of it all could never be truly comprehended, let alone be reported in the papers.

That kill had happened so long ago.

8

AURORA could barely contain her excitement on the relatively short drive home from her sleepover at Kate's, an excitement that had nothing to do with her family or her house, her cats or even her music. She had barely thought of her husband. If she'd been concerned about spending a night away from Jason, she could just as easily have forgone the champagne and driven home last night. But they'd been married for long enough that one night apart meant little more than a chance to do something different. She'd spoken to Stella and Grant on the phone before they'd gone to bed. Yes, they'd done their homework, and yes, they'd fed Mimi and Leo, and yes, they loved her. Jason sent some weird *Home Alone* GIF, confirming he'd been into the scotch. The only time she thought about her harp was during her brief description to Kate of the scantily clad actresses and moody models with their "fuck off" dark glasses who'd attended the wedding she'd played at recently.

What excited Aurora was the clock, nothing more than a fine wooden shell really, now lying in the back of the Toyota Camry beside the empty harp platform. The makings of a grandfather clock, just the middle, without any base or top carvings. She'd have to find patterns and build those parts. Equally as exciting as the shell was the case full of companion pieces she couldn't wait to go through in fine detail. There were books and brass dials and chapter rings, hour markers, coils, and pendulums. The case was so heavy, the sisters had enlisted a neighbor's help to lift it into the back.

The clock she did have of her grandfather's was the one she had rescued—perhaps *stolen* was a better word—from her Aunt Tanya's house the day after the old spinster's death. She knew no one else would appreciate it. It was a dignified Napoleon with melodious authentic Westminster chimes. She could vaguely remember her grandfather putting the finishing touches on that clock when she was barely six or seven. *Magnificent design*, Grandpa had told her. *They only made it long like this at the base so the bars could be extended along the floor of the case. See what I mean?* He always showed her the intricate workings inside.

Aurora had kept the Napoleon in a box at first when she and Jason lived in that ugly house up north, but when they moved into their high-perched coastal dream home, she'd had a special shelf built for it. It sat alone on that shelf at the end of the hallway, its chunky turned bun feet signifying strength and stability whenever Aurora glanced at it.

Now she would build a grandfather clock, one she knew would not sit comfortably in her own house. Perhaps I'll make it for

Kate, she thought. How fitting: a grandfather clock for the house their grandfather built.

She would take her time with it, of that she was sure. Her grandfather always said it was dangerous to immerse yourself too deeply in one thing. *In the end, you miss something*, he said. *You need to put things down, let them come into being organically.*

She wasn't sure she understood him at the time, but later, when she'd taken to her music studies in earnest, when she'd fallen in love with the harp, Grandpa's wise words had guided her. And when she began to seriously write music, his words became a mantra. Something of beauty could not be created in haste.

After Jason had helped unload her bounty, she'd covered the longcase with a sheet and put it against the back wall of the garage, the wooden case in front. She planned to unpack slowly, every day taking a couple of items from the case.

The first day, she unveiled a worn cardboard box with intricate patterns and detailed instructions inside. The box also contained a set of brushes. Aurora held each brush, feeling its weight and texture. She ran her fingers over them, imagining them in her grandfather's capable hands. As she did so, the happy memories returned: long summer days scrambling over the headland rocks searching for crabs and mussels, tasting the many spoils of Nan's kitchen labor, playing in the tree house with her sister, spending hour upon hour immersed in the wood shavings and intricate schematics of Grandpa's world.

She wondered why he'd left all these precious tools behind. Why not take one clock to his new apartment? Aurora surmised it was because his soul was shattered. She imagined him as he was then, mentally and physically exhausted after all Peggy had put him through, unable to bring himself to sell the tools of his trade, which might have seemed like cutting off his hand. Perhaps he found it easier to close the door on the shed and walk away.

Aurora pushed the pervasive thoughts of Peggy's destructiveness away. She was determined to resurrect her grandfather in the perfect clock she would build. In her mind, she would destroy all traces of Peggy's damage, restore Grandpa's image, and heal her own battered psyche.

On day two, the case produced a faded picture of a complex Aztec calendar. In the white space at the edge of the picture, her grandfather's handwritten note:

contained enough information to predict solar eclipses!

Aurora stared at the exclamation mark, imagining her gentle, cucumber-cool grandfather being excited enough to add that piece of punctuation so that now, years later, his granddaughter could experience the passion. She rejoiced in each thing brought forth from the case, even an old frayed cleaning rag he used to polish tiny brass screws.

Rather than taking her away from her music, the rekindling of her knowledge of clockmaking and the memories of her grandfather resulted in weeks of musical joy—communing in spirit with Mozart and Handel, losing herself in Debussy's "Sacred and Profane Dances" and Tchaikovsky's elaborate cadenzas, as well as working on a highly original orchestral composition of her own.

In time, she brought some of the intricate clock parts into her music room.

Grant was fascinated. "Are you really going to build a clock, Mommy?"

Stella was less enamored with the whole idea. "It's not even big enough," she said, when Aurora showed them the shell in the garage.

"This is the middle casing part," Aurora explained. "Wait till you see it with its carved stand."

The case was dark walnut, and she planned a classical Parthenon-inspired hood.

"Won't exactly fit the decor," was Jason's contribution. He was fond of the Napoleon, fitting in as it did with the art deco style of the house.

When she told him she'd probably give the grandfather clock to Kate, he relaxed.

At night, she would recall strange facts her grandfather used to recite. He told her how many million times the pendulum in a longcase swings from side to side in a year. Now she couldn't remember the exact figure he quoted, but courtesy of one of Grandpa's time-related facts, she always remembered how old her grandmother was when she died.

She made fifty-seven years and one month, Aurora. A milestone. She was alive for half a million hours.

At first, the clock parts elicited happy memories of time spent in the shed with Grandpa, but then she found herself questioning, as she had in the past, why she and her siblings had spent so much time there with their grandparents.

She did have some fond memories of her parents too, but they were different. Her father had been an overachieving architect with a strict, regimented lifestyle, and it was often hard to believe he was the son of the grandfather Aurora knew and loved so well. Still, despite his square-shouldered formality, her father did have moments of childish exuberance.

She recalled on occasion being bounced on his lap in tune with a jingle.

My nanny's ninety-nine, her father would sing. *She can thread a needle.* Aurora used to squeal with delight and anticipation as he drew out the penultimate line. *Eeeeevry time she winks her eeeye.*

Swift as a fox, her father would move his knees, and Aurora would slip between them, laughing with exhilaration as he caught her.

Pop goes the weasel!

And he loved to listen to her play the harp.

Overall, he was a serious man who, unlike his father, rarely laughed. Despite his formal distance, though, Aurora had never doubted her father's love. She did remember that he'd read to her once or twice, from weighty historical tomes, and there was a lullaby he'd often sing: "Oh, My Darling Clementine." In truth though, he was rarely home, and once she started going out with boys and forging a life of her own, he became more distant. When he made a speech at her wedding, she realized he barely knew her and she probably knew him even less.

Her mother fared somewhat better in Aurora's estimation, if only for the magnificent example she set: always nothing less than immaculately groomed, a lover of fine art and music, responsible for outings to the ballet and concerts and—the minute she detected Aurora's interest and aptitude—arranging weekly music lessons.

There was never time to merely play games in her parents' home. They didn't watch much television; they didn't listen to popular music. There was no idle reading of fiction, even though she and Kate knew where their mother kept a private stash of romance novels.

For Aurora now, reminiscences of the clocks and her grandfather inevitably unearthed nightmares of the false memories Peggy had spouted, courtesy of her psychiatrist, supposed retrieved memories of being tied up and hidden in a box, abused and beaten and sexually assaulted.

Aurora had fought against the images, and yet she could sometimes swear she felt ropes around her own wrists, felt a strap digging into the skin of her back, hands groping her. Over the years, the feelings had faded, but still, the pictures would gnaw at the corners of her brain.

Now, Aurora's body tensed again, and she found herself fighting for air. She reminded herself that all accusations had been disproved and Peggy now admitted they were never her memories at all.

Kate could play Pollyanna all she liked with her *It wasn't Peggy, it was the psychiatrist* and her *Drugs can do such terrible things,* and the whole holier-than-thou *We must learn to forgive her* pleadings. Aurora was beyond caring about the mitigating factors: the drugs, the drink, the psychiatrist. All she cared about was her precious grandfather and the fact that her idyllic memories of childhood holidays had been taken from her. One person was ultimately responsible for that. Peggy.

In the dark of night, Aurora's subconscious played with an alternative universe, pictures of her naked grandfather looming up at her, despite the fact she'd never seen him naked. Her sleeping mind sometimes conjured a Grandpa doppelgänger brandishing a whip and an evil scowl, even though she knew her grandfather would never have countenanced any form of corporal punishment.

Tonight she dreamt her grandfather was her lover. In dreamland, she yelled at her sisters to keep away. "He's mine!" she cried. She awoke confused and angry. Angry at Peggy for what she'd done, angry at Kate for stirring everything up again. Angry at Jason, who was shaking her, demanding to know who was in her dreams.

9

PEGGY knew it was only a matter of time before she would have to visit Kate in her grandfather's old house. Kate had already been to see her and Bo twice.

"You know, it wouldn't take long to walk there, Peg. I could meet you halfway."

Peggy had distracted her with a comment about Bo being a lazy walker.

"Well, anyway, you don't have to worry about the bus," Kate said. "I'll come and pick you up."

She'd assured Peggy there was no alcohol in the house. They wouldn't go anywhere else. She wouldn't see anyone else—meaning specifically Aurora. It would just be the three of them.

"You don't think there's a chance the house is going to stir things up, that you'll ever make up more false memories, do you?"

"Oh God, no." Peggy sounded more assured than she felt.

Kate's move into Grandpa's house did stir up memories. Of course it did. But they weren't those old fake ones.

After being arrested for theft one too many times, Peggy had been ordered into rehab, and after her release, psychiatric treatment had been her punishment. Supposedly helping her to get through her addictions, the appointed psychiatrist had, instead, taken her on a journey to a world of recollections that were untrue. Through prescription medication and regression therapy, Peggy had ended up in a place just as bad as the one she'd come from, in a courtroom accusing her grandfather of rape when the evidence and timelines proved the accusations to be impossible.

Now, after years of untainted blood and sweet breath, Peggy's real memories had returned. There were blackout areas to be sure, but they were of more recent times: somehow conceiving a child in a dark back alley, shooting up on a secluded beach, roaming the streets with an unnamed newborn, crashing her car with a two-year-old Bo in the back seat. Those things were told to her or sometimes came to her in serial flashes in the middle of the night. But her childhood memories were clear and would have been delightful were it not for the fact they were tarnished by what she had done.

She worried that seeing Kate in that environment, and walking with her through Grandpa's garden, could mess with her mind. There was also the possibility that the guilt, if it rose up to slap her in the face again, could trigger the old longing for a sweet elixir to dissolve her tears. She lowered her guard to explain what roiled and rumbled inside her.

"First of all," Kate said, "you are forgetting what you've been told by the real psychiatrists and psychologists and social workers. You were not responsible. She was at best inexperienced, at worst a charlatan. And you know now what evil tricks drugs and alcohol can play on the mind."

"Aurora still thinks it's my fault."

"Aurora just doesn't understand."

Peggy knew that. She'd known it for years. She would be fighting an unwinnable battle if she ever thought Aurora could forgive her. She also knew from recent therapy that her happiness and her recovery were in no way dependent upon outside sources. It was all up to her.

All Peggy's excuses to not visit Grandpa's house had been negated, which was why Bo was bouncing in the driveway in the middle of a crisp morning waiting for his Auntie Kate to arrive in her nifty VW Golf. Such a funny car to see Kate in, Peggy thought. Through all her high-flying years away from home, Peggy knew Kate had driven—variously—a Mercedes, a BMW, and a top-of-the-range Audi and, for a time, had even slid in and out of the shiny upholstered seats of a chauffeured limo. So to see her swing her long legs from such an unpretentious car made Peggy smile.

Kate and Bo played games in the front seat on the drive while Peggy sat in the back, sweating a little and trying to ignore Kate surreptitiously checking on her in the rearview mirror every two minutes.

"I spy with my little eye something beginning with *s*," Kate said.

Peggy noticed her sister drove a block out of her way so as not to go via the courthouse. She didn't have the heart to tell Kate she went past it on her regular bus trip to the hospital. Mercifully, the office of Peggy's other psychiatrist—her preferred one, the one Kate had helped her find—was a mere three blocks from home with not one bar along the route, but there had been no escaping the need to visit the court-appointed therapist every three months.

"Sky," said Bo.

"Nope."

"I need a clue!"

"Come on, Bo. You've only had one guess."

He poked his head around the edge of the front seat. "Help, Mom. I can't think of anything."

Peggy smiled. "What about steering wheel?"

"That would be *s-w*." Bo's tone hinted at his exasperation.

Peggy went back to her thoughts. There were lots of rational reasons Kate had been in the house so long and they were only now paying a visit. In the first place, Kate had secured a job with Lilly and Sandringham not more than three weeks after settling in, and as was the norm with Kate, she'd immediately thrown herself into fourteen-hour days.

Peggy worked just fifteen hours a week as a cleaner at the local shopping center, three four-hour days and a three-hour stint on Saturday mornings, when her employers deliberately overlooked her eight-year-old helper. At times, Bo stayed home alone on Saturday mornings, lolling about in bed with his books or watching cartoons. Sometimes he rearranged his room or put decorative name tags on the inside covers of all his books.

Work, Bo, psychiatrists...no excuse had satisfied Kate.

Don't you drive yourself mad with all that time alone? Kate asked.

Peggy knew it would seem odd to someone like Kate that she could spend so much time in the house by herself and not get bored. For one thing, since her recovery, Peggy had become a fastidious cleaner. She could spend four hours scouring all the taps and basins in the house with a fine toothbrush, and it once took her a full day to clean two wrought-iron outdoor chairs.

Life in her rented home was regimented, clean, safe.

But there were things that occupied her mind and body as well. She wrote in her diary twice a day. More correctly, she wrote in a bona fide diary every morning. That diary was kept in her writing desk, and although she trusted Bo, there was nothing in there she would have been ashamed of him reading.

At night, however, she wrote in an exercise book; this record she kept in the false bottom of a chest at the back of her wardrobe. In the dark of night, when all was quiet, when Bo was well and truly asleep, she would write her deepest, darkest thoughts. Sometimes, when she had particularly difficult things to write, she would walk to the park on the corner or to the beach, lest her writings taint her happy home. There were things in there even her psychiatrist would be shocked to read.

The burning to write in her secret books was like yet another addiction. She'd feel the anger roil inside her as the urge to get her hands on a pen raged; then her heart would race alarmingly as she scribbled, the poison spewing from her in a stream of hatred. Immediately after, there'd be a surge of relief as she returned the book to its hiding place, closely followed by shame.

Scrapbooks were piled high on the bureau, weighty portfolios marking Bo's milestones and achievements, for they were her milestones too.

Most recently, distance-learning studies kept her deeply engaged, but dipping her toe into the alien world of academia was not something she'd yet discussed with Kate or anyone else. Except for her psychiatrist, Dr. Leichardt. Only the doctor and Bo knew that she'd done a year of preparatory work, that she had sailed through an entrance exam, and that she was now studying to become an accountant.

"Shoes." Bo's voice showed he was becoming impatient with "I spy."

"No." Kate continued to check her out in the review mirror.

Peggy thought she might tell her big sister about her studies. She would see how the day panned out.

She was looking forward to seeing Grandpa's garden. No matter the season, it was a sight to behold: the splashes of pink from the flowers of the *Autumnalis Rosea* that Peggy always thought was called "Rosie's tree"; the creamy fragrance of the semi-evergreen honeysuckle shrubs; and the dark-green spine-toothed leaves of the evergreen japonica.

"Come on, Auntie Kate. I need a clue."

"Well. Let's see. 'Shoes' was very close."

"I know! 'Smiles.'"

"Now I ask you, young Bo. How is that close to 'shoes'?"

He laughed. "I wasn't thinking properly." He looked down at his shoes pensively for a moment. "Ah. You spy with your little eye something beginning with *s*? 'Socks'!"

"You got it, buddy." Kate turned off the main road, and the Golf snaked its way up the familiar winding street. "And in perfect time too."

"Which one is it?" Bo asked, reminding Peggy he had never been here before.

"You can't see it yet, but that's the garage straight ahead."

Peggy knew her delightfully thoughtful son would be itching to say something complimentary to Kate about her house. He understood how important it was to her. "Oh, great! An automatic garage door," he said as the black door concertina'd up inside, and Peggy smiled.

From the trunk, they hoisted the lunch basket Peggy had insisted on packing, along with the belated housewarming present: a set of scented bathroom candles. They followed their hostess through the side door of the garage, emerging onto a pathway, framed with camellias of every conceivable color combination, that snaked its way down to join the main steps leading to the portico. The purple, pink, and white flowers of the various Scottish heather ground cover made a soft carpet.

Bo inspected the furry tan buds on the Michelia.

"Just wait until you see them in bloom, Bo. They are glorious." Kate turned and placed her arm around Peggy's shoulders. "Do you remember, little Peg?"

Yes, she remembered. The sweet perfume of those precious white flowers was not something easily forgotten. The two sisters stood back and watched Bo seeing this garden for the first time. Peggy stared at the deep green of the rhododendron leaves and the bright pink splashes of color painted by a few early blooms, providing a contrast to the light pink stars of blossom on the distant cherry tree.

She held her breath when they walked through the front door and into the hallway, surveyed the lounge and then the French doors, and sighed. This wasn't half bad at all.

"I'm going to rebuild the wall here," Kate was saying.

"Really? Must you?"

Peggy loved it the way it was. Much more open and inviting. Just like Grandpa. Her eyes smarted. She replayed the mantra Dr. Leichardt had helped her to memorize.

It wasn't me. I didn't know what was happening. It wasn't my fault.

She had loved her grandfather, surely. Standing in his house now—Kate's house—she imagined he might be looking down on them and he would have forgiven her.

A tiny kernel in her brain fought against the calm, begging her to answer the question: Had *she* forgiven *him*? Why should she need forgiveness and not him? Her memories might not have been real, but they were sparked by something.

One part of her hated Kate for buying this house, hated Aurora for stubbornly refusing to acknowledge anything remotely unpleasant, let alone terrifying, about their early lives. She rubbed at her eyes erratically, subconsciously trying to erase the thoughts and images coming to her like flashes from a horror movie.

Her fingers itched to wrap themselves around a pen, to spread like vomit over the page the words she could not say.

10

SHE always looked for that glimpse of understanding, a flicker of fear in their eyes marking the moment of no return. Usually the drive of frantic sex meant they were looking right through her. She was a mere vehicle carrying them to their satisfaction destination.

It always arrived, that moment. The startled lightning bolt as they realized there'd be no coming back from this.

He was close, writhing beneath her, a slave to her whims.

But what was this? His eyes blurred. He stopped his frantic humping and looked at her, really looked, as though he were boring down into her soul. He whispered something, something about beauty.

Her mind wandered. She imagined lifting from him, saw herself uncuffing him and releasing the ties around his ankles. He'd place his arms at her hips. He'd pull himself to a sitting position and kiss her neck tenderly.

I love you.

For a second, she was sure it had happened, sure he'd whispered those words to her. The confusion rocked her and she stilled.

"You all right?" His voice was gentle.

She grabbed the tape. Slammed a strip over his mouth.

Lying fucking bastard.

Time for him to pay for his trickery. Time for him to know there was no way out. Lying and cheating would not help him out of this predicament.

Bewilderment flooded his eyes, locked with hers.

She searched around behind him.

When he saw the knife, his body began to spasm. He tried to move sideways, to curl away, to diminish himself.

But it was too little, too late.

She worked fast, at once feverish and single-minded. The blade caught on a rib and the pressure on that bone threatened to defeat her, but she lifted herself and used the full weight of her body to press forward and down. The blade slid away from the resistance and slipped, spongelike, deep into his body.

Her face was so close to his, and she saw his confusion turn to a flutter of acceptance.

When it was over, when those moments of frantic bucking and buckling had passed, when a final sigh escaped from those cruel lips, she sat for a few quiet seconds, drinking in the sight of him, limp and powerless.

Then she rallied. Remembered the work still to be done.

Cut. Snip. Shift. Snip. Cut.
She stood back to reflect. Grinned.
Man, deconstructed.

11

KATE felt drained.

The whole day had been filled with speculation about murder. About the possibility of the two recent murders having been committed by the same person. It had started with newspaper headlines attempting to build links. There'd even been mention of a case from a couple of years ago.

It was no surprise the press was keen to focus on the salacious, such as the use of handcuffs and anything they could find to link the victims to the underbelly of society. There were quotes from those in the loose and free surf culture, hinting at debauched beach parties. A neighbor of the latest victim seemed intent on telling anyone who would listen about the "depraved" clubs the man frequented.

The sexual undertones of the linked crimes had been hinted at by the mainstream press, despite the fact that the police seemed to be placing more emphasis on the knife skills evidenced by unspecified mutilation. For those reading between the lines, there was little doubt the killer showcased an entrenched anger.

Both Kate's bosses had sources within the police department, but neither of them was keen to share widely what they'd learned. They were more focused on presenting arguments about the legality and moral responsibility of the reporting, standard lawyerly banter.

The office discussions had moved to water-cooler nonsense about unsubstantiated claims. Then, of course, came the usual keyboard warriors on social media, flinging their wild conjecture out into the world.

Kate grew weary of the talk.

She was also sick and tired of her dysfunctional family, of a childhood she couldn't seem to make sense of.

She'd hankered to see Aurora and Peggy together, talking and laughing as real sisters should, dangling their legs over the stone ledge in front of the Climbing Pinkie roses, drinking tea, reminiscing. The reality, she knew, would be nothing like that. The conversation would be spiteful; they'd argue about what did or did not happen.

Should any of the sisters wish to dissect their childhood again, to finally discover why they had spent so much time at their grandparents, they'd have to do it without the help of their mother, who, since her stroke, had languished in the nursing home with no will to get better. Kate sometimes wished her father was still alive so maybe she could place some of the blame where it belonged. No sooner had the thought escaped than she tucked it back into the past where it was safe.

Whenever she'd tried to analyze her feelings about her father, she found herself stuck in a maze, struggling to find a way out. Yes, he was largely absent. Yes, he was reticent, perhaps cold. But was that enough to create the unease with which she approached her memories of him? When he died, she'd had the sensation of a taut rope snapping inside her, an uncoiled something that ricocheted around her insides until she felt she would go insane.

Most often, she tried not to think of him at all, to remain remote as he'd always seemed to be with her.

Mother, pre-stroke, had been so tight and stiff that no one could comfort her. Kate had never stopped wondering if it was grief that kept her mother bound like that or something else. Relief perhaps? In Kate's ignorance, she'd thought Peggy moving in with their mother might have felled two flies with a single slap, so to speak. Peggy had been, by then, eighteen months into her wild years, what Kate had thought at the time was little more than a bit of rebellious nonsense.

"She'll grow out of it," she'd told Aurora then.

Karina Rowling had her stroke just a few months later, and then came another of Aurora's phone calls, this time dropping Peggy's bombshell.

"She's off the drugs and booze," Aurora had said.

Kate's heart had lifted. "That's fantast—"

"Wait! She's off the stuff, and she's under the care of a psychiatrist."

"How wonderful..."

"For God's sake, Kate, let me finish! She's accusing Grandpa of hideous things. Molestation, abuse, physical, mental, and sexual."

"What?" It was all Kate could do to keep breathing. "What?"

"I don't have all the details yet. The way it's coming across, she thinks Grandpa tried to kill her."

"Grandpa? But that's..."

"Ridiculous. Yes. But somehow this disgusting excuse for a psychiatrist has used all sorts of radical techniques, and under a form of hypnosis, Peggy has dragged these obviously fake memories from somewhere."

Kate felt an evil breath at the nape of her neck. "Hang on, Aurora. Is there any chance there's some truth behind it?"

"No! Peggy's mixed up time frames, and it's clearly impossible."

"Nothing's impossible," Kate said, ignoring Aurora's tone. There was something cold, almost vicious there. Instead, she adjusted her law-skewed cap. "Let's not forget that victims can easily become confused."

"She's not a victim," Aurora spat.

"Any one of us could be a victim," Kate said cryptically.

"For heaven's sake, can you just listen? She's saying she was tied up and put in a box, that she was raped. How on earth could she blame Grandpa?"

Kate had felt the bile rise to her throat, swallowed hard. "What are we going to do?"

"We! *We?*" Aurora's hysteria was clearly building. "I don't know what *we* will be doing. Perhaps if you could get your ass over here, you might be able to talk some sense into her."

By the time Kate had returned, the legal wheels were in motion and she was allowed to see Peggy only in the company of the court-appointed liaison.

Kate's stomach dropped and her heart ached when she walked into the courthouse waiting room. Peggy, pale and sunken, sat flanked by a nurse and a psychiatrist. When Kate had tried to gently indicate the memories might not be all real, Peggy started to rock backward and forward. She screamed and cursed.

So Kate had done the only thing she could. She'd engaged the best legal minds available to represent her grandfather, who seemed shocked and terrified by what was happening. It was only their combined money—Kate's, together with Aurora's and Jason's—and their fervent assurances that had kept their grandfather out of jail during the trial.

It was hard enough to listen to the charges and the flimsy case the prosecution put forward, but the cross-examination of Peggy was brutal.

"And where were your sisters during these so-called attacks?"

Peggy's eyes had darted around the courtroom but failed to latch on to either of her sisters. "Sometimes they were out. Maybe in the garden?"

"And why didn't you report the abuse to your mother and father when you went home after the holidays?"

That line of questioning made Kate furious. Non-reporting was a typical victim response, and she'd told the defense lawyers there was absolutely no need to go for the jugular, as Peggy's accusations had already been disproved. But they charged like bulls, needling Peggy until she was defeated, until she folded further and further into herself. She'd begun to ramble about their father being dead when, at the time of the alleged abuse, he was very much alive. The confusion and agitation accelerated. Time had lost relativity. Peggy couldn't even remember her sisters' names. It was a mess.

Despite their grandfather's exoneration, there were people who would not acknowledge him, neighbors who for years had accepted cuttings from his garden and purchased glorious handmade clocks from him at ridiculously cheap prices, shopkeepers who went to great lengths to avoid serving him. Teenagers threw stones at his house; someone cut off the heads of his three remaining hens.

Kate tried to comfort him. She tried to stand in solidarity with Aurora, but there was something broken among them all, inside of them all, so she did what she always had: she ran away.

Aurora had fumed. *Yes, that's right. You go and cavort on that rickety old boat.*

The *rickety old boat* in question was actually a sturdy and majestic replica ship, built of jarrah below the waterline and Oregon above. Its twenty-plus sails were complemented with six-cylinder diesel motors, generators, and other comforting trappings of modern life. Kate had gone on a coastal jaunt, along with an idealistic and very sensual Frenchman.

As always when problems surfaced, she indulged in reckless behavior, drinking copious amounts of Cointreau and stumbling about on deck, eventually falling overboard.

They were moored at the time, not sailing the high seas as she sometimes imagined; otherwise the outcome might have been a whole lot different. She thought she'd stumbled, was sure she remembered that. Sometimes, though, she dreamt she'd purposefully jumped, thought she'd felt the breath of ghosts at her back.

Whatever the truth of it, she'd found herself somewhere too dark to comprehend. Something deep and innate within her had fought valiantly against her body's knee-jerk reaction to the cold, which was to gasp for breath when there was no air to be had. Her reactions, dulled by the devilish orange liqueur, left her rolling end over end for one turn too many until she was deep enough in that dark, alien underwater world to lose the direction of the surface.

For a time—Kate had no idea how long—she'd imagined surrendering to the realm of the sea and accepting a watery grave. She questioned if she was mired in sin, if she was deliberately quashing memories and truths herself. She questioned who her solidarity should be aligned with. She questioned her own worth.

Sanity had prevailed when the feisty, adventure-seeking, resilient Kate took over and she'd lunged back to the surface to drag in a lungful of sweet oxygen.

Even after that scare, she'd still not had her fill of foolish behavior, so she'd thrown in yet another perfectly good job to run away with an Italian stallion who broke her heart just a little more. By the time she'd gotten it all out of her system, her grandfather was settled into his new unit, and it had been too late for Kate to even think about raising money to purchase the house that meant so much to her.

Peggy was, by then, pregnant and off the rails again.

"Who's the father?" Kate asked her.

"Don't know."

"How will you care for the baby?"

"Don't care."

Aurora had given birth to her second child, a son who was the spitting image of his father, and there'd been no point in broaching the subject of Peggy with her.

Kate admitted that a better sister would have nursed Peggy through, tried to keep her off the booze that had reared its ugly head again after the court case and that everyone thought must have damaged the fetus. A good sister would have been there for the birth, would have offered to take the baby, to care for it. But Kate wasn't strong enough. She wasn't equipped to deal with booze and drugs and mental illness, let alone a baby—damaged or otherwise—so, once again, she'd retreated to the hustle and bustle of big-city life and thrown herself into the corporate arena. The movers and shakers in the world of law were always prepared to overlook her instability in the face of such raw talent.

She once received a note from a retired prominent judge, saying Kate's charisma in front of a jury was *nothing short of spectacular*. A copy slipped into the back of her résumé never failed to impress.

There seemed little point dredging up the past to analyze her motives. Yes, she could have been a better sister, done a better job of looking after her siblings. But it was done. Ultimately, the three of them were the product of their upbringing, and any guilt should be borne by their parents.

Every time she managed to put thoughts of her family to one side, they were replaced by the details of recent murders so that, tired as she was, she couldn't resist trawling the net for more details. The information available pointed to a sick mind, and that sick mind was lurking in their vicinity.

12

SHE wondered how long she'd have to wait for them to discover her latest handiwork. She had enjoyed the sensation caused by the discovery of Henry. The nightly news anchor, grim-faced, reported the murder in scant detail, but it was enough for her to relive the finer points. Again, it was nothing like the way she'd felt after The Man. That murder had been so thrilling.

Her days alternated between remembering and not. Sometimes, she'd read a news article and feel no connection to the murderer at all. Other times, she'd remember what she had done and search for details in the papers. A couple of articles referred to the killer as a man. *It would appear* he *could have been known to the victim... the young surfer was possibly lured by* him *to the deserted boat shed...* he *must have planned the murder.* He. He. He. For God's sake, she railed.

In lucid moments, she knew the investigators would have

strong evidence that the killer was female, despite her cleanup efforts. She wondered why the media hadn't caught on. Perhaps the police were playing their cards close to the chest.

Given the circumstances surrounding that old case, it had been understandable they'd all jumped to conclusions. The Man, as it happened, was a closet bisexual who had once been the subject of blackmail, so it hadn't been a huge stretch.

But Henry was different, and she thought she'd made it pretty obvious. Hello? His dick was cut off! Possibility this crime was committed by a female? She imagined there'd be little doubt when they discovered the latest one, also sans cock.

A few bright sparks had already caught on to the possibility—and, in one local identity's case, the probability—that the crimes had been committed by a female.

SATAN'S HANDMAIDEN OR THE DEVIL INCARNATE?

Congressman Paul Margate caused a stir at yesterday's media conference when he referred to the killer of promising young surfer Henry Macinaine as "Satan's Handmaiden."

When asked if he possessed information that would lead to such a conclusion, the congressman admitted to being privy to some of the case details and that evidence did point to the strong likelihood the killer was a woman.

Police officials still refuse to speculate on the gender of the murderer or on a possible motive.

The article had excited her and frightened her at the same time. As she mulled over precisely what information the police might have, she wondered if she had covered her tracks adequately. She wasn't foolish enough to think she'd been able to remove everything. A condom had been a necessity—the thought of a narcissistic man like Henry impregnating her almost made her hurl—and she'd disposed of it in the ocean. What might she have left behind?

She consoled herself with the possibility they had simply decided to use their pea-size man brains to deduce the feminine justice that had been meted out by way of a severed cock. Still, she was torn between her desire not to get caught and her wish for the police and the newspapers to find a connection between her victims.

It was some weeks before scant details were released about the latest killing. She wondered if he was from some important family, with relatives wanting to keep sordid details kept away from the media.

Years ago, during the time when she had followed the newspaper reports on The Man's murder, she'd thought a lot about him. She knew his name then. She saw it in print so often she thought it would be etched indelibly on her brain. But how forgettable he had turned out to be. She hadn't thought about The Man for many years and sometimes she doubted if any of it had truly happened. Certainly, for a while, she had no recollection of having played any part in the incident.

It was only when an all-encompassing hunger came upon her that she had begun to think of him again at all. She had hoped Henry's death would be far more satisfying and that he would have surpassed The Man. The truth of it was, she had to admit, he'd only caused the dry thirst for blood and the ache for the joy of death to increase within her. So she'd killed again and was already planning the next one.

She wasn't a bad person. Maybe if she went around killing good, noble women, then perhaps she would deserve the title Satan's Handmaiden, but the more she dwelled on it, the more she began to think of herself as a Good Samaritan.

God's little angel.

The sort of work she was undertaking was necessary. There was no point in sitting around bemoaning the male scum that walked the earth, causing havoc with their lies and their wants and their sick needs. There was work to be done, and she realized that while she had been trying to control her desire for blood, she had been leaving other—softer, weaker, more timid—women to carry the burden. No one else—at least not in her region—was stepping forward to take up the mantle, to weed out these men. She could see now that the work would be hers alone. It would be time-consuming, lonely, and sometimes difficult. Not the killing; the killing was easy. Oh, so easy. But the planning, and the covering of tracks. That was the hard part.

She also knew it was time to be smart. She sometimes had trouble controlling her urges. Every time she started to scope out a new man for a kill, a primal need overcame her. She imagined herself literally fucking them to death, these poor excuses for human beings, and the excitement of such thoughts would lead to the fantasy of sucking their blood. She loved the metallic taste of it, its viscous qualities. Often, she would black out and completely forget she even had a mission.

Sometimes she'd wake from a dream so real she had to check the news to convince herself it had only been a fantasy. In dreamland, she had the time and the privacy to spend days torturing her victims. These repulsive men would do anything to save their own skins. In dreamland, she sliced pieces of their skin using the ivory-handled filleting knife she'd long ago disposed of, and she would hang those morsels of fine prosciutto-like meat out to dry. She would pierce these men and suck at their blood and watch their fear turn to complete horror. In dreamland, no one heard them scream.

In her fantasies, she had rid the earth of hundreds of the animals. In reality, it had been only four, and that was nowhere near enough. The first one was so long ago it was now only a vague memory. She was so young then, and her only weapons had been a can of fuel and a match.

Her second victim, The Man, with his peccadilloes he shared with people other than his wife, had been a blight, a piece of rancid gum or stinking dog shit stuck to humanity's sole.

She'd tried to stop after that. But then, after a long break, came Henry.

Henry didn't have a wife and children, but he did have a mother who he no doubt abused with his selfishness. Even Henry's mother, who they showed on the television, with her dark glasses and her lace handkerchief and her twisted, anguished mouth... even she would one day secretly thank the person who'd killed her son. When the mother realized she did not have to watch him prancing around her house with coltish abandon, draining her energy with his chore-inducing way of life, she would smile. The mother would lift her lips in secret delight in the middle of the night, and maybe sometimes when no one was around to hear her, she might even chuckle, realizing she was a mother unburdened, a mother saved. Besides, Toots had been returned; surely a dog would be better company.

Weeks after Henry's death, and after the discovery of the other asshole whose name constantly escaped her, a local paper showcased an article—ostensibly unrelated—by some enterprising journalist. "Women Who Kill" was the headline, K.R. Carstead the author. The writer was also a hotshot profiler who spoke of the propensity for a certain type of woman to be easily led into becoming so deeply involved in men's fantasies as to be willing to rape and kill and maim for them, "Lonely Hearts" who were so desperate to be loved they would fall into relationships built on kinky sex and black magic and who were almost hypnotized when they performed their dastardly deeds.

How dare they? Why did these "experts" always jump to conclusions about the superior evil mind of the man? She would have to come up with a way to show them she was no one's handmaiden—not even the devil's.

She ran her fingers over the headline. "Women Who Kill." Was K.R. Carstead a man? If so, he was a dead man walking.

13

AURORA waited until Jason was at work and the kids at school before she opened the packs of walnut planks. Mimi caressed her ankles, slipping in and out and around Aurora's legs in a perpetual figure eight. Leo, fat and lazy, was curled into a gray ball on his blanket.

She laid the planks side by side, tenderly, noting their fine quality, the exact half-inch thickness. The grain of the walnut perfectly matched the basic cabinet her grandfather had already built. The timber was well aged, to be sure, but it was nothing that sandpaper and lacquer, good old-fashioned elbow grease, and a lot of tender loving care wouldn't correct.

She expected the project would take two to three months to complete, wonderfully timed for the perfect Christmas present for Kate.

Her grandfather used to make his own patterns for curved panels and rails, but knowing she lacked his eye and experience, Aurora worked from templates she ordered online. She'd been itching for weeks to start cutting but heard her grandfather's voice constantly.

Let it come organically, Aurora. Feel the wood. Smell it.

A friend of Jason's had lent her a bandsaw, which she now used to follow the line of the template. The sawdust smelled like Grandpa, a man who'd been big on Christmases; at least he had when Nan was alive. His workshop had been home to many other projects besides the clocks, and in the lead-up to Christmas, his majestic measures of time had been set aside for other projects. One year she remembered well was the year of the shadowbox or, more correctly, the knickknack shelf.

Can you help me in the shed later, Aurora? Grandpa asked one morning on the precipice of Christmas as they stood at the back porch watching Kate take some feed into the henhouse.

It was an unusual request; Aurora spent so much time in the work shed, her grandfather had never seen the need to invite her before.

This standing on the porch early in the morning, just the two of them, watching Kate feed the chickens, was yet one more of their holiday rituals. Grandpa always pushed his top lip out and blew on his mug of hot coffee, and Aurora would imitate him, despite her mug holding cold milk. The grandfather would rock on the balls of his feet, and the granddaughter would do the same. This was in the days before Peggy was born, or it might have been when Peggy was really young. Peggy didn't start coming with her older sisters until she was about two. Before that, the baby Peggy had accompanied her parents on their overseas jaunts.

Most mornings, breakfast consumed and poultry fed, Kate would hang off Nan's apron strings for a while, learning to cook, or they'd spend time in the garden while Aurora headed off to the shed with Grandpa. Hard to fathom that, now they were grown up. People generally thought of Kate as a bit of a tomboy: career-focused, childless, sporty, and adventure-seeking, while Aurora was the "girly" one. She chose an early career in interior design and found great joy in motherhood. Her musical instrument, the harp, was strongly feminine.

As children, the two girls and, a few years later, the three of them, had spent much of their time together: in the tree fort Grandpa built at the bottom of the garden or lying on the lush patches of grass picking out cloud shapes and inventing stories. Sometimes if Nan was busy in the garden and out of earshot, the girls would run inside to the hall cupboard and pull out the old electric floor polisher Nan had inherited from her own mother and refused to update. They'd let little Peggy stand on it as they whizzed it around the kitchen and along the uncarpeted hallway. When they were old enough, the sisters would spend hours at the beach, making castles with moats and digging enormous channels to capture the water. But most often when they were at the house, it was usual to find Peg playing with dolls, Kate either baking or climbing trees, and Aurora building things with their grandfather in the shed.

So it had been odd, that morning, for Grandpa to have specifically invited Aurora to the shed, and she'd looked up at him questioningly. He'd continued to blow on his coffee. She blew on her milk and mimicked his rocking motion and, only then, did she notice two of the fingers on his right hand were bandaged together.

"What happened to your hand, Grandpa?"

"Nicked it with the saw yesterday," he said, then laughed when Aurora tutted. He was always cautioning her to watch where her fingers were, check the angle of the saw, calculate its trajectory.

His taped fingers made it difficult for him to grasp the block plane to profile the fins he'd painstakingly measured and cut out with his "newfangled" miter saw. The interlocking fins would clip into each other to form a series of tiny block shelves to hold Nan's miniature hand-painted ornaments.

Almost thirty years later, as Aurora used a router to shape the first piece of walnut for the ornamental pelmet of her grandfather clock, she was amazed she could remember that day so clearly. Now, as she sanded the walnut piece, first with the orbital sander and then more gently by hand, she recalled how nervous she was when Grandpa had allowed her to even out the edges of the fins. Of course, he didn't have much choice. There had been just days to go before Christmas, and this was his gift to the woman who held his heart and insisted on inexpensive but thoughtful gifts.

Grandpa didn't really need Aurora the following day—he was able to hold the brush adequately to varnish the shelving—but, as always, he invented things for her to do.

"See how tightly you can work the clamp onto that block of wood," he told her.

Standing on top of an overturned wooden crate, she had grunted and groaned as she pushed the silver lever up to twelve o'clock and then leaned on it, pushing it clockwise down to half past, before pulling it back up and wrenching it down again. "What are you going to do with it Grandpa?"

"I need you to bang a nail into it."

She smiled now, bringing the walnut piece—gradually taking shape—to her nose, occasionally to soak in the aroma of her youth, recalling it was a few years after that Christmas before she thought to question what had happened to all those scraps of wood with nails hammered into them and how he'd had to show her the big box on top of the Meccano-like shelving unit where he put them *until we need them*.

Aurora couldn't remember a Christmas spent in her own home with her parents. There were a couple of Christmases when her parents had joined them at Nan and Grandpa's, but they were usually overseas. Sometimes, they were off doing good deeds for Community Aid: Father acting as a consultant on building projects like bridges and pipelines, Mother teaching English to children. Other times, they were lazing about on Hawaiian beaches or trekking in mountains. She knew her parents loved her, despite the fact they weren't overly demonstrative, but it seemed Nan and Grandpa loved the children more, or perhaps needed them more. Whatever the reasons, Aurora was never sorry. Many of her happy childhood memories revolved around her grandparents.

"Oh, it's beautiful!" Nan was besotted with Grandpa's workmanship that year.

"It's a shadowbox," Aurora said proprietarily, feeling somewhat responsible for its completion.

Kate jumped straight into things as she usually did. "That's not a shadowbox! A real shadowbox has a..."

Nan's eyes widened. "You are mistaken, Kate.

"Finest shadowbox I have ever seen," she said to Grandpa, and then she blew him a kiss from her big green club chair in the corner to his spot near the Christmas tree where he sat on a tiny stool wearing an oversize Santa's hat. Nan had told Grandpa of a shadowbox she'd seen and admired, and he had apparently misinterpreted her description. The knickknack shelving unit he'd made was his interpretation. Nan so much loved the man who made it for her that the knickknack box became a shadowbox, and if anyone used the wrong terminology, she would always "correct" them.

"What happened to Nan's shadowbox?" Aurora asked her grandfather years later when she went to visit him in his tiny apartment.

"It went to the Salvos. It wasn't really a shadowbox, you know."

She had been standing next to her grandfather at the kitchen counter and noticed that his hand shook as he poured the tea. "I know. But I thought you always believed it was."

"Kate told me it was a knickknack shelf," he said. "She showed me a picture of a real shadowbox."

Aurora was surprised that her older sister would have done such a thing. It seemed so cruel after so many years. "When did she tell you?"

"Day after Christmas."

She'd tried to remember the last time Kate had been home for Christmas. "Which Christmas?"

There was a touch of sadness beneath Grandpa's chuckle. "The day after I gave it to your Nan."

Aurora smiled ruefully. All those years, they'd called it a shadowbox so as not to hurt his feelings—even Kate!—and yet the error had been outed the day after Christmas.

She smiled again now as she packed up her work for the day: the first precious piece of walnut, now fashioned into a beautifully curved pelmet for the top of the clock, went into the old wooden case, together with the templates and wood offcuts; the other planks were wrapped in a sheet and stacked in the corner. She moved the portable workbench to its position against the wall and wrapped up the extension cord.

She could remember the presents she had received for Christmas in the year of the shadowbox. Her parents had left a gift for her: a painting of two Japanese children holding hands with a mustached man in a garden. Aurora had despised that painting; there was something about the man that made her skin crawl. Nan and Grandpa had given her a tool belt with a real chisel, screwdrivers, a red-handled hammer, and tiny boxes of assorted nails and screws. From Kate she'd received a Barbie-type doll—a scaled-down, cheaper version of the real thing—with white high-heeled shoes and a white ball gown, together with a pack to change the doll into a tennis player.

Aurora started to wrap the longcase in its flannel sheet, pausing as she did to inspect the perfect joints and run her hand over the rabbet her grandfather had cut so many years ago, providing the ledge on which a piece of glass could be accommodated. Tears stabbed at her eyelids.

Oh, Grandpa.

She had tried to reach out to him in the years after Peggy had shredded his heart, but he'd wandered around like a half-dead man, working his garden joylessly until he couldn't stand living in the house any longer. Well before his death, he had become a mere shell of his former self.

Outwardly, the rest of Aurora's afternoon was standard: an hour at the harp (her favorite addiction), dredging her memory so she could assist with Grant's math homework, browsing dresses on eBay with Stella, roasting a chicken and preparing a persimmon mousse for dinner, followed by the increasingly familiar argument with Jason.

"You're just not here with me, with us. Even when you're physically here, you seem to be a million miles away, like you were back when..."

"Leave it, Jason. Please."

She tried to explain that her focus was on getting the clock finished, but she knew there was more to it than that. While she was working on the clock, she was able to immerse herself in good memories, alleviating the internal conflict she often felt that had increased since Kate's return. It stopped her from fixating on the mess Peggy had made of everything, stopped her from thinking about Kate in their grandfather's house, opening up old questions. And it stopped her from thinking of other things that had no place in her present life.

14

PEGGY had begun to feel some fraying at the edges of her perfectly ordered life, and something in her laid the blame at the feet of her sisters. Before Kate returned, Peggy had come to a space and place in her life where she could enjoy a stroll along memory lane, where reminiscing had become less fearful. She knew she should be thankful that Kate had never given up on her like Aurora had, but at the same time, she was angry with her big sister for buying that house and stirring everything up again.

Unlike Aurora's, Peggy's Christmas memories were not about clocks or work sheds or even, for that matter, presents. Almost all her reflections of the festive season were centered on food.

Peggy loved food, and food was kind to her. It didn't matter how much she ate, her weight never altered, something that had always irritated Kate and Aurora. As a teenager, Aurora had ballooned and dieted with groundhog-day regularity. The only thing that had kept Kate from the puberty fat blues was relentless sport. Aurora's adult body was now kept slim because she ate like a bird. Kate's was lean and muscular because she was always in some state of action. Peggy's boyish lines, however, were natural, bequeathed to her by her maternal grandmother, a woman she had never met. Everything else about Peggy's appearance came from her father and her father's father. *Spitting image*, her mother used to say every time she looked at Peggy.

On her Saturday shift, Peggy chatted with the center manager, Mariana, for almost half an hour.

"You drink coffee, Peggy?" Mariana had called from her office doorway. "I've got a spare cappuccino in here. Took one whiff," she said, handing the cup to Peggy and motioning her to sit, "and almost puked."

Mariana talked fast like a New Yorker but without the accent. "Think I must be pregnant again," she said as she jiggled a tea bag inside an oversize mug with pictures of frogs on it.

In the time it took Peggy to drink her coffee, she learned Mariana already had three children and she'd not planned on having any more. "Don't get me wrong," she said. "I'm thrilled, actually. Just surprised." Mariana and her husband relied on what Peggy thought was a ludicrous scheme called the rhythm method for birth control.

"Yeah, I know," Mariana said wryly. "Not exactly high-tech, is it? But Dario is Catholic." She sipped her tea as she pushed the cookie tin across the desk, motioning Peggy to eat. "You look like you could do with a feed."

Peggy helped herself to a couple of gingersnaps.

"Coffee is the first thing I go off," Mariana said. "Then fruit. Give me another week, I'll barely be able to stand the sight of a banana or an apple."

Peggy was bemused. "All fruit?"

"Yup. Oh! Except dried. Love raisins and dried apricots."

Talk of dried fruit reminded Peggy of the Christmas puddings Kate used to make. She wondered if she made them still. Although Nan was a vague memory for Peggy, Aurora used to talk about how Kate spent so much time in the kitchen with their grandmother. Every September, Nan and Kate would bustle about mixing ingredients with wooden spoons in huge stainless-steel bowls. The next day, they'd hang little pudding balls wrapped in calico from hooks in the hall cupboard. For three months, all the towels and linen got stuffed into any other available storage area in the house, the shelving in the hall cupboard was removed, and the whole space would be chock-a-block with puddings. And every year at the start of the Christmas holidays, Kate and Nan would take one of the puddings and, just the two of them behind the closed kitchen door, unwrap the cloth with hushed whispers and sighs as they tasted the rich, groggy pudding.

Although Peggy could remember when Nan and Kate had made them together, she mostly just remembered Kate laboring over the recipe, making them exactly as she'd been taught.

"I've never had ones like that," Mariana said when Peggy described the miniature balls wrapped individually in calico and left hanging for months.

"Me neither."

Peggy jolted and turned at the sound of a male voice. It was the maintenance manager, he of the high forehead and alabaster skin, leaning against the doorframe.

"Hello, Denton." She'd only spoken to him once or twice but she never forgot his name. He was a dead ringer for an Australian journalist by the name of Andrew Denton who she'd seen on TV with Robert Plant and Jimmy Page from Led Zeppelin. Both Dentons shared a slight build and receding hairline, even wearing the same style of circular soft-framed glasses.

Peggy had dreamt about him a little over a week ago, and the memory brought a faint pink tint to her cheeks.

"What do you reckon, Denton?" Mariana plowed on, thankfully oblivious to Peggy's blush. "I think Miss Peggy ought to make puddings for our Christmas party."

Peggy remained outwardly calm, but the word *party* always set off alarm bells these days. Coupled with *Christmas*, it sounded like her worst nightmare. For years, she'd managed to avoid any hint of a party, and it hadn't occurred to her that joining the workforce would bring social obligations.

"Sounds perfect," Denton said, before abruptly shifting the conversation. "Did you hear there was another murder near the beach?"

"Another one?" Mariana sat bolt upright. "Near here again?"

Peggy willed her shoulders not to slump, tried to keep her expression neutral.

"Shit, Peggy. You've gone as white as a ghost." Denton pushed his lean body away from the doorframe and moved toward her seat. "I'm sorry," he said. "I shouldn't have started talking about killings."

Peggy held up her hand to keep him outside of her space. "I'm fine, I'm fine."

Mariana, generally not big on insight, continued on regardless. "Back to puddings. Just thinking about Christmas pudding, absolutely oozing rum and all things decadent, gets me excited."

Denton laughed. "Wouldn't matter how much rum you put in those puddings, Peg; it would never be enough to satisfy our Mariana. You should have seen her last year."

Peggy told herself to just keep breathing. Don't think about murders. Don't think about alcohol.

"Oh, don't start!" Mariana looked at Peggy sheepishly. "He loves telling stories about my drunken behavior."

Peggy's stomach became more squeamish by the minute. What on earth had possessed her to talk about alcohol-flavored puddings. For a second, she could actually taste brandy on her tongue. The back of her throat held on to it like a memory.

"All those stories are true," Denton said. "I'm the only one who doesn't drink. So I get to tell them all in excruciating detail of their sins. Like when Mariana told the big boss his lips were very kissable, and then there was the time she told Tom he was a boring old fart who should..."

"Enough!" Mariana held up both hands in mock surrender. "You won't have any more stories to add this year. I think I'm pregnant again, so it'll be no sauce for me."

Peggy took a deep breath. "I won't be able to come to the party, I'm afraid."

"But we haven't set the date yet," Mariana said.

"Anyway, one thing at a time," Denton said. "Congratulations are in order, surely?"

Mariana was easily distracted, as always. "It's not confirmed, but yes, I'm pretty sure. Number four. Here we go again!"

Peggy took the opportunity to glance at her watch and scramble from the chair. "God, look at the time. I'd better get back to work."

Mariana motioned to stop her, her chatty frame of mind unaltered, but Denton waylaid his boss with talk of supplies and problems with the new storage-room locks while Peggy slipped through the door, grabbed her bucket, and ran to the restroom.

She locked herself in a cubicle and rested her forehead against the cool, graffiti-chiseled wall, concentrating on every breath, listening to her heartbeat, wondering why—after four years—such exchanges could still be so hard. When would it become easy? When would she be able to socialize? Would she ever be able to flirt and banter and maybe share a meal with a man like Denton? Everything was tarnished by this insidious desire. Even something as simple as making Christmas puddings from her grandmother's recipe was impossible.

But that wasn't all there was to it, she admitted. She'd felt herself unraveling for a while, but she'd been doing fine at hiding it.

She got through the rest of her three-hour shift in a daze and slipped out the side door without having to interact with Mariana or Denton or any of the other nine staff members.

Later that night, almost against her will, she trawled through her box of letters and keepsakes, searching for her grandmother's recipe.

Bo was long asleep, thick clumps of hair standing at attention, thanks to his attempts to imitate Harry Styles. He'd used three huge handfuls of mousse and almost half a jar of the styling wax Kate had insisted on giving him, telling him it was what all the stars used.

Peggy had rescued the compact fabric-covered box from her mother's house years ago and had managed to hang on to it when she'd hawked everything she'd ever owned—including her soul—to keep high. The box had lived under beds and in underwear drawers and, finally, in her backpack with her few other meager possessions. Somehow it had survived, its tattered edges a testament to the places it had been.

She'd been through its meager contents twice tonight and was flabbergasted to discover no sign of Nan's Christmas pudding recipe. Peggy could distinctly remember the year Kate gave it to her. Nan had been dead for almost three years, and Kate had finally released her stranglehold on her self-imposed position of sole pudding maker and keeper of the recipe.

For two Septembers after Nan's death, Kate had gone shopping and then locked herself in the kitchen to spend hours making the puddings, carefully cutting the cloth, wrapping and boiling them and hanging them on the clothesline to cool and air before moving them to the hall cupboard. For days, she barely spoke. Grandpa used to try to cajole her from her misery, and when that failed, he'd tell her that, as the oldest, it was her duty to set an example to her sisters and to not wallow in self-pity. On Christmas Day, Grandpa would tell Kate that Nan would have been proud of her, and Peggy and Aurora would ooh and aah as they ate their pudding with hot banana custard and a scoop of ice cream. Both years,

Kate took one bite of her dessert before bursting into tears and fleeing the table.

Then, in the third September after Nan's death, Kate had unexpectedly invited Peggy to help. They shopped together and cooked together, and on Christmas Day when Kate ate all her pudding and didn't cry, Grandpa said it must have been due to a magic ingredient. *Sisterly love.*

Now the recipe had disappeared. It wasn't that Peggy needed the recipe; if she'd gotten it in her head to make the puddings, the ingredients would roll off her tongue in an instant. After all the years she'd spent with Kate creaming and measuring, wrapping and boiling, tasting and tweaking, she'd be able to whip up a pudding batch by rote. She had lost so many memories, yet the puddings were a part of her fiber. What was upsetting was that she couldn't remember how she'd lost the recipe.

She decided to take a walk, as she often did when Bo was asleep. She'd told him once: *If you ever wake and I'm not here, don't panic. Sometimes, I need to walk in the fresh air*. He'd only woken one time when she was out, and he'd sat in bed reading and eating banana bread.

Tonight, she went by way of the beach, working her way through Nan's pudding recipe in her mind, trying it out, wondering if she'd be able to purchase whiskey and sherry and if she could pour them into the mix without drinking any.

Surely, she thought, I am strong now. Surely.

Soak the raisins and mixed peel in the brandy and sherry overnight.

Contrary to Mariana's pudding reminiscences, Nan never used rum.

Kate had given Peggy a teaspoon of the sherry that temperate night when they'd prepared the fruit for Peggy's first ever pudding, and she'd screwed her nose up in disgust.

"Don't worry, Peg. It'll taste like Nan's did, once it's cooked."

How Peggy wished she could hate the taste of alcohol now. What a joy it would be to never have to battle those demons.

The recipe and the memories mingled as Peggy strode the familiar path that would take her to the beach in four blocks, and then over the dunes.

Add the baking soda, mixed flours, cinnamon, and spice.

As she reached the top of the dune, the salt air smacked her in the face, along with one of those unpleasant memories that lurched out of the past at her periodically.

"Whadaya got in here?" the man drawled.

Peggy was naked, spread-eagle across the bed, in a familiar and comforting state of drug-induced euphoria. She guessed they must have already had sex, going by the dampness between her legs.

The man—fat, she recalled, with a harsh, stubbly chin—was rifling through her keepsake box.

"Leave my shit alone," Peggy mumbled.

He ignored her and pulled out a picture of Peggy and her sisters, taken amid the daffodils in their grandfather's garden. "This you?" He waved the picture about.

"Put it back."

He flung it back in the box and then drew out the recipe, written delicately in Kate's finest penmanship.

"Nan's Christmas Pudding," read the fat man. "Well ain't that sweet."

Somehow, she found the strength to rise from the bed and lunge for him, but she moved too quickly. Her head spun, and she lost her footing and fell, hitting her cheek on the corner of the chair as she tumbled face-first at his feet.

When she woke hours later, she discovered the fat bastard had upended her keepsake box, written *cunt* in lipstick on her mirror, and stolen the last twenty-dollar bill from her purse.

As the ocean played a background symphony of crashing cymbals, Peggy finally remembered what had happened to the recipe. For reasons that had somehow appeared logical to a junky on the way down, she'd picked up that precious piece of paper and ripped Nan's recipe to shreds.

Peggy sat on the sand and cried for the lost paper, flushed down the toilet like lewd confetti.

She cried for the words written in Kate's hand at the bottom of the page:

In the words of Mrs. Wendy Rowling, our dear departed Nan, boil for one hour on Christmas Day and serve with custard and ice cream and huge dollops of love.

So that's where the recipe went. Peggy would have preferred not to remember.

A sudden, familiar urge assaulted her senses, stronger even than the need to breathe. She could almost taste it on her lips, coating her tongue, sliding its way down to her belly, the heat of the alcohol burning away old pain.

The ocean was a blur from behind her tear-muddied eyes as she tried to find a fond memory from within her meager arsenal to replace the image of that word—*cunt*—smeared in lipstick across her mirror.

In her mind's eye, she took herself into Grandpa's garden. She was sitting on the natural granite shelf that served as an outdoor potting table, listening to Kate reel off the names of roses.

"Is there one named after you, Kate?"

"Probably not. There are ones like Kathleen and Kaitlyn, though."

Kate's name was not derivative; she was just Kate. Neither was Peggy short for Margaret, as many people assumed.

"There's some named after you though." Kate told her there was one rose called Peggy Netherthorpe and another called Peggy Lee.

And Peggy could distinctly remember Kate's excitement years later when she bounded through the front door to announce the name of a rose garden in New York.

"Guess what I found out. Not just a rose, little Peg, but a whole garden! The Peggy Rockefeller."

"Peggy Rockefeller," Peggy whispered aloud to the ocean now.

As she walked back from the beach, she said the name of the rose garden over and over again so she could replace the memory of that ugly word on the mirror with the gentle one of her and Kate in the garden, so this deep yearning for a drink would dissipate.

She had to stay sober. Look how long she'd managed to. Look at the life she had now.

But, surely, just one drink.

No, she had to think of Bo. The idea of descending into that world again was horrifying.

She licked her lips. Swallowed hard. Started to map out where the nearest bar was. A house! She could break into someone's home, find a bottle of wine, let it coat the back of her throat, let it numb her again, make everything right in the world. Imagine what one drink would feel like now.

No!

15

SHE read voraciously: newspapers, web pages, blog posts.

She discovered that the person who was writing articles about women who kill—and the men they stood behind—was a retired psychologist who once provided academic information to the Justice Department but who had "sea-changed" a year ago.

K.R. Carstead, part-time journalist, wrote there was little doubt that Henry Macinaine's killer was a woman. Finally!

But they gaveth and they tooketh away.

Furthermore, the article stated, *the killer would likely be someone with limited intelligence and education who had been lured into evil by a strong, dominating man with a number of fetishes and a bizarre hold over women.*

"Prick," she spat at the morning paper.

K.R. Carstead was probably some ancient professor who couldn't get it up without delving into the deviousness of the deranged. She would find the bastard and show him a thing or two. She'd carve her initials into his body, swim in his blood. Drink it. She'd change his views on Women Who Kill.

It took a while for Google to come up with the goods. K.R. Carstead was born in New York, studied psychology and journalism at NYU and, before moving west, wrote a well-received thesis on the psychology of deprivation as well as other specialist papers on the effects of incarceration.

After days of sliding from one silken thread to another, the web finally revealed some personal details about K.R. Carstead. The psychologist was into bodybuilding, owned two cats, was a past president of the American Cat Fanciers Association, and was—most illuminating and fascinating—a woman. Her highly protected name was Kirsten Reanna Carstead.

"Now we're talking," she said as she stared at the only photograph of Carstead she'd managed to unearth, taken at a New York dinner celebrating all things cat. For someone so well respected and so often quoted, the psychologist had done a damn fine job of keeping her physical self in the land of the unknown. In the photograph, she appeared dwarfed by the fellow academics surrounding her, yet not overshadowed.

She revised her thoughts on Carstead. Dead woman walking.

She discovered easily where the psychologist lived, but it took two weeks of planning before she was able to visit Wentworth Street. She waited nearby for two hours to catch a glimpse. As it was, she was hard-pressed to recognize her. Obviously the one photo that made it onto the Net had been taken many years ago. The New York Carstead had been about forty, sporting a soft, blond-streaked pageboy hairstyle. She was not bad-looking in a bookish sort of way, her classic clothes hanging well from squared shoulders. Comparatively, the new Carstead, striding manfully, hunched against the wind and the weight of the world, was a muscly old witch who wore thick glasses and a startling outcrop of hair, much of it perched on the upper lip.

It would take a lot of planning, but Carstead was bound for death.

That night, she dreamed her dreams of swimming in thick rivers of scarlet blood, of making macabre intestine bracelets and wrapping them around her wrists. In her dark fantasyland, she carved her name into the backs of a hundred men, after she had snipped at them, mutilated them, disemboweled them. She dreamt of a dinner she prepared, of liver and sweetmeats, and she saw herself—dressed in virginal white—sitting at the end of a long table. Behind her, piled recklessly against the wall, were the bodies of beastly men, unrecognizable now with their smashed faces and severed limbs. She rose from her place at the head of the highly polished table and carried her plate slowly past twenty empty chairs to the other end. There sat K.R. Carstead, silent and pale.

"Eat," she whispered, but Carstead turned her face away from the proffered plate. It made her angry and, as she reached for a carving knife to chop out the tongue of the psychologist–cum–journalist–cum–expert on women who kill, a voice cried out from the doorway.

"Stop!"

She recognized the speaker immediately and froze.

Then another equally familiar voice cried out.

"Oh my God, what are you doing?"

She knew them so well. For them to discover her like this was her worst nightmare. How had they found her?

She turned slowly and was surprised to see that the stack of bodies had shrunk to four. Henry and her latest kill were piled on top of The Man; another body was underneath. She couldn't see who it was. It must have been the first one she'd killed. She could not recall his name, but she knew he'd burned to death.

"There's only the four of them. Please don't stop me. I have so many more to go."

Surely she could make them understand.

But they advanced on her, threatening to unearth her secrets, to expose her to the world, to put a stop to her important and extremely necessary work.

Now she would have to kill them too.

The thumping in her head was almost deafening as she advanced, and her hand shook as she raised the knife high.

They stared at her with such horror it startled her. Her hand began to shake more violently as she realized that she could not kill them. She turned away from them quickly and plunged the knife into Carstead's shoulder, repeatedly reefing it out and thrusting it back into the pulpy flesh, until she woke herself with her own guttural moans.

She opened her eyes and scanned the room, the bed, herself. She was wrapped in a tangled sweaty sheet, shuddering, terrified they had discovered her. She lifted her tightly clenched hand and was surprised there was no knife.

Just a nightmare, a dream. She calmed herself with a whispered mantra. A dream. They did not know. Her secrets were safe.

Just a dream.

But what had the dream been trying to tell her? Would she be caught if she went after Carstead? Was Carstead—being a woman—more powerful than those stupid evil men? Would the psychologist find a way to outsmart her?

She wondered if it was time to end it. She had managed to stop in between the one she'd burned—Mr. Briels, she remembered now—and The Man. Then, she'd stopped after The Man, at least until Henry and the follow-up. Surely that's what the dream had been telling her. *Stop the killing.*

Most days, she didn't remember she was a murderer. She went about her daily life like any normal person, and when the visions of things she had done did intrude, she brushed them aside as nothing more than fanciful musings. It was usually only in the dark of night that she would sometimes admit to the reality of the murders.

The yearning was increasing. This was a crossroads. She extricated herself from the tangle of sheets. If she was to stop, she would have to stop now. She would forget about Mr. Briels and The Man. She'd forget about Henry and the latest fool. For the rest of her life, she could pretend they had been part of a strange dream. Or she could take the opposite road and accept she had a calling, a mission she had no right to refuse.

In the cold, predawn stillness, she dressed hurriedly. She

needed to walk in the open air, to be calmed by the rhythmic push and pull of the familiar sound of the ocean, to think and meditate.

She passed the dark, sleepy homes of suburbia and wondered what sort of dreams the occupants had. Did they dream about their children and husbands, or was it their lovers, their secret desires, that held them enthralled in that "other world"?

She shivered, standing on the cold, dark sand, wondering about her own desires and wishing she could turn them off. Why was she compelled to act upon her need to see blood and mutilation and entrails? Shouldn't she be satisfied with the memories?

As she mused, she saw the specter of her fear rise from the ocean, a great rolling cloud of frightening animosity, and she remembered why she had to continue. All this time, she had been denying her mission in life. Perhaps she had hoped others would undertake some of the work, but no one else, it seemed, was prepared to step forward and do what had to be done. The world needed to be rid of this scourge that was man.

She recognized the source of her current unease. It was Carstead. Kirsten Reanna Carstead. It would have been so much easier if K.R. Carstead were a man.

She decided then, with the rolling waves and the shadow of her fear as the only witnesses, she would not kill Carstead after all. She would put the fear of the devil into her. She'd see if she could make her recant her fanciful musings about the killer being nothing more than a man's puppet, and if she could drive Carstead out of her world and back to New York, the psychologist could hang on to her precious life.

She walked home as the rest of the neighborhood woke, lifting their blinds to the dawn and innocently planning out their routine days, preparing breakfasts and packing school lunches, oblivious to the evil passing by their front gates.

16

KATE found herself deep in debate with her bosses and two colleagues. The "Women Who Kill" article was on everyone's lips.

"It's been said there might be other connected murders besides just these two," Blake Lilly said.

Kate took a seat by the window next to Blake. "'It's been said'? Who's doing the talking?"

He touched his nose. "Private source." As he spoke, he angled his phone so Kate could read the message on-screen. One name stood out clearly and caused a hard, erratic thudding behind her ribs.

"You've got a police insider?" one of the interns asked.

Blake chuckled. "Sounds like you've been watching too many cop shows. But, yes, something like that."

Kate zoned out. She could hear them talking, but the chatter was overridden by one name. That name had shocked her so much, she hadn't even managed to read the rest of the message on Blake's phone.

"What are your thoughts on this, Kate?" Blake's partner, Ethan, asked.

Kate had a few sources of her own and decided it was time to take a deeper interest, to find out why the previous owner of her house had been mentioned in one obscure article, what commonalities someone had found between that and these recent murders. It seemed no one else had latched on to that online feature article, and it certainly wasn't something Kate was about to voice, but it had clearly been noted by the police.

For now, she decided to deflect, concentrate on the reporting rather than the killing. "I think there's a conflict of interest there, for sure. Carstead could get herself into trouble unless she chooses a hanger for her coat. Psychologist or reporter—fine line she's treading."

Kate was treading a fine line herself.

She was lucky she'd proved her worth to Blake Lilly and Ethan Sandringham early on by punching a perfect hole in an eyewitness account, sinking the prosecution boat at a training meeting. Soon after, she'd represented a consulting engineer in a civil case from which he'd walked, untainted, via a technicality.

Kate was not a peg easily pushed into a perfect-fitting slot. On the one hand, she was highly intelligent, possessed an almost photographic memory and an ability to read people and situations in an instant. She was business-savvy, tech-savvy, and law-savvy down to the tiniest detail. On the other hand, she was prone to flights of fancy, to exaggerations. She would often immerse herself in the highly superficial, like the sex lives of the rich and famous. She'd burrow down rabbit holes online and follow conspiracy threads just for fun.

Subsequently, her uncanny ability to sum up situations in an instant, to think way outside the box, and to get solid results often amazed people who'd already marked her as a flake.

Her bosses, Blake and Ethan, would be surprised to know that Kate had instantly intuited which one of the partners didn't quite warm to her at the job interview. She had a fair inkling they would have fought over hiring her once the meeting concluded, but she hadn't been too worried about the outcome. Ethan, she knew, was solidly in her corner. Her spasmodic work history and numerous employers didn't faze him one bit. He knew that any concerns about Kate's longevity were far outweighed by her experience and sheer brilliance, as testified by her outstanding curriculum vitae. Brilliance, on the other hand, frightened Blake Lilly. He was a quiet, methodical man who preferred to surround himself with like-minded people. So, when she had a last chance to pitch at that interview, she'd faced Blake squarely.

It is my firm belief that the best work gets done by teams of different people. If you have a team where all the personalities are similar and everyone has the same interests and goals, you always get predictable answers to the same questions.

Ethan had smiled and nodded his fervent agreement. Blake had done nothing more than raise his eyebrows, but Kate had no doubt those words would have swayed him in the final analysis.

Once on board, she surprised Blake with how much they had in common. Both were in favor of abolishing the practice of challenging potential jurors, albeit for different reasons. Blake was constantly frustrated by the inability of lawyers to satisfactorily "read" potential jurors. On the other hand, Kate—who could interpret subtle nuances of posture and expression with an enviable innateness—was against the challenge because she felt it resulted in a jury that was less representative of the community than it would be if the law relied solely on the random draw. She also hated the assumption that jurors were somehow incapable of weighing evidence fairly and would favor "their own kind."

The other thing she had in common with Blake was money: his love of it and Kate's ability to generate it for his firm. Where his partner, Ethan, was in love with the law, Blake was a numbers man, and once he saw an increase in turnover, he became her number one fan.

Once she was able to call the shots, she shortened her office days and reclaimed her weekends for working on the house and tending the garden. She wasn't so sure now that culling her workload was a good idea. Too much time on her hands wasn't doing her any favors. Still, she left early and headed home to ponder the renovations.

After seeing the open-plan living area through Peggy's eyes, Kate decided to think again before rebuilding the wall. Peggy, who'd already visited twice with Bo, loved the openness of it, the increased access to the ocean views, the lightness.

On a cool but sunny morning, Kate sat in a club chair, her back uncharacteristically turned to the ocean. Warmed by the sunshine caressing her neck, she focused on a narrow, internal view. It was wonderful to be able to see the kitchen from here. She looked to where the service hatch with its custom-made knob had once been and remembered her grandmother there, straining to see the television as she clattered her pots. Later, Kate herself used to inwardly curse that wall and its sliding door, which had just been big enough to see the television and provide a glimpse of the whitecaps beyond.

Years dissolved effortlessly...

"Grandpa! I can see the whales!" Aurora's words were as clear in memory as they had been twenty years ago.

It was midafternoon, and Kate had been in her familiar spot at the stove, eager somehow to take Nan's place and to cook at every available opportunity.

Grandpa had jumped from his chair to join Aurora at the open French doors. He'd knelt beside her and she'd handed him the binoculars. Kate was jealous, watching Aurora's fingers gently brush their grandfather's shoulder as he complimented her on being such a good scout.

Kate had drawn away from the pot and walked out of the kitchen and into the hallway. She had smiled in anticipation as she'd opened the door to the lounge, only to find Grandpa had returned to his chair. She had so wanted to be a part of the tenderness she had witnessed, but it was too late.

"Show me," she'd said as she grasped the binoculars forcefully.

All these years later, she could remember the surprised hurt on Aurora's face as the binoculars were taken away from her.

Kate had grown angrier when she was unable to see the whales, something she'd not been prepared to admit to her younger sister.

"They're only tiny ones," she'd said gruffly, handing back the binoculars.

She remembered three other things about that day: Grandpa's confused scowl over the top of his newspaper as Kate turned back toward the kitchen, the thick film of congealed flour on the bottom of the pan caused by Kate's abandonment of the pot when she had not finished stirring the stew back to the boil, and the sullen insistence of both Aurora and Peggy that night that the fricassee of chops didn't taste as good as the one Nan used to make.

"You wouldn't even remember what Nan's chops tasted like," Kate had flung at Peggy.

"I do so."

Later, when Kate offered to read her a story, Peggy declined. "Aurora's going to read to me."

Then, when Grandpa had abandoned the news to join Aurora and Peggy in the bedroom for story time, Kate had been left bereft, staring unseeingly at the television and trying not to listen to the laughter echoing through the hall.

Now she could clearly see that, in her desire to restore the house to what it had been, she had been closed to other ideas. And the difficult memories that had stolen up on her so unexpectedly clinched the deal.

Aurora was always telling Kate her memories were coated with a rose-colored film, that she only remembered what she chose to. Kate had long ago decided she preferred a pink lens, so if the service hatch evoked less-than-joyful memories, then the hatch and its surrounding wall were just as well done with.

Strange fragments had come to her since she'd purchased the

house. Minute vignettes like the sighting of the whales and her feeling of exclusion were seeping out at odd moments. She didn't much like it, but she was old enough and wise enough to know that selective amnesia was no longer an option, and *idyllic* was not a term to be used in relation to childhood anyway. Instead, she would focus on the good memories and throw the bad ones out as quickly as they surfaced.

She slapped the side of the chair decisively as she stood. She would not rebuild the wall. She eyed the carved knob she held and wondered what she would do with it. She thought about sticking it on a wall somewhere and then noticed how the grain of the wood perfectly matched the new-old dining suite. She placed the knob in the middle of the table and popped the fruit bowl on top. Perfect.

Her shoulders carried less weight as she wandered out to the garden. Somehow, the wall had become a symbol of secrecy. Now that it was not going back up, perhaps her memories would flow more freely.

She remained determined, however, to hang on to her rose-colored glasses.

Her garden memories were surviving almost intact, and she smiled every time she relived them, frame by frame, in her mind's eye. The heady scents, the warm peaty earth, the textured leaves and multihued flowers, all combined to provide a deep sense of peace.

She spent the day chasing away the niggling less-than-precious memories that had begun to encroach whenever she was inside, with a bout of muscle-straining work in the garden. She finished spraying the roses and cropped back the ornamental grasses edging the southern pathways. Then, like a woman possessed, she set to work on the new vegetable patch, mixing in fertilizer and mulch she'd been brewing.

Once the vegetable area was raked even and ready to be planted, she moved on to attack the tiny patch of lawn, raking and aerating and reseeding some bare and damaged spots. As pleasant as it was sometimes to casually weed and snip and sculpt, other days, like today, it was the physicality that soothed her.

By the time she came up for air and memories, the sun was arcing its way to the western horizon and the temperature had dropped considerably. As exhausted as she was, she felt compelled to take her ritualistic jog on the beach. She alternated between hopping into the car to zip a little farther along the coast and sticking to the path at the bottom of the hill. Often, she preferred to go in the early morning, slowing to a walk on the way home and taking a secret delight in glancing into people's lives: a curtain pulled back revealing a boy peering into the almost-darkness, perhaps having been woken by a barking dog; a woman at the kitchen sink rinsing last night's cups, a buff blind pulled to half-mast revealing sagging breasts beneath a too-flimsy nightgown; a shift worker quietly pushing his car door closed, almost tiptoeing up his own front steps, hoping perhaps to slip into the warm bed and spoon his body into his wife's before she stirred.

In the early evening, though, it was comparatively noisy. Children were being called inside, dogs were still being walked, television stations were beginning to blare through windows still ajar.

By the time Kate hit the beach, there was only a lone fisherman lugging his rod and tackle box up the sandy, rush-lined path and, in the distance, a man and a dog, barely visible in the encroaching dusk.

The girls had tried to talk their grandfather into getting a dog once, Kate remembered now as she pounded her way along the wet sand. It was not long after Nan's death.

"We'll look after it for you, Grandpa," Peggy had promised. "We'll feed it and teach it tricks."

"And how do you plan to keep it out of my garden, little one?"

"We'll tie it up," Peggy had said.

"And we can train it," Aurora chimed in.

Kate couldn't remember if she had added anything to the debate. She recalled that they had all been sitting on the veranda, Aurora contorting her body between the railings as she always did, Peggy hopping about on one foot, putting off going to the toilet as she so often did. Kate remembered the feeling of wanting a dog but thinking it was not her place somehow to push for it.

Grandpa had explained it was too much responsibility. "It might be different if you girls lived here all the time, but you have another home, and you know your parents wouldn't be able to manage a dog with all their traveling."

"Go to the bathroom, Peggy," Kate had said, sick of the jumping and jiggling.

"Don't want to."

Grandpa had heaved himself out of the wicker chair. "Come on, little one."

Only now did Kate remember Peggy's anguish. Grandpa

hadn't missed it, and he'd immediately plonked himself back into the chair. "You take her, will you please, Kate." He'd shrugged and rolled his eyes in a *No idea what her problem is* kind of way. Kate wondered why she should remember such things now. She found it annoying that somehow Peggy's old problems were crowding her thoughts. It wasn't that she had ever doubted or ever would doubt that everything Peggy had accused their grandfather of had been fabricated. It had been proven beyond even a hint that the charges leveled against him were lies. The judge knew it, the police knew it, the psychiatrists knew it. Even Peggy knew that now.

So why was Kate remembering such insignificant things? Why were subtle nuances of expression taking on ominous undertones? She became lost in her thoughts, in a meditation so deep that it was dark when she made it back to the house, and she had to stare at the clock and double-check it with the digital one in the bedroom before she could believe she had been gone for three hours.

What on earth had she been doing all that time?

17

AURORA once had an affair.

Much as she told herself it was in the past, it sometimes came back to haunt her, creeping into her thoughts, arousing her body.

She'd played at the opening of Arnaud's first exhibition. Lost as she'd been in "On Wings of Song," she hadn't seen him enter—fashionably late. He said he would always remember how the Mendelssohn piece had been the background to his instant attraction.

I noticed these long chestnut tresses, he'd told her later, running his fingers through her hair. "And then I noticed the tiny flex of your bicep muscle and the soft pale skin of your inner arm." She still sported decent biceps, courtesy of the continual lifting of her orchestral harp into the back of her Toyota and complemented by weekly yoga classes.

Despite what Jason might think, she did not spend her days

reminiscing about her affair. When she was working on the clock, she was able to banish Arnaud from her thoughts, instead disappearing into a fugue of walnut shavings and delicate shaping, anticipating the big Christmas Day reveal.

That was, until Kate informed her over a cup of tea on an impromptu visit that she wouldn't be joining them for Christmas after all.

Peggy.

Aurora should have known her little sister would get in the way.

"You said yourself she wants to spend Christmas at home, just her and Bo." Aurora was aware of her whining tone, but damn it, she felt like complaining. Peggy was the addict who had torn the family apart. It was unfair for Aurora to sit with guilt for not being able to forgive her little sister.

"I know, I know." Kate had shrugged her shoulders. "But I can't bear to be with you and not with her. We were a family once, and I..."

"Oh please, Kate. Let's not dredge all that up again."

Kate tried another tack. "Besides, I want to spend Christmas in Grandpa's house, my house."

Aurora gave up. If Kate wanted to rattle around in that old house on her own because of some misguided loyalty to their sister, then so be it. "You could always pick Mom up from the hospital and take her home for the day," she suggested.

"I went to see her a week ago, you know."

"You did?" Aurora was hopeful. She still visited her mother once a month, but Karina Rowling showed no recognition, no emotion.

Kate dashed any hopes of a miracle with an abrupt shake of the head.

Their mother was an empty shell.

Just like the longcase. Aurora had made that mental comparison on her last visit to her mother but then shook the thought away. The longcase had beauty and style and a future, she decided. Her mother had none of that. Aurora confessed—only to herself—that one of the reasons she continued to visit her mother was for appearance's sake. She couldn't bear for the staff in that facility to look down their noses at her, to think she was neglectful.

A week before every visit, she called to ask what her mother needed. Then she would shop for fresh underwear, new easy-care slippers, and good-quality shampoo that she suspected was later stolen by some of the young orderlies if the state of her mother's hair was anything to go by. She'd turn up with some chocolates for the staff, expensive magazines for the common room, flowers for her mother's bedside table, and still, always, with a glimmer of hope that her mother would be once more complete, the tower of strength Aurora had always loved and admired, the stylish, classic woman who so many others aspired to be. She supposed she would continue to go every month until some merciful god remembered Karina Rowling vegetating pointlessly and decided to end her suffering.

To Aurora's surprise, Kate had visited their mother three times since her return. Peggy, on the other hand, had never ventured near the place, not once.

"I've made you a Christmas pudding," Kate said in a conciliatory tone, after draining her teacup.

"I hope you've made more than one." Aurora pictured the size of Nan's miniature puddings. "I've got to feed my mother-in-law, for starters."

Selfishly, it was one of the reasons she'd hoped Kate would spend Christmas with them, so she wouldn't have to talk to Jason's mother all day about quilting and the proper way to raise one's children.

Aurora had been feeling morbid: ever since Kate had come home, now that Peggy's name was constantly mentioned, since memories of her childhood, her grandfather, and her parents had wheedled their way back in. That house, Grandpa's house. There were things rattling around there that didn't deserve air. Maybe, too, it was working on the clock that caused her angst, her beloved grandfather sitting at her shoulder. She recalled the pained look on his face when, years later, she'd asked why their parents had deemed it necessary for them to spend so much time at his house.

"It was at my insistence," he'd said.

"But why?"

"I can't answer that, Aurora."

Aurora's recent angst was also about Jason. He'd been making her claustrophobic again with his *Where are you going*s and *What time will you be home*s. He'd started asking which events she was playing at, when he hadn't bothered in years.

"Why this sudden interest?" she'd asked.

"No need to get touchy. If you paid attention to the news, you'd see there's a killer on the loose and..."

"Don't exaggerate, Jason. And I'm not touchy."

He'd even wanted to come walking with her last week.

"For heaven's sake," she'd said, dragging on her jogging pants. "It's too early in the morning for you." She knew it wasn't about the murders; he was jealous. Did he really think she'd go off to meet her lover in sweatpants and no makeup? "Go back to sleep."

Now she sighed with a sense of longing as she threw a sheet over the almost completed clock, wondering for the hundredth time what she would be doing right now if she'd taken the opposite fork in the road when Jason had begged her to end her affair and stay with him and the children.

It didn't help her attack of the blues now that she had to play at a funeral the following morning. No amount of money made funerals an enjoyable experience for her, but money was never her motivation for playing at functions. When she played, she liked to see people transported, mesmerized; she didn't want to see them cry, unless it was with joy. So, she never imagined she was providing much of a service at a funeral. It wasn't a performance as such, and she often wondered why people didn't have prerecorded music. But, of course, most of the time, it was for the same reason that they didn't have a cheap coffin and why they wanted the church to be bursting at the seams, why they wanted superbly catered suppers when no one felt in the least like eating anything but comfort food. Appearances.

The funeral of the longest-running and most popular editor of *The Daily* was an occasion, in every sense of the word. People would be climbing all over themselves to make sure they would be seen—and seen in the right dress, and the right hat—at the church. Everyone who was anyone and all those that aspired to be someone would be there.

They were a bunch of vultures. The majority of them had hated Melissa Bellington, partly because she was a woman at the top of her game in a male-dominated field and partly because she was darkly beautiful and had expensive tastes she was well able to accommodate. Perhaps most of all, the men despised her because she either refused to sleep with them (which made them a minority) or she had gladly slept with them and then stomped all over them on her way to the top. The women despised her because she'd either slept with them or their husbands, and, if not, then it was clear both they and their husbands were as ugly as sin.

What was particularly funny to Aurora was that Melissa Bellington's loved ones had chosen "Greensleeves" to be played as the coffin was carried from the church, a piece purported to have been written about a promiscuous young woman, maybe even a prostitute, with the green of the lyrics being a reference to the grass stains her dress would sport after she got laid outside at parties.

It was one of those stories Kate lapped up, laughing raucously when Aurora gave her updates.

After dinner, she watched television with Stella and Grant, and when they'd retired to their rooms—Grant to sleep and Stella to don headphones and listen to pop music—Aurora played her harp until Jason fell asleep in front of the television as he did with remarkable regularity.

She grabbed her sleeveless parka and headed to the beach.

"Dangerous," Jason constantly muttered. "Walking off in the dark like that."

He'd been particularly annoying since all the publicity about recent murders. Try as she might though, Aurora couldn't shake the idea that Jason was more concerned about who his wife might be meeting than about any fear for her safety. He'd complained that, ever since Kate had returned, Aurora had been distant.

She didn't care. Despite being alone when she practiced in the music room and when the children were at school, it wasn't the same kind of solitude she enjoyed on her walks. Out strolling, she sometimes thought about Arnaud, something she stopped herself from doing on "home soil."

Arnaud had told her he got a spontaneous erection watching the natural curve of her fingers as she swooped to pluck the strings and he imagined her featherlight touch on his cock. He had stared at the red silk fabric of her gown fanning out at the sides, her legs covered but for the ankles spread wide. Weeks later, she had posed for him, exactly as he described but minus the red dress. She spread her nakedness for him so he could see her sex like a succulent mollusk under the smooth wooden frame of the harp.

Whenever she thought of it now, she blushed. It was difficult to reconcile herself—the self she had been both before and after Arnaud—with that wanton naked woman. She had fallen in love with him so deeply and quickly she'd almost lost herself.

When Jason had inevitably discovered the affair, she'd been mortified. Oh God, would she ever forget him standing, stony-faced, outside Arnaud's car when they emerged from their steamy cocoon?

Arnaud had made himself scarce, Aurora had apologized to Jason, packed her bags, prepared speeches for the children, tried to justify her actions in her own mind. But Jason surprised her by backing down, by demanding promises from her and begging her to stay. It wasn't that she was over Arnaud, but she'd been unable to withstand Jason's appeal to her sensibilities. In the end, she'd chosen to honor her responsibilities to him and to her children. At the same time, she'd ached for Arnaud and for a life of art and music and wild, wild sex.

She'd reverted to her good-girl status, but now that Kate had returned and seemed to expect her to continue to wear that crown, she found herself fighting against it again.

Her brisk stride narrowed as she neared the beach, and when she reached the sand, she removed her shoes and socks. Other than in the dead of winter, it was a feeling she could not resist, that sensation of the sand between her toes.

As she walked, she meditated and emptied her mind, an ability she thought she might have inherited from her father. She'd seen him do that often: go off into the darkness in a daze, to return hours later rejuvenated and happy.

She reminisced about her father often these days. Perhaps it was the sadness of seeing the shell that was her mother wasting away in the nursing home that sent Aurora's mind wandering back through the corridors of her youth. Yes, Daddy had been distant, but Aurora found that fond memories were returning now as the years passed.

She'd always attributed her harp skills to her mother's diligence in getting her to and from her lessons, in her insistence on Aurora's adherence to a practice schedule. Now, she acknowledged that thanks were due to her father too. She recalled his deep appreciation for music, something she had in spades, either by way of his genes or his nurturing, she wasn't sure which.

Her meditations and ruminations kept her out longer than expected, and the house was dark but for the hall light thoughtfully left on by Jason. She imagined him lying awake, fuming over her tardiness, trying to keep his eyes open so he could glare at her silently, but failing and falling into his customary scotch-induced slumber.

18

PEGGY raked a brush through her straight blond hair and applied another layer of lipstick as Bo came to the bathroom to tease her yet again.

"Woohoo. Sexy!"

She laughed, despite her nervousness. Or because of it. "Give me a break, Bo. He'll be here any minute."

"Wait till I tell Auntie Kate you've been on a date."

"Don't you dare tell Kate anything." She turned her face sideways to check the line of her makeup. "Besides, it's hardly a date when you take your eight-year-old son with you."

Bo was still for a moment, pensive. "Are you sure you want me to come, Mom? I could stay home and watch TV."

"Please don't do that to me, honey." She raced to him, wrapped her arms around him. "I would be too nervous to go without you. I wouldn't be able to do it."

The doorbell rang, and Peggy was instantly rooted to the spot, barely able to mumble a response to Bo's "Do you want me to answer it?"

She listened from the door of the bathroom as her eight-going-on-thirty-year-old son introduced himself to Denton, seated him at the kitchen table, and poured three glasses of homemade lemonade into tall glasses.

"I see you've introduced yourselves."

"That we have," Denton said. "You look nice."

Hmm, "nice." Peggy would have to think about that.

"Thank you," she managed, glancing down at her white three-quarter pants, navy slip-on shoes, and navy-and-white striped top. Denton looked rather "nice" himself, in a cream cotton shirt and jeans.

"Casual," he'd told her, when she asked where they'd be going. She was pleased that her definition of *casual* coincided with his.

She had no idea what he had planned, but it didn't frighten her—the not knowing—half as much as she thought it would. She'd been put at ease by the knowledge—imparted to her secretly and with great difficulty by Denton—that he was a recovered alcoholic. He'd handed her that gem a week after their conversation about the work party, at the same time he'd given her a recipe he'd found online for the perfect alcohol-free pudding. From then on, they'd talked or texted daily, Peggy arriving early for work so they'd have plenty of time to share a coffee before going their separate ways.

He'd been working hard on getting her to come to the Christmas party. "You can't be a hermit forever, you know."

"I can't imagine how I could possibly do it, Denton." Every time she tried to picture herself surrounded by happy, laughing people drinking their scotch and their wine and their vodka, her stomach cramped and she would begin to shake.

"By continuing to avoid it," he'd told her, "you might be making the problem bigger."

Denton at least understood how difficult it was. He'd been clean for nine years.

But he didn't know about Peggy's other demons, the painful, frightening visions that had returned.

"How long did it take you before you could socialize again after you gave up?" she asked one morning.

"It was only about three years. And it turned out to be much easier than I thought."

He'd described his first foray back into the world of alcohol; coincidentally, his "coming out" had been at a Christmas function too.

"I knew some of the people and I knew they drank a lot, so I made a conscious decision to arrive late."

When Denton had been a drinker, he'd had enough people tell him what an asshole he was when he was drunk, and much later, his own flashbacks had confirmed it. "So I kinda thought if I was such a tool, then maybe most other people were too."

"Were you right?" Peggy asked.

"Half and half, I guess."

She tried to imagine walking into a crowded room of party animals as Denton had done.

He said he'd been surprised that a couple of people who knew him well and knew of his struggle had made the effort to remain sober, some not drinking at all, others sitting with one warm drink all night.

"But to see some of the others in full swing was actually the best thing to happen." He'd been totally stunned at the personality changes, the nastiness, the ridiculousness. "I never felt so glad to be sober."

He'd almost convinced Peggy to go to the party. At the least, she'd consented to make little puddings as gifts for everyone, and Denton had promised to take them for her if she chickened out and decided to stay home at the last minute. Without alcohol in them, the puddings needed to be made much closer to Christmas Day.

All that was still ahead of her. For now, Peggy concentrated on their outing. Despite what she'd said to Bo, it was a date. She acknowledged, though, that any date with an eight-year-old along had to be a safe bet.

If they drove past any bars on their way to the wharves, she didn't notice. She was far too busy taking in the occasional glimpses of Denton's profile from her back-seat vantage point and listening to him banter with her son. From time to time, Denton's eyes would twinkle mischievously from behind his wire-framed glasses as he'd take his eyes off the road to glance over his shoulder at Peggy.

For his part, Bo kept up an easy chatter and she was enthralled, listening to her son easily answering questions and holding his own on a range of topics. There was the predictable—for a couple of males—like the latest Audi and who played the better Batman: Robert Pattinson or Christian Bale. Bo was a sucker for Batman movies, despite many of them being released before he was born.

"What about Val Kilmer?" Peggy's contribution was met with groans. Apparently, Kilmer's portrayal wasn't worth discussing.

The other reason she'd wanted Bo along was to stop talk of the recent murders. Peggy was sick of hearing about it. Profiles of the victims, quotes from their families, pleas from the police for people to take care, be aware, report suspicious activity, keeping everyone frightened.

Turned out to be Bo who brought the subject up anyway. His teacher was a friend of the mother of one of the men recently killed, a young surfer.

"Someone said they hacked off his limbs."

"Oh, yuck, Bo!" She was amazed at the sort of things kids talked about.

Later, at the end of the pier, Bo and Peggy unpacked Denton's picnic basket and went into raptures over the goodies, unearthing them like archaeologists finding buried treasure: prosciutto and olives and freshly baked sourdough, sliced vine-ripened tomatoes that smelled of rich spring earth, a delicate jar of fig jam.

Bo pulled out a foil-wrapped pack of cheese. "Hey, Mom, it's your favorite!" He pulled back one side of the foil and waved it under Peggy's nose.

It was indeed her favorite. She glanced over Bo's head to where Denton sat pulling glasses and a bottle from the cooler.

She'd barely started to formulate her question—How did he know it was her favorite cheese? Or was it merely coincidence?—before Bo was on his feet, dropping the creamy white cheese onto the blanket.

"What are you doing?" he cried in anguish.

Events unfolded like a postmodern movie clip made up of different angles and extrusions of time. Peggy registered the shock on Denton's face as he began to raise his hand protectively, Bo almost falling over as the sole of his sneaker made contact with the dropped cheese, Peggy reaching out to stop—what?—she didn't know. Bo lunged at Denton's other arm, grabbed the bottle, and hurled it off the end of the pier.

"How could you bring that?" Bo's voice was shrill and frightened. "Why?"

Peggy's heart was beating way too fast. What the hell was going on?

Denton was, on the other hand, strangely collected. "Calm down, Bo."

Was that the hint of a smile she detected?

"Why?" Bo repeated. "After I told you."

Denton took off his glasses and ran his hand over his great expanse of forehead.

"It was grape juice, Bo. Non-alcoholic."

Peggy's glance fell to the fluted glasses with the beautiful etched stems, slowly comprehending their significance to Bo, and she smiled at her darling overprotective son. She almost laughed out loud but swallowed the hysteria, not wanting to hurt his feelings.

Soon, though, Bo saved her the difficulty of holding it all in with his own laughter. He snorted and pointed at the water gently lapping at the pier. He pointed at the glasses. He jumped up and down like the eight-year-old boy he was but so rarely displayed.

Denton's shoulders were shaking with mirth and Peggy's carefully applied mascara streaked her cheeks.

It was only later, when the raucous belly laughs had been reduced to smiles and the occasional giggle, and when Denton had purchased some cans of flavored mineral water from one of the moored boats selling fish and snacks, that Peggy remembered Bo's admonishment to Denton. *I told you*, he'd said. What had he told Denton? The only time Denton and Bo had been alone was when Bo had answered the door, but even then, Peggy had been able to make out through the open bathroom door almost everything they had said.

"Bo, what did you mean when you said you told Denton? What did you tell him?"

She didn't miss the surreptitious glance that passed between the man and the boy, and when Bo failed to answer, she turned to Denton.

"What did he tell you?"

Denton took a sip of his mineral water. "I'm not sure what you mean. I didn't hear him say..."

"It's all right," Bo interrupted. He patted Denton's arm before turning to Peggy. "I called him last week."

"What?"

"I'm sorry, Mom. But you wouldn't tell me anything about him, and I was trying to look after you."

"How did you know his number?"

"I called the shopping center and asked to speak to him. At least I knew where he worked."

Peggy was beyond surprised. It wasn't something she imagined Bo doing, going behind her back to call a man he'd never met to say...to say what?

"What did you say to him?"

"I didn't tell him any secrets, Mom, honest."

"That's true, Peggy." Denton conveyed a silent *Tread carefully* message with his glance, which Peggy caught easily, despite not knowing him intimately.

She forced a nonchalant shrug. "I know you'd never do that, Bo. It's fine." She pulled her son in close and wrapped her arm around his tiny shoulders. "I don't mind. Not at all. I was surprised, that's all."

"Bo called to ask me if we would be driving very far on this outing," Denton said. "He told me he suffers from a bit of travel sickness and would hate to throw up in a stranger's car."

Peggy's son smiled at her with those beautiful eyes that mirrored her own. She was the only girl in many generations who'd scored the Nordic blond hair and the cornflower-blue eyes of her father and grandfather evident in pictures of a long line of male ancestors, and she was glad she had given them to Bo. She was pleased almost beyond description that she had not dimmed them with her drinking through pregnancy. These days, she knew about fetal alcohol syndrome. The fact that her son's growth was not stunted and that his mind was quick and sharp made her believe there truly was a God.

"It was only then," Denton said, "that Bo also thought he should mention your allergies."

"My allergies?"

"Oranges and alcohol, he told me."

Bo shifted uncomfortably. "I might've..."

"That's right," Peggy interrupted him. "Oranges and alcohol."

She was happy to adopt an allergy to oranges to save face for Bo. What old shoulders her son had.

It didn't take long for the joyous vibes of the day to disappear. At home, when Bo was asleep, Denton returned to the subject of the murders.

"Probably not a good idea to go walking late at night," he said.

"Please drop it." She was aware she sounded snappy. She could see it in the expression on his face. When he said he was tired and should head home, she made no move to keep him there.

The minute he was out the door, she was scrabbling for her diaries, those hidden exercise books.

FUCKERS! She scrawled over the pages.

One word, over and over, almost carved into the thick paper. FUCKERS.

19

SHE sat on an inner-city park bench, reading the daily paper.

> **YOUNG FATHER FOUND MURDERED**
>
> **Loving husband and father of two Frank Spelt had no known enemies, according to his family.**

Liars.

Lies about his character. Words about his move to the States from England. Quotes from his wife, Carol. Quotes from his neighbors. Lies upon lies and no clues as to who was responsible.

No mention of a serial killer. No connection to the others.

She crumpled the paper and shoved it into the park's recycling bin.

Of course, there was no reason to connect those particular dots. There had been no time for her to give the body her usual loving hatred, to show some of her signature moves.

The opportunity had presented itself, and the loudmouth had been asking for it.

She'd heard his annoying cockney twang, long before he came into view. She'd crouched at the edge of a small rise where she could see him clearly, sitting on a boulder along the path, yammering into his cell phone.

"Well, you've got no choice in the matter, Carol. I'm the one bringing home the Johnny. You wouldn't be able to clothe and feed the kids without me."

As he drew breath, she'd inspected the surroundings. It was early afternoon, cloudy with a chill in the air. No one visible on the paths.

"Don't fuckin' interrupt when I'm talking. I'll kick you out of that house altogether. Maybe I'll keep the kids with me. Wouldn't be too hard to prove you're an unfit mother."

Shivers had ripped through her body as she thought about the woman, Carol, putting up with this shit of a man. Husband, she assumed, given the mention of keeping kids.

"Get a grip, bitch. You'll do what I say, when I say. And you'll quit your fuckin' complaining."

He jabbed at his phone to end the call.

Bastard!

He put a rolling paper between his lips, pulled a wad of tobacco from a plastic pouch.

The rock was in her hand before she registered it. Adrenaline coursed. A furtive glance up the pathway, left and right. Then she'd charged.

That first thump to the back of his head should have knocked him out, but he'd turned, tried to launch to his feet.

She'd slammed the rock down again fast. It crunched into the top of his skull, and he fell forward to his knees. Went onto all fours. Swiveled to face her, just as she slammed her arm down one more time, the force behind the rock breaking his nose. He fell sideways and she jumped on him, slamming the rock down repeatedly.

"Not so all-powerful now, you fucker!" The words erupted from her in a fierce whisper.

Blood bubbled from his mouth, along with a moan.

Another check of the path. All clear. She slammed the rock once more into his face. One eye sprang from its socket like a grotesque Halloween toy.

She'd dropped the rock, grabbed his arms, and dragged his dead weight into the scrub. She ran back for the rock. Little doubt he was dead, but she slammed it into his head a few more times for good measure. She took some branches to cover her tracks until she was deeper into the brush. She removed her shoes, carried them in one hand as she made her way to the cliff's edge and threw the rock into the sea.

She'd walked carefully, calmly along the ledge until she spied a well-worn path. Scuttled down to the rocks, where she ripped off her sweater and used it to wash the blood from her hands.

By the time she made it home, her heartbeat was normal. The

sweater was in a trash can far from the body. Although she was somewhat disappointed she'd had no instruments of torture or dismemberment with her, her appetite was sated. She'd rid the world of one more useless creature, freed a woman named Carol.

She'd sung in the shower. Smiled at the memory of that sprung eye, hanging out, looking for redemption.

Fucker.

Her mission continued.

Dead fucker.

20

NICK Timms felt the weight of the world on his shoulders this morning.

The tall, broad-shouldered detective found himself heading up an investigation that appeared to be ramping up and going nowhere at the same time.

What had seemed like a possible thread between two recent murders had now become a highly likely connection among three, with this latest discovery of a body in the brush near the cliffs.

Journalists were turning into vultures. There was a fine line between the public's right to know and the fact-reporting that could jeopardize the case. Or cases, as it now appeared.

Officer Selford tapped at his glass door, and he motioned her in.

"I've been working through those media articles like you told me to, boss, and that stabbing murder at the house in the heights last year was mentioned a couple of months ago by a *Daily* reporter."

"In what sense?"

"Hinting at a possible connection with the more recent ones."

"Damn it, how on earth would *The Daily* have latched on to it? There was a complete embargo on that."

In fact, Nick was far from sure there was a connection, but if there was even the hint of a possibility, he wanted to keep it quiet. Certainly, it had nothing like the same postmortem brutality of the other murders. It was, from the outside, a burglary gone wrong. The wife had heard some noises, thought it was her husband going outside for a smoke, and gone back to sleep, only to wake later to cold sheets where her husband should have been.

"You really think there could be a connection?" the officer asked.

"Not ruling anything out," Nick said. "But it was a stabbing; that's about as close as it got to being connected."

The victim's wallet had been taken, along with his watch. Seemed like small fry for the poor guy to lose his life over. Plenty of statements on file already. Wife was cleared. Every lead they grabbed took them up dead-end alleys.

"Guess it's time to go back to square one." If there was a link, then it was up to the team to find it. And, if there was no such link, they needed to show the press and the public that they'd considered every possible lead. "Bring Jake and the crew in for a meeting, will you? We'd better look at doing another search at that property."

21

KATE woke early. Decided against opening her laptop and scanning the news. It was Sunday; she should give it a rest.

She opted instead to lean back against a pile of pillows in bed, sipping a green tea and enjoying the view.

She tried to relax, and although her body itched to drag on her tracksuit pants and oversize T-shirt, tear down the hill, and run through the suburban streets to the beach, a tiny part of her knew that even she needed to have some downtime occasionally, to think about where she was going, reevaluate, recharge.

Since moving back, she'd taken to swimming again, vigorously. Swimming in city apartment pools had been nowhere near as exhilarating as jumping into the cool, rollicking ocean.

She had an extra incentive to dive into the sea, one she was not always consciously aware of, since the night—years ago—when she'd found herself pitched from the bow of a yacht, floundering in the cold, dark ocean. The emotions would sometimes come flooding back, the fear of never finding the surface, that momentary release when some part of her brain had decided to give in to it all. Then the returning panic as she fought back, determined not to die. Now, every time she swam in the ocean, she felt she was winning the war against that watery fear she dared not own.

These days, she usually wore her one-piece swimsuit beneath her running gear, and when she reached the rocky end of the beach, she'd kick off her shoes, peel off her outer clothes with swift economy, and charge into the surf. Just ten minutes or so of straining her body against the waves, or swimming with sure, hard strokes to the point and back, were enough to set her up for the day, to make her feel invincible and mighty.

This morning, from her vantage point in the main bedroom of her grandfather's home, Kate could see the white dots of the windsurfers' sails, and she thought she might have to buy a sailboard again. Just as quickly, she dismissed the idea, realizing it would curb her running. She'd have to get some roof racks for the Volkswagen, and she'd only be able to windsurf on the days she drove from home. She couldn't exactly run two miles with a bloody great board and sail under her arm. In Monty Python–esque fashion, she pictured herself strapped onto the board and skimming down over the smooth grassy hill at the front of the house. Instead of pounding the pavement on her normal route to the beach, she saw herself sliding around the great trunks of ancient pine trees before flying off the edge of the cliff and out into the deep cobalt sea beyond.

She chuckled and shook her head. See what happens when you lounge about, lazybones, she thought.

From the minute she could walk, Kate had been a doer rather than a thinker. Dark-eyed Mario once told her she must have been a thinker as well; otherwise she wouldn't be a lawyer. She'd tried to explain to him that, despite the amount of necessary reading, the Law was a profession for doers. It involved acting and flamboyance and movement. It required a mind that could hold facts and regurgitate them effortlessly. Sure, lawyers had to think, but it was a different type of thinking, not deep and introverted, instead quick and intuitive. If she was a deep thinker, she'd told him, she might have opted for teaching or psychology or any number of other professions.

And here she was, thinking about Mario again.

Maybe it was because of Bo's question yesterday. *Are you going to have kids?* More than that, perhaps it was the expression on Peggy's face and her later eagerness to convince Kate she would make a great mother.

"I've got everything I need, Peggy."

They'd been standing in the kitchen, and Kate had waved her arms in a wide arc to encompass the lounge, the open French doors, the veranda and the incredible ocean views.

"Children need..." Kate had been about to say *Children need a father* but stopped in the nick of time. "Too much time and attention." She thought Peggy might have picked up on the stumble, the hesitation. It appeared not.

Talk of children brought Kate back to Mario again, someone she might have imagined building a family with. What a prick he'd turned out to be. But, oh, what a lover. And therein, Kate thought, lay the rub. She'd been home for months and hadn't come close to anything resembling a lover—good, bad or indifferent—and she certainly couldn't imagine she would ever meet a soulmate. She had actually been naive enough to give Mario that title once. But it turned out he had thought of her as little more than a trophy, an intelligent girlfriend who lent some legitimacy to a wasteful dilettante, and as he'd told her on plenty of occasions, she also happened to be a damn fine fuck. No, Kate didn't want a soulmate or a husband or even a boyfriend, for that matter. But a *damn fine fuck* on occasion wouldn't be bad.

She pushed her teacup to the back of the bedside table, piled the unread decorating and gardening magazines onto the far side of the ridiculously gigantic bed, and slunk back under the covers to remind herself of the slender strength of her body and her own sensuality.

Later, she fell into an uneasy sleep and woke, teary, at ten thirty. She dragged herself from bed, groggier and more lethargic than when she'd first woken at five, and shuffled to the kitchen.

She opened her laptop. Shit. Reports of another murder.

God, when would it end?

She slammed the lid of the laptop shut, stormed into the sewing room, and sat on one of the new single beds. She looked up at the carved cherubs and cupids with bows and arrows, so familiar from the many nights she'd spent in this room as a child. She peered through the crisscross windowpane at the forest view barely altered in the intervening years.

She shivered, from the tingling cold of ghosts of the past, and was drawn to sit on the hearth of the unused brick fireplace. It had a soft mocha velveteen curtain strung across its wide mouth, presumably put there by Mrs. Beige. The fireplace hadn't been used when Kate was a girl either, but in those days it had been filled with Nan's beautiful porcelain dolls dressed in intricately designed, handcrafted outfits and surrounded by a large colorful screen. Kate had been allowed to touch the dolls only under Nan's supervision, but after her death, Grandpa had told her she could play with them. By then, she'd been too old for dolls, so she used to let Peggy play with them as long as they all got put back in their rightful place.

Kate wasn't fond of the curtain and wasn't sure why she hadn't removed it before. In fact, the sight of it was making her nauseous, a little like she'd felt on the day she arrived. There were two eyelets screwed into the mortar at either end, and the curtain was hung between on a strip of stretchy wire. Kate pulled one end to free the hook from the eyelet, releasing the fabric.

As the curtain fell away, a fierce pain stabbed at the left side of her head. She pushed the heel of her hand to her forehead as she peered into the dark, cavernous fireplace, and then there was something akin to a flashlight shining, or a spotlight in an otherwise darkened theater, and for a split second she saw Peggy's face: not grown-up-mother Peggy, nor alcoholic, drug-addled Peggy; it was the little frail, innocent Peggy of over twenty years ago.

In that fiercely blinding flash, Kate saw another shape, to the left and farther back. Another person. It was too dark.

She felt she'd been blinded. The agonizing pain caused her to cry out. She crawled from the room, collapsing totally in the hallway, grasping the side of her head.

Mercifully, she passed out.

22

AURORA had always been the good girl.

Of the three sisters, she was the responsible one. It was Aurora who'd sensibly married a man of some substance with a promising career. She'd researched pregnancy, birth, and child-rearing long before she took the plunge, so she was as prepared as it was possible to be for carrying babies in her womb and bringing them into the world. She'd given both her children a solid educational grounding before sending them to the best schools available. She'd kept involved in their ongoing education and extracurricular activities, such as soccer and ballet. She'd been the one to comfort Grandpa through the most difficult times imaginable; she had found the right facility for their mother when Karina Rowling lost her ability to function normally. Aurora's house was beautifully decorated and immaculately kept, her clothes and those of her family stylish and understated. She drove a reliable car and prepared nothing but healthy, nutritious food for her family.

The good girl, always.

Apart from that brief period that started with her performance at a decidedly upmarket gallery opening. On that night, as she'd sat straddling her harp in a siren-red backless gown and stiletto heels, she'd clapped eyes on Arnaud van Jules, and for seven scorching months, she had forgotten all about her good girl status.

She'd thought of Arnaud again this morning as she waved Jason off at the airport. Arnaud had been so different in his pale aesthetic from Jason's swarthy Mediterranean appearance.

She wondered if Arnaud still had that glorious, shatteringly naked painting of her. She would close her eyes sometimes and marvel at her wantonness. He had officially named the painting *The Harpist*, but he'd named the harpist—Aurora—"my succulent mollusk" so she could never think of the painting without thinking of that private name he had for her during the months of her double life.

"My wife posed for me naked once," Arnaud had told her. "It was only then I saw how icy cold she really was."

Aurora had been unable to avoid Arnaud's wife—Kara—with her steel-gray eyes and angular chin, and she agreed, silently, that *icy cold* was an apt description.

"Jason is a little cold too," Aurora had confided, realizing it to be true only as she spoke it.

"Why did you marry him?"

Aurora had held her breath then, staring at Arnaud,

unashamedly allowing her eyes to feast on his nakedness, as he laid down his brush and walked toward her.

"I married him because I hadn't met you," she'd said as she prepared to disengage from her harp.

"Stay," Arnaud whispered. "Keep still."

He'd moved to stand behind her, picked up the clip he'd torn from her hair just hours before, and roughly piled her thick locks high on her head. Then he'd massaged her neck, pulsing his fine artistic fingers over her delicate skin. She'd had a fleeting image of him strangling her and had almost willed him to do it, so fierce and demented was her lust. Let him kill me now, she'd thought, knowing she would die smiling after being loved by a man like Arnaud.

When she remembered that strange notion, Aurora snorted at the ridiculousness of it, the melodramatic nonsense her crazy desire for him had aroused.

As she drove behind the delivery vehicle carting the grandfather clock to Kate's, she allowed her mind to wander.

"Play Mendelssohn for me," he had whispered that day, the afternoon he'd stopped painting her to massage her neck, in the stolen hours when he'd first called her *my succulent mollusk*.

Her strong arms had instantly angled. She bent her head slightly and arched her fingers as she swooped to pluck the strings. Her timing faltered as his hands moved to her breasts. "Don't stop," he whispered. "Keep playing, my love."

How she'd managed to continue to play when his hands had slid over her body, she could not fathom now. But she did Mendelssohn proud, she recalled with a soft smile, right up to the point when Arnaud had pushed two long fingers of his right hand deep inside her while his left hand massaged her to an orgasm that left her breathless.

They didn't have many whole afternoons together. Sometimes they would not see each other for weeks, and those weeks were painful. There were times when all they had were stolen moments in Arnaud's sports car that would leave them both battered and bruised from the shift stick and door handles and spaces too confined for their wide desires. They couldn't use the back of Aurora's station wagon because either the harp or its wooden pallet on rollers was always there, and she stopped short of making love inside her car proper.

"It's different," she told Arnaud. "I ferry my children around in that car."

Regardless of how desperate and fast and feverish the sex between them sometimes was, Aurora and Arnaud had always spoken slowly, weighing their words, as if knowing that everything they uttered was important in respect of each other. When time was so limited, every word had been significant.

As she got closer to Kate's house, she tried to jettison Arnaud from her thoughts.

"Jeez, Mom, you just went through a red light!" Stella's admonishment jarred Aurora fully from her reverie.

"It was yellow," she replied with more confidence than she felt.

"Does Auntie Kate know the clock's coming today?" Grant asked.

"She's probably guessed. Anyway, she'll know in a couple of minutes," she said as she pulled up behind the truck.

"I assume you've heard the latest," Kate whispered the minute they were inside.

Aurora nodded and cocked her head toward the children as the deliverymen shuffled the sheet-laden clock through the front door. She wasn't comfortable having these sorts of discussions in front of Grant and Stella. In fact, she didn't like talking about it at all. It was everywhere these days, around schools and in the grocery aisles; everyone seemed captivated, fascinated by the darkness. She'd noticed the way people's eyes lit up when they brought up the latest article or detail. Aurora tried to avoid it all.

The unveiling of the clock was epic.

"Honestly, Aurora, it is the most beautiful gift I've ever received," Kate said through her tears.

They found the best position for it, adjacent to the dining room table and framed by the foreground trees and background ocean displayed by the windowpanes on either side. Aurora worked on leveling the clock precisely, while Kate took Grant and Stella on a tour of the garden.

After eleven, when the children were asleep, talk inevitably led to the murders.

"There was something in one of the articles that mentioned a murder up this way," Aurora said.

Kate's face seemed to pale. "They're talking about the previous owner of this house."

"What the hell? You told me the previous owner died. You didn't say he was murdered!" Aurora didn't know how to feel about this latest revelation. "How was he killed? Where?"

"Don't be such a drama queen," Kate said. "They found his body outside. He'd been stabbed."

"And you didn't think that was something you should mention to me?"

"You practically fainted when I told you the previous owner had died here, so I thought it was better not to say anything else. You're too sensitive; that's your problem."

"I am not that sensitive!" Aurora was aware of her sulky tone.

"You know what," Kate said. "Let's not talk about it anymore. The previous owner has nothing to do with us. These murders are just making people nervous. Let's the two of us just have this night to let our hair down, to have some fun."

Aurora had trouble letting it go. She knew she was probably still pouting, and it didn't help when, in the absence of murders, talk turned to another of Aurora's least favorite subjects. Peggy.

Kate made yet another pitch, the excuses cascading, piling up around Aurora.

Poor Peggy.

It wasn't her fault; you know that.

She just had a rough go.

She's not like you, Aurora. You don't understand.

As if it were Aurora's fault, as if Aurora couldn't have just as easily gone off the deep end. As if Aurora didn't wake up every day choosing not to fuck things up, as if it all came easy to her and simply didn't to Peggy.

"You know she was always going to be the wayward one," Kate said. "Just as I've always been the mischievous one. But you, Aurora, you were just always the good girl."

Aurora wanted to scream. Instead, she took a sip of Kate's expensive champagne.

"I had an affair."

It slipped from her lips with perfect ease.

"What?" Kate ran to the hall door, opened it, cocked her head. No sounds. Grant and Stella were clearly asleep. She closed it softly and scooted back to the arm of the club chair Aurora sat in.

"When?"

"A while back." Aurora was not sorry she'd blurted it out, was pleased, in fact, to see the shock on Kate's face. She wanted to say, *See, I'm not a Goody Two-shoes; I too have had a life.*

"Holy shit, Aurora! You've blown me away. This calls for more champagne!"

The sisters talked until the early hours of the morning, or, more correctly, Kate fired questions, and Aurora answered them… most of them.

Had she known what the coming days would bring, Aurora wouldn't have spent the night talking about something as frivolous as her past affair.

23

PEGGY'S doorbell chimed at exactly the same time that the phone pinged.

In a strange synchronicity, she looked down at the message as she pulled the latch on the door.

It was from Kate: don't answer the door to anyone.

Too late. If Peggy had heeded Denton's warning about a murderer on the loose, maybe she'd have been a bit slower about it.

"Detective Nick Timms," the man in the suit said, flashing a badge. He indicated the woman at his side. "Police Officer Selford."

"Bo? Is my son hurt?"

"This is not about your son, Ms. Rowling."

Peggy remembered to breathe. Bo was at school. Of course he was all right. She stared at her phone again, swiped the screen closed over Kate's message, pocketed it.

How long had it been since she'd had police at her door? The petty thefts and solicitation that were all part of an addict's need to survive. Assault. She'd thought those days were gone.

Her heart pounded wildly as she led them to the kitchen but settled just a little when it was clear they were there to talk about Kate.

"Tell us about your sister's state of mind before she purchased the family home," the detective said.

"It wasn't really the family home. It belonged to my grandparents. And I don't know about her state of mind. She didn't live close by."

"She didn't talk to you about moving back?"

"No. I didn't hear from her much back then."

"Oh?"

Peggy wasn't biting. She was well aware of police tactics: prodding for the answers they wanted, silent gaps they wanted you to fill. She wasn't falling for it.

"When was the first time you heard from her?" the detective asked.

"The day she moved into the house."

Peggy waited for the inevitable questions about her past; she imagined they'd have a thick file to wade through. But those questions never came. It was all about Kate and the house.

"Ms. Rowling, were you aware the previous owner of that house was murdered?"

Peggy felt winded. She knew her calm exterior had evaporated.

"No." Her answer was almost a whisper.

"Your sister never mentioned it to you?"

Peggy rallied, used anger as her armor. She was angry with this detective, angry with the officer scribbling away at his side, angry with Kate for involving her in this. "No. She never mentioned it to me. And why should she?"

"Does the name Damon St. Marks mean anything to you?"

"No."

"Interesting." Detective Timms moved forward in his chair, as though he was about to pounce. "You don't recall it from newspapers? The nightly news?"

Peggy shrugged, trying for a nonchalance she didn't feel. She wanted to vomit. She wanted to run. She wanted to be as far away from the police as she could be.

"I don't watch the news. Rarely read the papers. Still, I might have heard the name, I suppose. But you asked me if the name meant anything to me, and my answer is no."

The detective continued with his questions, the police officer continued to scribble in her pad, Peggy continued to show outward composure.

When they finally left, she slumped back at the kitchen table, exhausted and confused.

"Why didn't you want me to answer the door?" she asked when Kate finally arrived.

"I just didn't want you to get a shock."

"I still don't understand," Peggy said. "Did you know this murdered man?"

Kate explained that it was because of Damon St. Marks's death that she was able to purchase the house, that she'd never mentioned the murder to Peggy because it was unpleasant, that yes, she'd told Aurora, that there was nothing to worry about.

"Are you sure?" Peggy asked.

"Come on, little Peg. This is me. I'm a lawyer, remember. It's just one of those strange facts that come up in an investigation, and the police obviously wanted to follow up on it. You know, in the wake of what's going on."

By the time Kate left, Peggy felt reassured. At the same time, she felt she'd have walked over hot coals to get herself just one little sip of alcohol. Stress and sobriety were strange bedfellows.

Within minutes, she was back at her other addiction: the secret diaries. As she spewed words onto the page, she thought of that police officer writing in her notebook, imagined her shock, should she happen to stumble across Peggy's notes.

She flicked back through some earlier pages, astounded at what she'd written, feeling like her brain sometimes split in two.

Fucking cathartic. She vaguely remembered writing that, the anger she'd felt.

"Maybe it would be cathartic for you to write about your experiences," the court-ordered psychiatrist had said.

Sarah Chamberling was a snob. Peggy had a nose for insincerity after her incompetent psychiatrist made her increasingly wary of the mental health field, and she thought Dr. Chamberling reeked of it.

She had to admit, her life would make for a strange tale: a childhood that some might see as idyllic, marred slightly by the lengthy absences of her parents and the early demise of her grandmother but compensated for by her grandfather's love; an early taste for spirits leading to alcoholism by the age of consent; drugs, soft then hard; sex, early and unknowing, then abandoned, irresponsible, careless, and dangerous.

If she were to write a book, she'd describe the horror of a fat old man who always smelled like lighter fluid, whipping her with a belt because it was the only thing that aroused him. She would write about the pimp who gave her half-price drugs if she would perform lesbian cameos for him with other stray addicts he brought to visit. She could write chapters and chapters about how she'd shattered what was left of her family, alienated both her sisters—one of them for life—and how she had destroyed her grandfather's world.

Her new psychiatrist, Dr. Leichardt, was nicer than Dr. Chamberling, and he was much easier to talk to. She could tell him anything—well, almost anything. He encouraged her to write her thoughts in her journal. *Get them out into the open*, he'd say. *Let the air circulate around them; they will eventually disintegrate.*

She kept Dr. Leichardt in her thoughts as she tried to write about her feelings, but, once again, she ended up scrawling angry words across the page. The air around her was thick with hatred and fear.

She returned the books to their hiding place and spent the rest of the day cleaning. Something about scrubbing away dirt and making surfaces shiny always soothed her. By the time school was out, she had put alcohol and murders and childhood and wayward sisters out of her mind.

In the early evening, when she'd finally been able to put the police visit aside, she opened the carefully folded sheet of paper Denton had given to her:

The Food Lover's Festive Pudding (1 doz. puddings).

"Someone is bound to notice the absence of alcohol," she'd said when they discussed the puddings.

Denton had shrugged away her concerns. "I doubt it. You can't always taste the rum or brandy or whatever. Anyway, you could lie. Or tell them you love food too much to sully it with alcohol. I always say that when someone wants to force wine into my glass at dinner."

Peggy's hands shook inexplicably as she measured out the fruit:

One cup each of dates, raisins, and dried apple.

She told herself to get a grip. She cooked every day; there should be nothing different about cooking a Christmas pudding.

"Stop shaking!" She hadn't realized she'd shouted until Bo ran into the kitchen.

"What's the matter, Mom?"

She decided to enlist his help. He rolled up his sleeves and emptied the measured fruit onto the chopping board in front of her.

"You chop and I'll measure," he said, the movie he'd been watching now serving as nothing more than a soundtrack to their work.

Three cups of white sugar and two cups of brown, four cups of water.

Bo poured the sugars and water into a large pot, and together they mixed in the chopped dried fruit.

Peggy smiled at her son working so diligently and conscientiously beside her, and later when the miniature puddings were wrapped and submerged in boiling water and Bo had gone to pick up the threads of the movie, she carried her diary—her legitimate one—to the kitchen table. She rewrote Denton's recipe and interspersed it with a description of the last hour. They were passages she could read later, pages of her life that would one day, she imagined, be given to her son so he'd know how important he had figured in her life, what a savior he was for her dented and battered soul.

Her thoughts returned to her other diaries. By the time she would start to think about her own mortality, she expected those logs would be long gone. She imagined, in the not-too-distant future, she would stop having those fearful thoughts that should never see the light of day, the ones she was compelled to write down (the very act of writing them helping to exorcise at least some of them).

Cathartic.

All right, she confessed, maybe Dr. Chamberling had a point. But Peggy still thought it was a silly word.

When she no longer needed them, she would burn that collection of exercise books and, hopefully, along with them, every trace of the evil thoughts lurking within her. **I should have killed that fucker**, she'd written about the dealer who'd made her beg naked in a back alley for her fix. The act of writing *fucker* was somehow empowering now in her clean, grown-up state as a mother and responsible citizen.

I should have kicked him in the nuts and taken his clothes and left the cunt naked and vulnerable on a side street.

All the could haves and should haves, all the pages filled with cruel revenge went some way toward alleviating the pain she felt whenever she remembered the things she'd done, the danger in which she had placed herself, all to get stoned.

When she had flashbacks that she found difficult to reconcile with reality, the only way to cope was to write in her secret angry diary. When she remembered the night she'd drunk a man's piss because he'd told her it would be like straight scotch, given he'd not eaten and had drunk half a gallon of the nectar, she spent almost an hour in the bathroom vomiting. After that memory, she'd filled a whole two pages with the word *motherfucker.*

And when she'd seen some trailers about an old movie in which Jodie Foster's character is raped on a pool table, she suddenly and way too clearly remembered the drug-fueled night she'd spent with three heavily tattooed bikers in the back room of their shared house–cum–meth lab. The flashback had forced her into the shower in the middle of the day, where she sat on the cold tiles with the water raining heavily over her hunched figure, scrubbing her body raw with the laundry brush.

When she had these flashbacks, it was only the exercise book in the fake bottom of the metal box that allowed her to go on. Without its pages to unload to, she doubted she would ever be able to face herself in the mirror, let alone look her son in the eye.

In the lead-up to the Christmas party, her fears and memories escalated to the point where she could barely stand to look at the words she'd written.

As it happened, she spent weeks working herself into a frenzy over nothing. Denton somehow contrived to rearrange the whole Christmas party concept. Given that Mariana was pregnant and her husband was away, Denton had floated a completely different kind of party. What might have been a night of cocktails and fancy hors d'oeuvres with loud music and dancing, jokes, and innuendo instead became a family-friendly day with games and challenges. There was still way too much alcohol drunk by a few: Susan from the laundry room threw up in a back room, and the bookkeeper had a drunken argument with his wife. But, all in all, it proved to be no challenge to Peggy. Denton's beefy workplace colleague wore a Santa suit and handed out presents, among them the miniature puddings from Peggy. And when one of the presents she received was a bottle of red wine, Peggy accepted it gracefully and placed it on the table.

The day ended less than idyllically, when Peggy mentioned the drama she'd had a few days before with police at her door.

"Why wouldn't you tell me something like that?" Denton wanted to know.

"I'm telling you now."

"Why didn't you tell me at the time?"

Why indeed? Peggy couldn't think of a suitable answer.

24

SHE didn't get a chance to see K.R. Carstead again, but she did manage to contact the local cat show society, and through trawling the internet and stalking Facebook group pages, she gleaned two interesting and useful pieces of information: Carstead's oldest cat—a slender, muscular Abyssinian—was named Donatella, and the other one was a Japanese Bobtail who answered to Noodle.

Handy information.

She needed to get rid of Carstead, and the easiest way she knew was to use cats. But cats were gentle creatures. They were not men. Killing men was easy; they had an acrid, musky smell when they were afraid, and it was a scent she found quite delicious.

She bided her time, putting up with galling headlines like "Satan's Handmaiden Still on the Loose" and "The Men Behind Killer Women." She read online articles about women who had killed supposedly only to please the powerful men in their lives, women like Susan Atkins, who'd stabbed Sharon Tate sixteen times, under the powerful influence of Charles Manson; and Rosemary West, who'd helped her husband to torture, rape, and murder at least ten women.

It frustrated her that Carstead and the other writers should tar Henry Macinaine's murderer with the same brush. She had acted alone in that murder, as she had with the others. No man stood behind her or beside her; no man would be a match for her talents. It irritated her that, having concluded long ago that The Man's murderer was an out-of-control jealous boyfriend, they would never connect him with the others and work out that the same person killed all of them and that the killer was a woman.

While she was pleased there was not a hope in heaven or hell of her ever being a suspect, it was irksome that her good works would go unthanked. But there was more to it. She wanted the authorities to know the work had been done by a woman who was definitely no man's stooge. What she did, she did for women all over the world. She was ridding humanity of just a tiny portion of the scum clinging to its surface.

It took longer than anticipated to put a semblance of a plan into action. She had to admit to finding pleasure in her ingenuity.

Kirsten Carstead had seen some atrocities in her academic life of studying individuals under great stress. She knew the depths to which the human mind could plummet. She knew even her own personality was not immune to the horrors that one could inflict on another. If her own abusive mother had not died of a heart attack in her early forties, Kirsten wondered if she could have been pushed to the crime of murder. As it was, she had been saved from putting herself to the test, but she was under no illusions as to what others might be capable of.

Nevertheless, the package with the note she received in the mail at the end of a tiring week was one she was totally unprepared for. Maybe if she hadn't been so exhausted, she'd have analyzed the contents a little closer, rather than jumping to conclusions.

After opening the bag and unwrapping the cold, wet, organic-smelling substance within, it took almost a minute for her to register she was holding a cat's paw. She retched as she threw it onto the carpet and then screamed as Donatella jumped from her favorite spot on the arm of Kirsten's chair.

"Leave it!" she cried.

Donatella hissed.

"Leave it!"

Kirsten threw a pillow at her beloved Donatella, and then, as Noodle came slinking in languidly from the kitchen, she reached down and grabbed the item. Racing to the back door, she flung it into the rosebushes and doubled over on the stoop, retching again.

Donatella pawed at the back of her legs, uncharacteristically trying to get out the door, and Kirsten pushed her back before wiping her mouth and retreating inside. She dead-bolted the back door and switched off the kitchen lights before pouring a whiskey and heading back to the lounge.

She was not surprised by the page she pulled from the

accompanying envelope, covered in cut-out words from newspapers and magazines. It was like a B-grade horror movie in its predictability. Even the content was somehow expected.

> *YOU will stop with YOUR theories about WOMEN WHO KILL. And YOU will go back to NY where YOU belong. If you don't DONATELLA and Noodle will be NEXT.*

Kirsten's ex-husband had left her because he said she was too hard—*a tough nut to crack*. How wrong he was. Her father thought she was mad for ruining her body with *all that silly weightlifting*. Her new colleagues thought she was a lesbian, not something that bothered Kirsten, but not a truth. People thought she was brave to have traipsed off to a new life when New York had been too small for both her and her ex to be comfortable in.

No one in Kirsten's new circle of acquaintances was aware of the reasons she had run away. An ex-con who blamed his three-year incarceration on her professional evidence had wreaked such psychological terror upon her, she'd caved. She'd fought him for over eight months through the correct channels: reporting him to the police countless times, taking out restraining measures against him, putting extra security in her apartment and her workplace. Nothing had been enough. Despite all the security, he had sprung from behind her car in an underground garage with a knife in his hand and animalistic urges written clearly upon his ugly face, and she'd been saved by something as untrustworthy as fate. Fate had sent a fresh-faced man back to the garage, searching for his wallet, and fate had allowed her the seconds of that distraction to get into her car and drive away. Then, fate had helped her to get out of New York within two days.

So, despite what others may have thought, Kirsten was under no illusions as to the level of her bravery.

And now she had felt the softness of that cat's paw. She had read the note from some sick individual who knew her cats' names for God's sake.

She had no urge to be brave; there was not an ounce of fight in her. Lily-livered.

Kirsten would have been astounded had one of her clients or subjects ever told her they folded so quickly in the face of something as comparatively minor as some animal parts and a crude note. *Why didn't you call the police immediately?* she would have asked. *Why do you think you did not fight?* She would no doubt wonder at their lack of adrenaline, their unwillingness to present arms, even the absence of normal human curiosity that would warrant an investigation. Nothing.

Well before the second package arrived, the following week, Kirsten had made plans to leave this unwelcoming place, where people found her love of lifting weights and body sculpting somehow threatening. For months, a colleague had been urging her to move farther south, where the climate was kinder, the lifestyle more laid-back. It was time for her to retire, after all. She had enough money. She had nothing left to prove.

The day after receiving the package, she'd groped around in the bushes in the early hours and discovered that shock had led to an illogical conclusion. Upon a second viewing, she recognized it for what it was: the paw from a fluffy toy with its stuffing removed and replaced with mincemeat. It didn't matter; the intention of the sender was clear.

Belatedly, she took the fake paw and the note to the police.

There was no need to open the second package. She didn't want to see any facsimile of any part of any animal. She knew what the sender wanted, and she was happy to pay the price. The package went from the mailbox to her car and straight to the station, where Nick Timms seemed happy to take it, along with another statement from her.

If she could do nothing more to save the sick and twisted minds of humans, then she would save Donatella and Noodle, and she'd save herself.

25

KATE experienced what she thought to be another blackout on Christmas Eve.

The stress she was under had been exacerbated by the police visit. She'd had to let them trawl through the garden again; she'd had to explain her motives for buying the house, provide alibis around the time of Damon St. Marks's death. They'd questioned her three times, and she still wasn't sure if she was rid of them.

She certainly didn't mention the blackouts to the detective, and she hadn't mentioned them to Aurora, who'd become apoplectic over the whole drama. Her questions had been almost as intrusive as those of the police.

Kate could not recall having blackouts in the past, but since she'd returned home, it had happened multiple times. After the last one, when she'd seen the shadow of Peggy and passed out in the hallway outside the sewing room, she'd taken herself to the doctor.

"Fit as a fiddle," Anika Winslett had described her. The doctor, as it turned out, was the younger sister of one of Kate's high school friends. It made Kate feel old that someone's kid sister could be a fully qualified, bona fide doctor.

"Any chance of pregnancy?"

To which Kate had snorted. "I wish."

"Clock ticking?"

"Let me rephrase that," Kate said. "I have no desire for children. I just wish there was some remote possibility of having sex."

The standard questions drew standard responses. Sleeping like a log (not too far from the truth). Not overly stressed (a lie). Eating well. Moderate intake of alcohol. True and true.

"Psychological problems?"

It was the only time Kate hesitated. Eye of the beholder, she supposed. It all depended on your point of reference. Compared to Peggy, for example, Kate was in perfect mental health. Unlike her littlest sister, she'd never had a drug or alcohol problem. She hadn't needed to see a psychiatrist or a psychologist. She'd never experienced false memories.

But then, maybe compared to Aurora, she might not be considered so stable. Unlike Aurora, Kate had no children, no marriage, no enduring relationships. She didn't sit for hours playing a musical instrument perfectly, nor did she build replica clocks to honor the memory of her grandfather. Kate changed jobs like some people changed hairstyles; she fell in love with unattainable men.

So, okay, she didn't have a perfect life. But psychological problems?

"No." It was a truthful, if tentative, answer.

She had a good job that allowed her to own her own house, provide monetary assistance to the nursing home that cared for her mother, regularly contribute to the tertiary education trust funds of her niece and nephews. She had a good rapport with her sisters, got on well with coworkers and acquaintances. She didn't take any medication apart from the Pill—fat lot of use that was anyway. She was exceptionally fit and robust, always had been.

Blood tests proved negative, and when Anika suggested Kate might need to see a specialist in case there was some underlying brain disorder, Kate experienced a few seconds of horror as she remembered Peggy—disheveled and wild-eyed—turning up at the courthouse to perpetuate the lies against their grandfather.

No, she told the doctor. *I must have been overdoing the renovations a bit. I'll be fine.*

Now, on Christmas Eve, she wasn't so fine.

It had been a solid workweek, but the office staff had knocked off straight after lunch, and when Kate arrived home two hours earlier than she'd anticipated, she had done what she always did when she had unexpected free time: she jogged to the beach. Once there, she'd dragged off her T-shirt and tracksuit pants and dived into the swelling waves with abandon. There was nothing like the feel of those waves surging against her, the powerful sense of self it gave. It was exhilarating.

She remembered walking slowly back along the beach then, allowing the cool sea breeze to dry her body naturally. She recalled sitting on a perfect ocean-smoothed boulder, watching the surf build.

When she next became aware of her surroundings, she was standing on the first step at the top of the path at Grandpa's house—her home.

She knew where she'd been, had no doubt of the way she would have jogged home. What sparked her concern was the chill in the air and the gradual realization that it was almost dark. Glancing at her watch, she was astounded to have lost two hours. What was happening to her?

In years gone by, Kate would have been the first to tell someone they needed to seek psychological help should they display the symptoms she was experiencing now, but after everything that had happened with Peggy, she wasn't able to place her trust in the psychiatric profession.

She'd have to figure it out herself.

The house. Okay, it didn't take a genius to deduce it had only started since she'd come home and moved into the house. Then, the police turning up at her door and questioning her about the previous owner's murder, well, that had certainly ramped up the stress.

As she showered, she allowed her mind to revisit the whole Peggy mess. The fact that Grandpa had been innocent of all he had been accused of was proved time and time again. The memories Peggy imagined had been examined in minute detail and measured against any sane person's criteria. There was no legal or moral doubt in anyone's mind—including that of the original accuser—that there was not a shred of substance to the accusations leveled against the girls' grandfather.

Kate took a glass of wine to the front veranda, still trying to understand the lost hours. She allowed her mind to free-fall.

Funny how Peggy—the wild, reckless sister with her addictions and her demons—was now so settled. She was a brilliant mother to young Bo, incredible as that seemed. When Kate visited two days ago, Peggy had informed her she was studying for a degree.

"That's unbelievable," Kate had said when she'd found her voice.

Peggy had blushed. "I know. Who'd have thought I had half a brain?"

"Oh, Peg, I didn't mean that. I mean…accounting! That's what's so incredible. I just wouldn't have picked you as the type."

Peggy had laughed then and talked about her courses.

"Mom got ninety-two percent on her last assignment," Bo said proudly.

Kate ruffled his hair. "Well then, young man, you're going to have quite a bit to live up to, aren't you?"

Sitting on the veranda surveying the ocean, Kate smiled and shook her head, still in a state of shock that wild little Peggy was studying to be a mild-mannered accountant. Not that all accountants were necessarily sedate, Kate reminded herself. She recalled an extremely passionate fling with an accountant who collected Saabs, had a pilot's license, and liked to have spirited sex in public places.

And there had been Aurora's revelations of an affair. Aurora: married, settled, perfect children doing well at school, go-getter financier husband moving up in the world. Aurora, with her steady style of fresh-cut flowers, art deco design, sedate dinner parties, and quiet culture. Aurora, the adulterer.

Kate's tension eased, and she laughed out loud when the

grandfather clock began its deep, melodious emphasis at the top of the hour, slicing through her melancholy.

She wondered about herself, her place in the scheme of things now. She'd always been the tomboy: career woman, sport and exercise junky, adventure lover. She had to consider her own self-assessment. It had been easy before, when Peggy was wild and Aurora was the good girl. Now that their personalities and positioning had changed, where did this leave Kate?

Kate, who was having weird childhood flashbacks and losing time, had also been having strange dreams about her parents. Not for the first time did she ponder the type of parents Karina and Andy Rowling were. Where Aurora had fond memories of their life at home—their other home, not Grandpa's house—and often talked about them, Kate didn't have many. Most times, when she thought about her parents, it was to wonder why they had bothered to have children in the first place when they appeared happy to offload them at every opportunity. When she thought about life with them, she more often recalled her school days and her sporting prowess. Her mother had always seemed proud of the athletics trophies, the basketball medallions, the swimming medals. But the most she could recall from her father was a disinterested *That's nice* or *Well done, pet.*

She had never sought her father's affection. She'd known instinctively Aurora was his favorite and Peggy ran a not-too-distant second. Mother didn't have favorites, but she was remote nevertheless. In Kate's mind, most of the good times had been in the school holidays when her parents were far away chasing their dreams.

The most distinct memory she had of her mother was when

Karina Rowling stumbled upon Kate furtively reading to Aurora from the pages of a romance novel:

Suddenly she drew back from their soft embrace and looked up into his smoldering eyes. Would he kiss her now, she wondered, and her lips ached as her eyelids lowered. Instead of bringing his lips down upon hers, he lifted her hand and kissed her knuckles formally, and she shook with desire.

"Just imagine that," her mother had whispered from the doorway.

Kate jumped and dropped the book, and Aurora scuttled back to her bed, distancing herself from any controversy as was her way, even at the age of nine.

"Keep reading, Katie. Your father's not home yet." Kate's mother was the only person who ever presumed to call her Katie. It was a name others probably found too soft and girly. Kate was just Kate.

That was the first inkling she'd had that her mother and father were not a solid unit, not always in sync, united against the world. Perhaps it was the first time Kate had thought of her mother as an individual in her own right.

Aurora had inched her way back as their mother sat cross-legged on the floor and Kate read another whole page from *Lady Sarah's Desire*.

After half-heartedly admonishing Kate for sneaking around in her room, Karina Rowling told the girls they could take the book out sometimes when their father was at work if they wanted to read it. But the book lost its luster for Kate. It wasn't really the book she'd wanted; it was not a story that particularly interested her. What she had enjoyed was the challenge of sneaking the book out and not being discovered.

Aurora told Kate later that she'd tried to read it herself but it had proved too difficult.

Funnily enough, the fondest memory Kate had of her father also involved a book. She'd been younger then, five or six, when she'd come across her father lying on the living room floor beside the stereo, reading a big fat book. Soft orchestral music filled the room, the only genre Andy Rowling could abide.

She moved close and sat timidly beside him. "What story are you reading, Father?"

"A true story, about a brave and wise man."

"Can you read some to me?"

He hadn't turned to her, or given her request consideration, or beckoned her to sit closer. He'd merely started reading aloud mid-sentence, about civilization, about the empire, about *"the sincerity of Churchill's sentiments..."*

She'd zoned out. She'd expected this *brave and wise man* to be wearing feathers and riding a horse. She'd pictured a king in a jeweled crown. By comparison, a man who spoke about *The British Empire* and *the survival of Christian civilization* was sadly lacking in Kate's eyes.

She stared at Churchill's crooked mouth and bowler hat on the front cover and thought instead about the following day's athletics competition, from which she planned to emerge with a bounty of ribbons.

At some point, she'd become aware her father had gone back to reading silently, and she quietly removed herself from his presence.

Strange, insignificant memories.

Something more concrete came to Kate in the middle of the night, roused her from a deep sleep, had her sitting bolt upright in bed. Something her grandfather once said.

"Be careful at home, Kate. Keep your sisters close."

"Why, Grandpa? What do you mean?"

Her grandfather had shaken his head. Sighed. Said something about responsibility that he'd shirked? Failed? She'd totally forgotten about it, and now, the memory was so fine, its edges so frayed by time, she couldn't quite grasp it. She was sure she could remember his last word on the subject before he'd retreated to his shed. *Evil.* That was the word.

Evil.

26

NICK Timms went from elated to despondent within the space of a week.

When Kirsten Carstead brought that fake cat's paw and crude note in, he'd thought they finally had something.

Then, when she'd turned up with yet another envelope, his excitement had mounted.

That second envelope was no more imaginative than the first. Another pretend paw, another piece of paper filled with unremarkable cutouts.

At first, he'd been sure that a killer that deranged was bound to have left some clues, but forensics had come up with nothing of any substance. Generic paper, standard glue used in classrooms and by craft workers all across the country. The paws came from a cheap, common Garfield-type toy. Officers were canvassing shops within a two-hundred-mile radius but coming up empty-handed.

One of the senior detectives had floated the idea of Carstead herself as a suspect. She was, after all, the one who'd been paid for her expertise, who'd been writing in-depth articles on serial killers, who'd often been quoted by the local papers.

Despite Carstead's name being added to a very small list of suspects, Nick knew she had nothing to do with it. He'd known her for years; she was completely legitimate.

Instead, it was Peggy Rowling's name that kept popping into his head. The interview with her had sparked his interest when he'd clocked her immediate discomfort. From the moment she'd opened the door, she had seemed alternately focused and distracted, truthful and evasive, angry and calm. As though her personality was somehow splintered. At one point, her eyes had darted about the room as if she was searching for clues or answers. Or a place to hide. Soon after, she'd glared at him with something akin to menace.

When they'd returned to the car, he'd asked Officer Selford for her thoughts.

"She gave me the heebie-jeebies."

Not quite how Nick would have articulated it, but he understood the feeling.

That evening, he'd reread parts of Peggy's file, going through some transcripts of past interviews and her disturbing court testimony. There was no doubt she'd been completely unstable then. Perhaps she still was.

He couldn't shake the idea that the deranged nature of the

letters somehow pointed toward her, so he quietly enlisted a young officer, Samuel Wisper, to go back through the files, looking for any correspondence sent to the court, to the sisters, to the psychiatrists.

"You find so much as a letter or a picture, you bring it straight to me," Nick said. "Not a word to anyone else."

Wisper came back with a note, written by Peggy Rowling, to one of the interviewing officers at the time. In a mix of lower- and uppercase: *please help ME. I can explain EVERYTHING if you just get me a DRINK.*

Nick started to feel his heartbeat was ticking like a metronome, reminding him that time was of the essence.

"You look tired, Nick," said Detective Tony Walsh. The two of them had been working closely on the murders.

Nick was beyond tired, beyond exhausted. "I can't wrap my head around the psychopathic nature of this killer. Here's someone—clearly a woman—who kills indiscriminately, brutally, with no regard for any of the victims, with no regard for society as a whole, and with no reasoning."

Tony grabbed his jacket, rummaged around in the pockets for his ever-present nicotine gum. "Come on—you know there are always reasons within the brain of a killer like this. It might not be apparent to the rest of us, but it's there, some kernel that the killer sees as an excuse."

"I know you're right." Nick slammed the folder over the warning letters sent to Carstead. "You know what, though? I'm beyond caring about reasons or excuses. I just want to find them. I don't want any more blood on my hands."

Tony shrugged into the sleeves of his jacket. "Don't make this about you, Nick. You're not some superhero who can prevent monsters from walking about."

"But it's my job. If I can't prevent it, as head of this investigation, if I can't put the brakes on this monster, then who can?"

When Tony left, his words remained hanging heavy in the air of Nick's office. Every killer had an excuse. Maybe if Nick could concentrate on the possibilities, it would lead him to unmask this one.

27

AURORA spent an hour after Christmas Eve dinner wrapped around her harp in the front music room, losing herself in a background of her choosing while Jason roped the children into begrudgingly helping their grandmother make a stuffing for the next day's turkey.

She'd just hung up the phone after a strange fifteen-minute conversation with Kate. Ever since she'd been put through all that questioning by the police, Aurora had been trying to avoid answering Kate's numerous texts, responding with a thumbs-up or an xo, until Kate had finally called.

"Merry Christmas," Kate had said by way of introduction but had then continued on in a vein that was many things: melancholy, maudlin, introspective. All the things that were just not Kate and far from merry.

Kate said she hadn't been sleeping well, had been having

childhood flashbacks, was feeling a little down. "I don't remember much about life at home with our mother and father," she'd said. "Why do you think that is?"

"I have no idea," Aurora said, moving to the music room, away from Jason's furtive listening. He'd been on high alert, complaining nonstop about Aurora's dysfunctional family ever since Detective Timms had paid her a visit.

"Maybe," she said to Kate, "it's because you've always romanticized the holidays and Grandpa's house so much." She laughed then. "Your house, I should say."

"Do you have lots of memories of our parents then?" Kate had persisted.

"Of course."

"Good ones?"

"Sure." Aurora had trouble disguising her annoyance. After a heavier than usual schedule of engagements, lugging the harp in and out of the car had taken a toll. Kate had made a point of saying she didn't want to be involved in any more Christmas get-togethers, yet here she was on the phone on Christmas Eve, wanting to talk family.

"Did Grandpa ever talk to you about why we spent so much time at his house, instead of at home with our parents?"

"No he didn't," Aurora said. "And I don't know what it is you're trying to get at."

"Did he give you any warnings?"

"Warnings? No. What would he warn me about?"

"Maybe we weren't safe at home."

"Seriously, Kate, you're starting to sound a bit unhinged. Why don't you come here?" Jason would be apoplectic, but too bad. "You're probably a bit lonely. Come and spend time with us. With family."

But Kate wasn't swayed.

While Aurora agreed with Kate when she'd said it seemed strange their parents didn't spend more time with them, she also didn't think that was necessarily such a bad thing. Karina and Andy Rowling were different types, that was all. They were formal parents, not ones for overt shows of affection. They had treated their children like miniature adults, where Nan and Grandpa had relished their childishness.

"None of that makes them bad parents," Aurora said.

"But I'm sure Grandpa didn't think they were good parents either."

"Just stop it!" Aurora could feel the pressure rising again. "Grandpa is not here to answer to anything you've got to say."

"I know but..."

"You're starting to sound an awful lot like Peggy right now, Kate. And I'm not up for it. Not after having the police around here, delving into our lives."

"It's not my fault. They were investigating the murder of the previous owner of this house. It's what they have to do."

"If that's all they were investigating, I don't see why they felt the need to question me." Aurora was screaming inside. She wished Kate had never bought that house, had never come back to live.

If she was honest, she was more than a little fatigued by Kate's drama. Once again, she retreated to her music, her harp, where she could lose herself, lose time.

She knew she'd been their father's favorite and imagined that would have been irksome to Kate, the firstborn, the ignored. Only now did Aurora realize that was probably why Kate held on to the memories of Grandpa's house with such determination. It no doubt stopped her from remembering she was not the favored daughter.

Aurora stopped playing and massaged her upper arms. She felt a coldness envelop her. Surely Kate would not have stooped to murdering the previous owner just so she could get her hands on the house?

Don't be ridiculous, she said, inwardly berating herself. Even the police didn't believe that, surely!

Their father had never had much time for Peggy either. Peggy had always managed to block their father's view of the television when he was trying to watch the news or clutter his side table with her doll's clothes. She was always either hopping about, fidgeting, or talking to those dolls of hers in silly made-up voices. Still, he hadn't been quite as remote with Peggy as he had been with Kate.

Aurora had been a calm child. She sat still. She listened. She did what she was told. So what if she had been the favorite daughter? She had earned that right with her poise and her good behavior.

Oh, my darling, her father would sometimes sing to her late at night before bed. *Oh, my darling, oh, my daaarling Clementine*.

"She's not Clementine!" Kate had yelled once from the doorway. "She's Aurora."

Go away, Kate, Aurora had willed, annoyed beyond words that her older sister would dare to interrupt their father's serenade.

Her father had echoed her thoughts precisely as he often did. "Go away, Kate."

Even though Kate had disappeared quickly, the magic was broken. "Oh, My Darling Clementine" was one of their father's favorite songs, so Aurora knew he was happy when he sang it. He almost always sang it to her, which had proved to her childlike logic that he loved her very much.

Favoritism aside, she still found it difficult to believe that Kate didn't have fond memories like that.

Aurora's reminiscences, along with her rendition of Handel's aria, were abruptly halted when Grant burst into the music room.

"Stella's being rude to Grandma." He plonked himself on the mat by the window.

As predicted, Stella was not far behind her brother.

"Tattletale!"

"That's enough, Stella."

The entrance of Jason and his mother sidelined any further tattling or whining.

"Oh, lovely! Christmas carols!" Helena Dwyer didn't stop to think carols might be the last thing on Aurora's mind.

"Aurora's not a fan," Jason started in heroically, knowing his wife's preference for anything else.

"It's fine, Jason," she said. It wasn't as if she'd ever had much choice in the matter. The Christmas season was a busy one, and she'd never been able to escape carols. If it would keep Helena quiet for a while, Aurora was happy to oblige.

She launched into a beautiful, soft "Silent Night," and naturally, Helena seemed to think it her duty to sing along in a slightly off-key soprano, and when she urged her tone-deaf son to join in, a headache of gigantic proportions encroached. After "The

First Noel," Aurora insisted on bedtime for Grant and Stella, which allowed her an hour of busyness before she was left with no choice but to sit in the lounge with Helena and Jason sipping *to-gag-for* eggnog and tasting Helena's latest recipe—a sickly white Christmas tart.

"I'm surprised you're not having your mother here for Christmas," Helena said.

Aurora didn't miss the hint of reproach. "If you saw my mother now, you'd understand. She really doesn't know what's going on, and she is so frail it's difficult for her to move about at all. A car trip would likely put her in intensive care."

If Helena weren't so self-centered, she might have taken some time out of her not-very-busy schedule to pop into the nursing home.

Helena, Aurora could tell, was miffed at having no further opportunity for censure. With a barely disguised sigh, Aurora asked about Helena's quilting group and then tried to remain focused as she was given the rundown on all the latest gossip. And when, twenty minutes later, the one-sided conversation turned to the actual sewing, Jason was allowed the distraction of a book.

Aurora was not predisposed to uncharitable thoughts and was determined, especially on Christmas Eve, to remain happy and hospitable to Jason's mother, but the effort was draining, and when Helena finally wearied and readied herself for bed, Aurora was so desperate for fresh air, she relented and atypically invited Jason to join her for a walk.

They held hands as they strolled, and she found herself reevaluating what constituted true love. It was not so long ago that she was sure Arnaud was the love of her life, notwithstanding her years of marriage to Jason and the two children. In the throes of that delicious longing for Arnaud, she had tried to remind herself why she'd married Jason: because he was stable and strong and wealthy, and because they enjoyed music and the theater together.

She'd made the right choice. It had taken time, but she could now see her affair with Arnaud for what it was. Lust and desire and the sense of adrenaline-fueled adventure had driven her to the madness that almost destroyed her family.

Reminding herself of the sacrifices Jason had made, of the strength of his commitment to her and his willingness to forgive her, if not his ability to totally forget, she felt a surge of love and gratefulness. As if sensing her feelings, he squeezed her hand and they strolled, in companionable silence, the suburban blocks she so often walked alone.

She was tempted, for half a moment, to suggest a walk along the sand but decided it would encroach too much on her own private space.

Later, in the depths of the night, after they'd made love, she listened to her husband snoring softly and smiled.

She thought of the beautiful clock she had built in Grandpa's name, standing proudly now in his old home, and of the case of treasures she'd still not explored fully. Today, she'd dipped her hand in and grasped a tarnished brass draftsman's compass that was cool and weighty in her hand and carried memories of her grandfather bent over the drawings splayed out on the workbench.

Instead of dwelling on the ache that the absence of Arnaud sometimes caused, she played over in her mind the musical composition she had been working on that was ninety percent complete. And rather than mourn her long-dead father and grandparents and the vacant shell that was her mother, she sent a silent thank-you to the universe for her healthy, robust children. She even felt kindly disposed toward Jason's mother, understanding the older woman's loneliness.

Aurora fell asleep with a smile on her face, but strange dreams came back to haunt her: a naked man with a leprosy-eaten face, brandishing a whip and a frightening sneer. The man laughed. Louder and louder. His mouth widened. She peered into the dark cave of a mouth and recoiled in horror and disbelief at what she saw there.

She wanted to scream but woke with a soft cry instead, instantly forgetting the substance of the dream.

Jason's snoring had reached a crescendo, so she threw the sheet off her sweating, shivering body, slipped on a robe, and tiptoed to the music room.

Very softly, she strummed and sung to herself in whispers: "*Oh, my darling Clementine, you are lost and gone forever.*"

She felt the ghosts of them all, icy cold against her neck.

28

NICK Timms was beyond exhausted, his team overwhelmed.

The bloated body was just the beginning.

It took some time to reconstruct Robbie Aston's last day. He had left home sometime between 6:30 and 7:15 a.m. His girlfriend, Tamara, had been awake at 6:30; she'd heard him shaking his protein cocktail in the kitchen, and then she'd gone back to sleep. When her alarm woke her again at 7:15, Robbie was gone.

Nothing unusual in that. Robbie had been on another one of his health kicks. He'd fatten himself up all year like some sort of grizzly bear, diet and exercise like a madman through autumn, then eat and drink practically nonstop from the beginning of the holidays until after Christmas.

Every year without fail, January would become the beginning of the "new Robbie Aston." Tamara told the police Robbie had been at his diet for almost two weeks this time. No alcohol, no fruit.

His food consisted of protein, protein, and then more protein. He became obsessed with the amount of protein he was eating, urging his body cells to start munching into the stored fat. The bathroom trash can was littered with piss-dipped ketosis sticks.

Sometime after seven, Robbie was spotted at the far end of the north beach by a couple who recalled having seen him a few times over previous weeks. The middle-aged couple ran every day—they were in training for the half-marathon—but they didn't see the young, prematurely balding man with his expensive running shoes and determined demeanor every day. They surmised they had seen him five or six times over the course of the twelve to fourteen days, something that surprised Tamara, who thought he ran the same way every day and could guarantee he had not missed a morning run since the day after Christmas. Went almost every night, too, she told them. She hadn't worried too much about it, knowing it would just be a matter of time before he'd give it all up again and eat popcorn on the couch with her as they watched latest-release movies.

That was the Robbie she loved, Tamara told the police, which gave the two uniformed officers something to laugh about later. Tamara was a good twenty pounds overweight, and they were not the least bit surprised she'd want her man to have some love handles and a strong interest in food.

Robbie was usually back before Tamara left for work at 8:15. On that particular Tuesday morning, she'd left earlier, *just ten minutes or so*, and therefore had no idea whether or not he had returned unharmed from his run and gone out again or if he'd just not come home.

Two days after the investigation started, a cab driver came forward to report he had taken the man in question to an address three suburbs away on that same morning.

Was he sure it was Robbie Aston?

Not a doubt, he said. Same chubby cheeks, same receding hairline. "And he had a gold Rolex—fake—that he kept twisting around his wrist."

"How could you see it was a Rolex, fake or otherwise?" he was asked at the station.

"He sat right next to me, in the front. Told me where he wanted to go and then kept fiddling with the watch."

The detective was skeptical. "And even while driving, you could read the Rolex insignia?"

"I know a good watch—or a facsimile—when I see one," the cab driver said. "And I know a poser too." Working on the assumption that his fare was trying to draw attention to the watch, the driver had put him out of his misery and commented straight away.

"Rolex," the man had responded to the driver's "nice watch" comment. "Girlfriend bought it for me in Thailand."

Fake, thought the cabbie. "Handy girlfriend," he said aloud.

The taxi driver was one of the last people to see Robbie Aston alive and, despite coming forward voluntarily, became a prime police suspect. The middle-aged marathon trainers weren't excluded. Maybe they'd chatted with the guy on previous days. If they had, they would certainly have noticed the fancy timepiece as well. Maybe they watched him from the other end of the beach on the morning in question and knew exactly where he was going in that cab.

Anyone who got to see the body, however, discounted a Rolex watch as a motive, despite its missing-in-action status.

Tamara was quickly excused. Despite a possible motive (if she'd discovered her man was visiting an address three suburbs away when he was supposedly running, jealousy could have reared its ugly head), Tamara's alibi that she'd been at work before the cabbie had dropped Robbie off stacked up. Four colleagues at the stationery wholesalers where Tamara was employed vouched for her attendance at the warehouse every minute throughout the day.

Robbie had paid the driver with cash pulled from his wallet.

He never usually took a wallet, Tamara told the police, but she confirmed that, on the morning in question, he must have. The wallet was nowhere to be found.

Cab drivers all over the city were questioned. No one recalled a fare fitting Robbie's description in the past, so it would seem the visit that had replaced the run may have been a one-off. Someone he had met on one of his previous morning or evening jaunts perhaps?

So, who, precisely, had Robbie Aston gone to visit?

The duplex where the cabbie had dropped him off was inhabited by a seventy-five-year-old woman with no teeth in unit one and a sixty-two-year-old widower in unit two.

"I did see him get out of the cab and come through the gate next door," the old woman told the police. "I was going to open the door and tell him Mr. Eckleston went away last month to visit his daughter, but as soon as the taxi left, the man turned around again."

The woman said he acted in a suspicious manner, glancing at

his watch and peering up and down the street, crouching when a car went by.

"He looked back this way. I was worried he'd seen me sneaking a peek. I thought he might be a robber or a rapist, so I moved away from the window."

When she'd gone back a couple of minutes later, the man was gone.

Robbie Aston's body was found three days later, half a block away from where the old woman had seen him. There was no wallet with the body; neither was there a Rolex watch—real or fake. Under normal circumstances, the missing wallet and watch would have automatically led police to consider robbery as the primary motive. The condition of the body suggested otherwise.

The real estate agent who stumbled upon Robbie Aston's corpse when he called to the house for a routine presettlement assessment thought no human could be capable of inflicting such horror.

Jake Meyer, one half of the pair of officers first on the scene, shuddered at the thought that one man would or could cause such damage to another man's body.

Officer Rose Selford averted her face and assured herself that no woman was capable of such violation.

Detective Nick Timms, the first senior officer to arrive, stared sadly at the mutilation and reminded himself that some humans were capable of superior evil, and gender was no barrier. He'd seen a few too many bodies in recent times that had been left with—or without, as it were—what was becoming a familiar calling card.

29

SHE was exhausted. After ten days of watching and planning and two hours of frenzied execution, she could sleep for a week.

She'd been lucky and was now more convinced than ever that she was invincible, her mission righteous and necessary.

She'd known him years ago, and they'd run into each other, literally, one night on the beach path. They'd strolled along the deserted sand and talked. She'd told him about her loneliness, her need to be held. He'd told her about his struggle with his weight.

The next day, she'd followed him, and when she was sure they were alone on the headland rocks before the sun had risen properly, she'd coaxed him into the bushes and kissed him. In a matter of minutes, he had her down on the soft carpet of moss and pine needles, pushing his sweaty cock in and out in a strident, urgent rhythm.

She had followed him a couple more times, watching him as he desperately searched for her in the same places. She was good at being invisible.

The next time they met, she was coming from the opposite direction. It was late at night. She'd given him the key then. "Day after tomorrow," she'd told him. "Don't let anyone see you. Go around the back and let yourself in. If I'm not there, don't worry. I won't be far away."

She knew the universe was guiding her when she'd seen the real estate agent leave the key in the mailbox almost two months ago. She'd been casing areas close to home but far enough to not be in her own backyard, so to speak. She'd simply taken that key and waited. Presumably, the agent hadn't given the missing key a second thought and was soon back to taking people through the house. She didn't have to wait long before an Under Contract sign was slapped over the big red For Sale lettering, and then it was just a matter of finding a victim.

Serendipity had led her to Robbie, overweight, miserable Robbie, stuck with a fat girlfriend and a dead-end job. Such an easy mark. She'd had a crush on him years ago, she told him, but had been too shy to tell him.

The flattery had the effect of making Robbie immune to a true image of himself, transforming him internally into a man who was desirable.

On the day she'd nominated as his last, he had been waiting at the house with eagerness and excitement evident on his face.

"I've thought about you every minute since last week," she'd told him, locking the back door and flinging herself into his arms. "I think I'm in love with you."

He'd fallen for it completely and immediately.

She'd told him as soon as the money from the sale of the house was in her bank, she was leaving her rotten husband, and she'd watched his eyes light up at the mention of how much money they would have to "run away with and start a new life together."

Oh, foolish, foolish little fat man, she thought.

She gave him some of the pills she said were for weight loss. "Honestly, you don't need to do all the exercise," she'd told him. "I lost fifteen pounds in one month."

She'd straddled him and sank over him, taking him into her depths there on the soft gray carpet in the almost empty room. His orgasm was fast and frenzied, and he cried out her name. She rolled him over and massaged his back and his ego with talk of what a magnificent lover he was, and thanks to the sleeping pills, he dozed helplessly.

As he snored softly into the carpet, she removed the rope she'd previously stashed in the built-in box by the hearth.

She thought of gagging him first, but terrified she might not have given him enough drugs for his hulking body, she decided it would be easier to explain a bit of rope around the wrists if he happened to stir. In any event, she had his wrists and ankles tied securely and was bending his legs to hog-tie him when he stirred.

"Shhh," she whispered. "I am your mistress. I've got some surprises for you."

He groaned softly, but she thought it was a groan of someone more asleep than awake. Probably thought he was having a wet dream. She grabbed the duct tape from the firewood box, eased a strip over his mouth.

It took a while for him to wake properly. While she waited, she started cutting small-scale crosses into his buttocks with a filleting knife.

He snorted and bucked beneath her. Right about now, she figured, he'd be wondering why the fuck he couldn't talk. What was she doing to him? How had she tied him?

She jumped to the side as he rocked. It didn't take him long to realize the rope around his wrists was also holding his ankles together and that same rope was wrapped around his neck. Every movement impacted his breathing and the blood supply to his brain. He couldn't roll over, couldn't beg for explanation or mercy because his mouth was covered with tape.

"Oh dear," she crooned. "Is poor little Robbie frightened?"

Then she set to work in earnest, lecturing him as she bent over him with her knife. "You should have thought about the possible consequences before you started telling me about your lazy girlfriend."

She cut and she sliced and she talked.

"This is what you get for fucking like a rabbit in the bushes with me when you should have been running all that fat off you."

She cackled and sniped and carped at him until, eventually, she realized Robbie was a long way beyond hearing anything she had to say.

Then she finished her work in silence.

30

PEGGY and Bo sat on one side of the kitchen table, Denton on the other.

"Denton's got a proposal for us, Bo."

Denton took a deep breath, then launched into his spiel. He and Peggy had been seeing each other for a couple of months now. They got along well. Denton thought he and Bo got along pretty well too.

What started off reasonably, soon degenerated into a whole lot of *ums* and *aah*s, with Bo appearing more confused by the second until Peggy saw the whole thing as though she were watching a comedy skit and burst out laughing.

Bo chuckled. "Do you want to translate, Mom?"

Denton went quiet, red-faced, and that made Peggy laugh more.

She caught her breath, tried to keep a straight face. "Denton is trying to see what you would think about him staying over on weekends."

"I was getting to that, Peg."

Bo coughed and lowered his voice theatrically. Peggy could tell he was trying to mimic one of the television newscasters, but he sounded more like his schoolteacher. "Well, you'll have to leave the suggestion with me, Denton. I'll think about it and get back to you."

Denton's color deepened.

Peggy could hold back no longer, and she squealed with mirth, with Bo joining in.

Despite his embarrassment, Denton began to laugh too. "Is that a yes then?"

"I vote yes," Bo said.

Peggy gave him a big happy, drug-free toothy smile. "And you know my thoughts on the matter."

They'd had their stolen moments. Some nights, when they were sure Bo was asleep, they would sneak into the bedroom to explore each other's bodies, to assess their needs and wants and play the courting game. It was all so new to Peggy. She had never known what it was like to explore sex properly without the armor of drugs or alcohol. She certainly had never known what it was like to feel a man's love, real love as opposed to mere desire. And she was lapping it up.

"Seriously," she said to her son later when Denton had gone home. "Are you okay with this?"

"Yep. Why doesn't he move in completely?"

"Whoa, hold up there," she laughed. "Let's see how we all get along in close quarters first."

By Saturday, there was an extra toothbrush in the bathroom, a spare set of keys on the key-shaped rack Bo had made at school. And on the first morning, the first challenge.

"Back soon, Bo," Peggy called from the laundry door after hurriedly pushing her feet into running shoes.

His standard *okay* rang out above the pinging noises of the *Wii Sports*.

"Hey, wait up!" Denton called from the bathroom, and her blood stilled. They'd had a minor tiff earlier when Denton showed her headlines about yet another killing.

She'd remained adamant. She wasn't in danger, and she was used to walking on her own. "It's you men who have to be careful," she'd said. "It's not females that are dropping like flies."

She was used to walking on her own. She'd stopped short of telling him it was alone time and that she needed it, figuring he understood so much else about her instinctively, she shouldn't need to ram it down his throat.

"I'll keep you company," he said, but she pretended she didn't hear as she escaped through the side door. She'd talk to him about it later, she reasoned.

But she'd barely walked thirty yards before he was beside her, swinging into step, attempting to match her stride. *Leave me alone*, cried a silent voice within her. She tried not to look at him, lest he sense her anger.

"Where are we off to?"

She couldn't believe a man so sensitive to her body could be so unmoved by her emotions.

"I go where my mood takes me," she said, trying to emphasize the *my* and the *I*. Just because she'd agreed to let him stay for the weekends didn't mean they had to spend every moment together surely?

By the time they'd walked a block and a half, Denton's jauntiness had dissipated and they strolled another couple of blocks in silence. When she turned into the side street to start back home, Denton decided to detour.

"You go on, Peg. I'll get some milk and the paper, and meet you back at the house."

Her initial sense of relief segued to guilt by the time she got back. She took off her shoes in the laundry room as always and came through to the kitchen to see Bo, having finished his boxing match on the Wii, sitting at the kitchen table reading a book.

"What happened to Denton?" he asked.

"He went to get milk and the newspaper."

Her abrupt response was not missed. "Didn't you tell him you like being on your own when you walk?"

"She did." They both jumped guiltily to see Denton in the room. He'd come quietly through the side door. "I was too dumb to understand."

"I'm sorry, Denton." Peggy couldn't believe he'd only stayed one night and she'd already succeeded in hurting him. This relationship caper was going to be a hell of a lot harder than she thought.

"No, please don't apologize, Peg. I'm the one who should be sorry for being so insensitive."

It was Bo who alleviated the tension.

"Women, eh, Denton?" he said, rolling his eyes comically, and Denton cracked up.

When she walked Denton to the car, the first weekend of cohabitation over, he confessed to being concerned about her walking the streets alone. "I know," he said, holding up his hands in mock surrender. "It's been you and Bo for a long time, and you've managed perfectly well without any fool pretending to protect you. It's just with this madman on the loose, you know..."

The recent murder had been in every paper and on everyone's lips, to the point where even Denton said he was convinced people were inventing more and more ghoulish details because the police investigators were keeping so much close to their chest.

"Isn't it supposed to be a madwoman?" Peggy said.

The latest news reports indicated the murderer was most likely female.

"Not with what they are saying about the latest body." Denton didn't seem to think a woman would be able to do such things.

She thought about her exercise book in the locked box with its demented scribbling and all the filled books beneath it. "Don't you think women are capable of evil?"

"Jeez, I don't know, Peg." He sounded tired, and Peggy was distressed to think she was the cause of his blue mood.

"Tell you what," she said trying to sound cheery. "Next weekend, we'll walk together."

But Denton wouldn't hear of it. He understood, he told her. He liked his own private time too. "Let's get the ground rules right now," he insisted. "In case we get married one day."

They'd laughed then, over the silliness of it all. And he kissed her deeply there on the sidewalk, and suddenly she didn't want it to only be weekends. She didn't want him to go back to his own place to sleep alone. She knew then she'd even try to forgo her solitary walks if he decided to move in permanently. She thought she'd give up her frenetic midnight scribbling too. She'd have to if they were ever to share more than a night or two in the same bedroom.

Later, close to midnight, with Bo asleep and the neighborhood silent but for the odd barking dog, she furtively removed her exercise book from the false bottom of the locked box, as she still did at least three or four times a week, and wrote out two pages of angry words. *Fuck them all,* she wrote, remembering all those awful men who had taken advantage of her drug-addled or drunken state. *Bastards*, she scrawled, wondering why some men had to be born such assholes.

She used to think they were all the same, but now she was not so sure. Certainly, she couldn't imagine Bo ever growing into an evil man. Denton either. He was kind and considerate, even-tempered, gentle. But, she wondered, had he always been so? If she'd met him when they were both drunks, would he have cheated and lied and abused her like the rest?

When Kate had called on Christmas Eve, Peggy's initial elation that her big sister might have changed her mind about spending Christmas together had turned to confusion once she realized Kate had been drinking. It was not that Kate had ever professed to be a teetotaler, just that Peggy would not have expected to be the one to get a phone call when Kate had obviously had more than one too many.

"Aurora said she had good memories," Kate said, indicating Peggy wasn't the only one getting some Christmas cheer from

Kate. "She said Father often read to her and sang to her. And Mom took her to art galleries and helped her with her music. I used to feel I was in the way. Didn't you?"

"No, I don't think so. I've got good memories."

"Like what, Peggy? Tell me what you remember."

Peggy thought it was insensitive of her older sister to ask her, of all people, about her memories, but she endeavored to comply, if for no other reason than to drown out Kate's slurring demands.

"They always returned from overseas with great presents," she told Kate. "Mom knew how much I loved my dolls, and she used to get clothes tailor-made in Thailand for my Mimi doll." Peggy remembered the playhouse in the backyard that their father had gotten the handyman to build, the beautiful wallpaper Mom had shown her how to put up. She remembered Dad meeting them at the bus stop sometimes on a Friday when he took the afternoon off work. *Playing hooky*, he called it. She remembered her pretty pink bedroom at the top of the stairs that was nicer than the spare room she shared with Aurora at Grandpa's house.

"We didn't have all those fun times like we used to have at Nan and Grandpa's," Kate insisted during that phone call.

Peggy had squared her shoulders, thought about Denton and Bo sitting in the den waiting for her with the movie on pause. She thought about all she'd endured. She was a strong woman. She should not have to deal with her older sister on the phone on Christmas Eve talking about memories.

"Kate, you call it Nan and Grandpa's house, and you forget I was only four when Nan died. To me, it has always been Grandpa's house."

"Oh, well, yes but..."

"You've suddenly chosen to forget the problems I've had with my memory. You obviously don't realize that an alcoholic has a separate alcohol antenna, and I can tell you've had a reasonable amount of Christmas cheer. You're also talking to me about what Aurora remembers. Considering Aurora likes to pretend I don't exist, it's a bit insensitive of you to interrupt my Christmas Eve with my son and my boyfriend to tell me about her memories."

She didn't miss the huge intake of Kate's breath. "Oh, I am so sorry, dear Peggy! Can you forgive me?"

"I'll forgive you tomorrow," Peggy said. "When I call to wish you a happy Christmas. Do me a favor and don't drink anymore tonight. Night night."

She'd hung up quietly and tiptoed back to the den, only to find both Bo and Denton staring at her, having obviously listened to the lot. Bo started to clap, and Denton joined in. "Hear! Hear!"

"Ah, cut it out," she said, smiling. But she was pleased she'd been able to respond to Kate assertively. She pointed at the television screen. "Press play."

Weeks later, with Kate forgiven and life back to normal, Peggy called her big sister to tell her about her new arrangements with Denton. *I think I'm falling in love*, she told Kate, knowing the words were a lie as they slipped from her tongue. She was already head over heels in love with him.

31

KATE could feel pieces of herself shattering. She needed to work hard to compartmentalize her fears. The police, Peggy, Aurora. The news of yet another killing. There was no doubt in anyone's mind now that there was a serial killer on the loose.

She was grateful to have a somewhat lighthearted case she could sink her teeth into so she wouldn't slide into a funk, fixating on things she couldn't control.

Despite knowing her way around family and criminal law, she'd always preferred civil cases. She loved working where the big bucks were, in the corporate sector, at the top end of town. The stakes were high, the egos enormous, and the distances to fall lengthy and steep.

This case was a double whammy: a defamation case but with a salacious twist. Restaurateur Richard Banna was suing the publisher of *The Taste* for defamation, after a food critic gave his restaurant a roasting. The publisher—Kate's client—was none other than the bubbly and entrepreneurial Adella Banna, ex-wife of Richard Banna, the plaintiff.

"But wait. There's more," Kate told Aurora over lunch at their waterside table. "The journalist who wrote the piece is Adella Banna's boyfriend."

Despite their recent arguments over the house and the death of its previous owner, despite their continued angst over Peggy, they'd kept their usual lunch date, and Kate was trying hard to keep things light.

Aurora squealed with delight. "You have got to be making this up!"

Kate was thrilled to see her sister relinquish her Goody Two-shoes guard for long enough to enjoy a bit of gossip.

"You're looking very stylish today, might I add," Aurora said.

Kate had paid particular attention to her appearance for court. That morning, she'd tucked her short chestnut curls—freshly cut—behind her ears. She'd carefully applied her makeup with a subtlety that rendered it almost undetectable. Her plain black pants and crisp buttoned-up pale blue shirt smacked of business acumen. Shiny Doc Martens showcased her sensible nature and, she hoped, marked her as a straightforward woman of action.

Kate was ten years younger than her petite client, Adella Banna. Predictably, Adella wore three-inch heels, a tight skirt, and a lavender blouse that was half a size too small. Her bleached-blond hair fanned her face flatteringly, but her makeup was overdone.

To Kate's horror, Adella wore false eyelashes and shiny purple lipstick.

"Didn't you hear me yesterday when I suggested you dress sedately?"

"I've toned myself down a bit," Adella said.

Kate stepped back a couple of paces, spread her arms expansively toward her client, and grinned. "You call that toned down?"

Adella laughed good-naturedly.

Kate was relieved the extra care she had taken would partially balance her client's excesses.

The plaintiff, Richard Banna, was way too handsome for his own good. His silk shirt and diamond-studded tiepin screamed money, his lazy, droopy eyelids hinting at privilege and a barely veiled sexuality that bordered on dangerous.

His string of fanciful, overpriced restaurants had humble beginnings in the family restaurant he and Adella had opened over twenty years ago. The success of that early restaurant came courtesy, in no small measure, of Adella's blood, sweat, and cooking expertise, skills some would say surpassed those of her classically trained husband.

Kate had read the "offending" review many times, could probably recite it by heart if she had to. Despite her dislike of the journalist Stephano Corelli, his piece was written in an entertaining and witty style.

Does Richard Banna have his fingers in too many pies?

Someone's fingers definitely seem to have

> **been lurking around in the venison and caramelized vegetable pie brought to my table on a recent Friday night. In fact, there was a dirty big hole in it and a perfect thumb-shaped red-wine-jus imprint on the otherwise pristine white plate that proved how the hole appeared in my pastry.**

The thumb-produced hole in Stephano Corelli's pie was just one error in a meal punctuated with them. Mistakes like *overcooked rubbery mussels that I could guarantee were not—as stated on the menu—local and the "freshest you'll find outside of collecting them from the rocks yourself."* Thanks to Adella's diligent fact-checking, Kate had a witness who'd delivered an urgent order of frozen imported mussels not two hours before Stephano sat to eat.

"I've already seen your name in the paper," Aurora said over lunch, taking a generous swig of her chardonnay.

Kate had been surprised they were getting any press coverage at all, given *The Daily* was filled with horror stories about the latest murder, but today she was determined not to speak of the murders with Aurora.

Kate laughed. "Yeah, did you read that one referring to me as the *no-nonsense Gen Y lawyer*? Someone has gone horribly haywire with their math."

"It's those childish tomboy shoes you wear," Aurora said.

"Ha! It could be just that I'm looking damned fine for a thirty-six-year-old."

"Almost thirty-seven."

"Almost thirty-seven means I'm still thirty-six." Kate laughed. "And, as I said, not looking too bad."

"Which, by the way, is not going to last if you insist on working yourself into the ground."

"I'm doing what I love," Kate said.

"I thought it was the house you loved. If you keep this up, you'll never get to spend any time there."

"I'm not working as much as you think."

Aurora huffed. "Well, I tried to get a hold of you on Sunday morning. No answer. You weren't there yesterday morning either, and you weren't there last night. I don't know why you bother with a landline."

"You should have called my cell then."

"You never answer it. And you've got that silly notification saying you don't listen to messages left there."

"Touché."

"You're as bad as me, Kate. Except I've got Jason yapping in my ear every five minutes about how I shouldn't be walking late at night in case the bogeyman gets me."

It was difficult to avoid talking about the latest murder. And this wasn't just any murder. Even though the published details were relatively scant in relation to the scope of the crime, it was clear this murderer showed such a total disregard for the human psyche that it was difficult to comprehend.

That night, Kate read the paper in more detail instead of skimming, in particular reading the reprint of part two of K.R. Carstead's psychological profile.

EVIL THAT KNOWS NO GENDER

Despite what I and many other psychologists have written in the past about "Women Who Kill," there is another disturbing entity besides those who are nothing more than robots for the men who control them.

We are talking here about psychopaths to whom a human life holds no more value than, say, a blade of grass.

Generally, narcissistic psychopaths not only fail to feel guilt but are usually incapable of such an emotion.

Long thought to be the domain of men, it is now known that severe psychotic personalities favor no gender.

The article did not specifically refer to the murder and mutilation of Robbie Aston, but its publication's timing implied a connection.

"It makes for tough reading," Kate said when Peggy brought up the subject over the phone. "Can you believe a woman could do such a thing?"

"I can't believe you of all people would think women aren't capable of this type of crime," Peggy said.

"What do you mean by that?"

"I mean your feminism, your belief in equality, all that. How can you say we are all capable of holding the same jobs, earning the same money, having the same privileges and then in the next breath express surprise that women can be as mad and as evil as men."

"Hmm. I know you're right. I just wish I could stay in denial."

Kate kept close to her chest the extra information released by the investigating officers, unpublished not because there were any police or court regulations but merely because it was deemed too confronting for the public to read about.

The victim had been discovered with a gnarled piece of driftwood protruding from his anus. His ears had been burned with candle wax, and matches protruded from his nostrils. His buttocks were scored with evidence of tic-tac-toe games, and tiny diamond shapes of skin had been removed from his back to create an intricate pattern.

32

SHE was constantly surprised by her ability to forget about her true maniacal disposition, for months, sometimes years. Even during her periods of remembrance, she could talk fluently and easily, smiling behind her mask of respectability, while images of destruction and carnage flashed across her inner eye. In the normal course of her day, while she undertook standard tasks and thought about what she might eat that night or what latest television series could be worth watching, she would have been unable to comprehend what she'd done.

Until recently, her remembrance periods had been rare and brief. She forgot about Mr. Briels for years. And, while she'd never completely forgotten about The Man, it had certainly slipped her mind that she was his killer. Often, she would recall the murder in purely academic form, as though it had been nothing more than a headline. But lately things were changing. Murderous memories of Henry Macinaine, Robbie Aston, and the others continued to pop into her head—in full Technicolor—at odd times, taking her by surprise. She'd think about the man who'd told her she was beautiful, who may or may not have said he loved her before she sank the knife into him. Then she'd forget them again.

As she went about her days, an unacknowledged portion of her brain was on constant lookout for opportunities and victims. She had such an enormous job ahead of her: ridding the world—or at least her corner of it—of as many evil men as she possibly could.

But she knew it was imperative not to be caught, as it became increasingly clear that no other woman had the courage to take up the task, even though every last one of them was grateful for what she was doing. To remain beyond suspicion and avoid being trapped, she knew she would have to wait. After so many years between kills, she'd allowed the passion to overtake her, and the connection between the recent murders had been more than hinted at. She had thought the disappearance of Robbie's wallet and watch would lead investigators to concentrate on robbery as a motive, but then she chuckled at her stupidity. A robber would hardly have taken the time to carve intricate patterns and perform such delicate—and not so delicate—surgery on the victim.

Despite having talked herself into waiting at least a couple of years before her next kill, when the opportunity presented itself again so quickly, she knew she would be foolish to pass it by.

"What's a pretty lady like you doing out all alone?"

He was on foot. Drunk.

"It's such a beautiful night," she said to him. "Much too nice to spend it indoors."

"Unless," he slurred, moving into step beside her, "you were lucky enough to have someone to be indoors with."

She laughed flirtatiously.

"Seriously," he said. "Don't you listen to the news? You shouldn't be walking alone."

"I would have thought it would be far more dangerous for a man to be out at night."

He stumbled slightly and held his arms out to steady himself. "Whadaya mean?"

"Well, it's men being murdered, isn't it? That's what I've heard."

He seemed at a loss for words, the wind taken from his sails. But he rallied. "I've seen you before. You live around here?"

"A couple of blocks away," she said. "You?"

"Live just around the corner in Walter Avenue."

Bingo.

It was too easy. Yes, she'd love to join him for a drink.

He was so drunk—or self-involved, she wasn't sure which—that he didn't even notice or care what she was wearing, what she'd been doing.

Sure, she was a fan of heavy metal. Mmm, she was hungry too. Maybe she could whip him up some pancakes. "Don't you just love pancakes after a night out?"

She could see his mind ticking, as he tried to assess his situation. How many drinks had he had? Was he sober enough to perform? Pancakes and coffee should fix him up. Who knew he'd get so lucky?

They saw no one as they turned the corner. All the blinds and curtains were drawn in the houses they passed. Not one car visited the street.

Once inside, he poured her a strange green cocktail.

"Where's yours?" she asked.

"I think I've had enough," he slurred. "I'd better put the kettle on."

"Good idea." She followed him to the kitchen, pretending to take a sip of her drink. "Do you have eggs?"

She eyed the unwashed dishes, the filthy wall tiles, the oil-splattered oven door.

Filthy pig.

Surprisingly, eggs were forthcoming. And milk. Butter. Alas, no flour.

"Never mind. We'll have an omelet instead."

She found an onion, as well as a huge knife that she wished was a fraction sharper.

"Why not use this one?" He held up a small black-handled vegetable knife, and she screwed up her nose and pouted.

"I like this one. Not overly sharp though."

Predictably, he offered to sharpen it.

Show-off.

Man the hunter, she thought as she watched him drag the blade of the cleaver through the sharpener. Soon he would know it was he who was the hunted.

Soon enough.

For a moment—after he'd passed the sharpened knife to her and she'd deftly moved behind him and reached up and sliced the blade across his neck in one swift angry motion—she felt sorry for him. Perhaps he was not a bad man, per se. Perhaps he was lonely. Not all men had to be evil monsters. But then, as he ineffectually reached toward his throat and, simultaneously, buckled under the shock of what had just happened, she reminded herself that all men were evil monsters. She had a job to do, and it was not for her to wonder about what atrocities the men had been involved in; her responsibility was to rid the world of the scourge.

There was no time for him to cry out. Later, she would wonder what she'd have done had he flailed about, if her swipe had not cut deep enough and he had been less drunk and more able to protect himself, to struggle for survival. When she thought of it, she chastised herself for being so foolish and reckless, for putting her life in jeopardy and, at the very least, for compromising her mission.

But for now, she was happy to step to the side and watch his face drain of color as he endeavored to lift his hands and failed. She laughed as he fell to his knees with a grunt. She ran behind him and swung in a high arc, double-handed, ramming the knife down squarely into the top of his head. The blade was momentarily stuck, but as he slumped forward, she ripped it out with all her might, and then as he lay prone on the cold, hard tiles of the kitchen floor, she rammed the knife into his back over and over, watching the blood spurt and smear, knowing it was probably contaminating her hands and her clothes.

Filthy pig.

She lost herself to the mania. She wasn't sure if she blacked out. A fog surrounded her. She was a child once more. A man's hands, pulling at her clothes. *Please don't hurt me.* Eyes piercing her depths, eyes that she loved, eyes that loved her but not in the right way. *Please stop.*

The fog cleared. She looked at the knife, at the man on the floor, at all the blood. She stepped away in panic, pulled a filthy tea towel from the rail, and wiped the handle of the knife. She wiped the countertop and the floor and the sink and the onion. She wiped the doorframes, her eyes frantically darting around the room to see what else she might have touched. When she thought she'd swiped every trace of herself from the scene, she fled, the carton of eggs and the tea towel tucked incongruously under her arm. She ran into the night and prayed to God to keep her hidden, to save her secrets so she might continue to fight the good fight.

Behind her own closed doors, in the quiet, under cover of darkness, she divested herself of her stained and bloody clothes, hiding them in her favorite spot at the back of the freezer to dispose of later, along with the eggs, which she had no idea why she'd taken. She sat in the bathroom for a while, silent and shaking. She closed her eyes and drifted.

As the neighborhood began its morning stirrings, she showered and washed and scrubbed the pieces of that awful evil man out of her hair and her nails, and she put on her standard mask and set about her normal day.

This is what she thought then: she alone knew the tiring nature of her work, the trials and tribulations, the enormity of the task ahead.

Soon it was all a dream. After that, it was forgotten. For a time.

33

NICK had never once been disappointed to see a perp brought to justice.

Until today.

Detective Tony Walsh, who Nick had been working closely with, called to say the suspect they'd been pursuing in the Damon St. Marks case had finally confessed.

Despite the mounting evidence against the vagrant Lawrence Gray, Nick had been holding on to the hope that Kate Rowling was, if not the murderer, then closely involved.

Her obsession with that house had seemed disproportionate, so killing someone to get her hands on it had somehow become realistic.

It had been hard for Nick to convince himself that she was not in the mix. But it quickly became clear there was no connection between Kate Rowling and Lawrence Gray.

Gray was quickly ruled out as a suspect in any of the other murders, and as Nick crossed his name from his Persons of Interest list for these recent cases, he was reminded of just how paltry a list it was.

"Could there still be any connection?" Rose Selford asked at the team meeting.

"Lawrence Gray? No. Seems it was just a coincidence," Nick said.

"So we're back to square one?" asked Jake Meyer.

"Let's just keep an open mind," Nick said. He didn't want to voice what was really on his mind. He couldn't let go of the idea that those Rowling sisters were involved in some way. He had a feeling that the three of them might know something.

Kate Rowling had not disguised her nerves well enough for Nick when the team turned up to search her backyard, but she'd recovered and had been quick to bring her lawyer status to their attention. Did she think that gave her an added layer of protection?

He'd also not missed Aurora Dwyer's discomfort when he'd questioned her about the murder at her older sister's house.

Added to that was Peggy Rowling's murky past and unhinged behavior, which had sent Nick back to the old police files.

He'd read back through everything he had on them, which, really, amounted to what they had on the youngest sister, Peggy.

Tony Walsh had been closely involved in the abuse case involving the grandfather years ago and said he wasn't convinced, despite the ruling, that there was not something evil about that man.

As he read through Peggy's file, there was no doubt in his mind she'd been touched by evil too. She might be all clean and suburban now, but there was surely more to unearth there.

Still, it wasn't the place for wild theories and suspicions. "It's time for good old-fashioned police work," he said to the team. "Let's start at the beginning again and go from there."

"And where's the beginning?" Rose Selford asked. "Is it Macinaine the surfer? Or are we reopening that old case?"

Nick had been unsure of a connection, but since the discovery of Robbie Aston's body, with its distinctive knife markings, it was now a definite possibility that the body found in a hut years back was connected. The duct tape, the knots, the crosshatched cuts.

"Tony's team will work on that," Nick said. "We'll start with Henry Macinaine and work our way forward to Robbie Aston." He shuffled some papers, collecting his thoughts, before scanning the room and looking into the eyes of each member of his team. "I want a clean slate," he said. "No preconceptions, no hunches. Just stick with the facts. I know we've denied the press's hints at a serial killer, but clearly we can't hide it any longer."

Nick was playing his own hand close to the chest. He didn't believe in coincidence. He couldn't shake the idea that one or all of those sisters were involved, and he was going to remain quietly alert to anything that led in their direction.

34

AURORA emerged from the waves, straightened her trim body, and flicked back her wet and heavy mane, all in a series of effortless movements.

On these balmy mornings, the gentle ocean soothed her. Like walking, swimming was a form of meditation, clearing her sometimes cluttered thoughts and easing her joints and muscles into perfect order.

She wrapped a supersize beach towel around her waist, shrugged her arms into her T-shirt, and pulled it over her head, then slipped on her sneakers.

It was a slow walk back over the dunes and through the quiet suburban streets to her home. The sounds of neighbors waking to the day ahead formed a symphonic backdrop to her thoughts.

A dog barked, sharply, three times.

She'd been toying with the idea of Kate's birthday. After all that nonsense with the police about the previous owner, after their delving into Peggy's sordid past and asking questions about their grandfather and their parents again, perhaps it was time the sisters tried to unite. To leave all the past behind.

God only knows how I'm going to get through this, Aurora thought, remembering her vow to keep Peggy out of her life for good.

That night, as she practiced in the music room, with Leo and Mimi curled at her feet, she surprised herself by having a thought about her little sister that wasn't venomous.

It had to be done. But what would she say after all these years? *How have you been?*

Before she could back down, she picked up the phone and scrolled through her contacts for Peggy, wondering as she did so why she'd never deleted her little sister.

"Peggy, it's Aurora."

She heard the sharp intake of breath.

Somehow, Aurora managed to find words. How terrible it must have been for Peggy to find the police at her door. How irresponsible Kate could be sometimes. How frightening all this business was with the serial killer, how unsettling for everyone.

Peggy spoke softly in her replies, with an economy of words. Aurora imagined she was probably in shock.

"I thought maybe we could try a little get-together for Kate's birthday," Aurora said. "Test the waters. What do you think?"

After so many years, as easy as one short phone call, the day arrived. They sat together, the three sisters at a small table by the window, and toasted Kate's birthday with flutes of orange juice.

And they talked, stilted conversation at first, some gentle unearthing of memories, just the happy ones.

Inevitably, some of the not-so-happy ones found air, and Aurora had to talk over them both. She was still furious with Kate for purchasing that house, for embroiling them all in a murder investigation.

"Which has been solved," Kate said.

"Be that as it may, look at what you've put us through."

"Come on, Aurora. It wasn't Kate's fault."

Somehow those words were the catalyst. "It's never anyone's fault, is it?" She looked at Peggy then and felt all the old hatred surge. How their family had been ripped apart.

"I'm sorry," Peggy said. "I didn't mean..."

"Come on, girls." Kate reached for Aurora's hand, for Peggy's on the other side.

Aurora's heart was thudding erratically. Why had she thought this was a good idea?

Peggy cut the tension by sliding an envelope across the table.

Aurora examined the handwriting on the pale blue envelope. Opened it to discover a beautiful handmade card.

> *Peggy and Bo Rowling, together with Denton Price, are pleased to announce the wedding of Peggy and Denton to be held in the Japanese Garden at the Royal Botanic Gardens.*

Aurora felt everything that was taut inside her begin to loosen, to soften. "Oh, Peggy! Getting married?"

That, in itself, was some sort of miracle.

Kate held her own invitation as tears flowed.

Each of them was lost in their own thoughts of what might have been, what might still be.

Aurora lay in bed that night thinking of her grandfather, wondering if he would have been selflessly relieved that his youngest granddaughter had managed to triumph against her bitter demons, to find someone to share her nights with, to love and be loved as he had always hoped.

And what would he think of Aurora?

She gave up her tossing and turning and quietly slid from beneath the down quilt, careful not to wake Jason snoring softly beside her. She was always mindful, although Jason could snore his way through an earthquake. She wandered down the hall to the main bathroom and examined her face under the bright, unforgiving light. What would Grandpa say about this face? Would he say she had held so fast to her hatred for her younger sister that it had wedged filigree lines beneath her eyes? She placed her fingertips in front of her ears and gently pulled the skin to see the softer face that had been hers not so many years ago: an unmarked alabaster palette waiting for life to paint its lines. When she let the skin fall back naturally, she noticed the lines fanning up from her top lip, hinting at a look of prudish distaste. Would Grandpa tell her they had formed from the effort of keeping her heart hardened against Peggy? And the slight downward turn of her bottom lip where it once turned up in smile. Grandpa would surely berate her for being forlorn and downcast. Aurora knew that beauty came first from within. The best of genes and all the lotions and potions in the world would never compensate for a rigid heart.

Returning to slide softly under the covers, she fell asleep with damp eyelids, understanding that Grandpa truly would want the best for *little Peg* and, deep down, Aurora wanted the best for her too.

"You will come to the wedding?" Kate asked the next time she phoned. "I know things got a bit heated the other day, but..."

"Yes, I'll come," Aurora said.

After the call, she retreated to her music room, played Enya's "Watermark," before segueing into her own, as yet untitled piece. She had been close to finishing it when crafting the clock had taken priority, followed by the usual "silly season" of parties and weddings. The work would start to taper off soon. Fall was not an especially busy time for weddings. Strangely, if spring and summer nuptials proved too difficult, the brides' next choice was inevitably winter. Fall seemed to be the forgotten season, but it was Aurora's favorite. The superb golden tones, the crisp mornings, the slowed pace. Perfect times for composing.

She stopped playing suddenly and ran her hands over the smooth wooden arch of her instrument.

The Forgotten Season, she scribbled at the top of the music sheet. A most suitable name for her composition, fitting perfectly as it did with the four divisions that had formed organically almost beyond her awareness. She began to see the piece in her mind's eye, as an art display. It was like a tetraptych, four complementary pieces hinged into a single work, the eye being led from winter through to fall. The musical composition led the ear in the same way, the autumnal finale perfectly suited to the naturally round sounds of Aurora's touch.

She most definitely would go to Peggy's wedding. She would smile and hold only goodness in her heart. It was time to bury the past.

35

PEGGY was not even slightly nervous.

She wore an ivory vintage dress with a high neckline and three-quarter sleeves, a single red rose adorning her hair, and as she walked between Bo and Denton across the little red bridge spanning two sides of the Japanese garden, she knew she was finally leaving one life behind—that old life of alcoholic memories, loneliness, and constant temptation—for a new one, filled with infinite possibilities.

She'd left all the organization to the boys. Thankfully, they'd stopped short of buying her a dress when Bo said the one Denton chose would make his mother look like an ice cream cone. But they organized the invitations, booked the gardens and the after-party venue, the entertainment, and the catering.

Peggy had never liked being the center of attention, even when she was little, and especially not once she had to learn to cope without drugs and alcohol. But somehow this was different. She didn't imagine herself as the main attraction. She was more interested in how gorgeous Bo and Denton were in their individualized outfits: Denton in black pants with a red shirt and white vest, Bo in white with a red-and-white-checked vest. And she was interested in the guests, delighted to see that Aurora really did come, with Jason and with those beautiful children who Peggy barely knew: Grant and Stella.

At lunch, when they'd celebrated Kate's birthday, Aurora had indicated she would come, but Peggy had been convinced she would renege, especially after their heated exchanges. She'd not really believed it until she got the formal reply, which she'd had to read three times before believing it.

> *Thank you for your kind invitation, which we are pleased to accept.*
>
> *Jason, Aurora, Stella, and Grant Dwyer*

On this, her wedding day, Peggy's own attention was taken up with watching Bo and Denton; blowing a kiss to Aurora and bowing her thank-you; trying to get a good look at young Stella, who everyone said was so much like Peggy; willing Grant to raise his head so she could see if he looked as much like Jason as Kate said he did; grinning at Kate, who winked and let out a wolf whistle, just as she'd always threatened to do on Peggy's special day.

Denton's parents and his sister had flown from Chicago. Peggy had met them only the day before, and it was easy to see why

Denton was such a gorgeous, loving soul when she saw the way his family interacted with each other.

Karina Rowling was there in the gardens, at least in body, early onset dementia now aggravating the deeply entrenched effects of the stroke. Peggy was pleased now that Kate had insisted their mother would be too tired and addled to attend the celebrations later.

Kate said it had been enough to get their mother dressed and into the car to take the short drive to the Botanical Gardens for the service, and there had been nonstop whining the whole time.

"She insisted on calling me 'Nurse' and kept complaining about the chill in the air," Kate had said when they'd first arrived. "And every time she looked out the window, she complained about all the foreigners."

"I'm sorry, Kate." Peggy wished she hadn't insisted on her mother's coming.

Kate had responded in her usual no-nonsense manner, a few moments before the wedding was scheduled to start. "Don't worry if I make a late arrival to the reception. I'll get Mom back into her PJs, and I'll get there as soon as I can."

"You're not going now?" Peggy had said.

"Shit, no! I wouldn't miss you tying the knot for anything, little Peg. I'll take her back once everyone starts heading to the reception."

With all that was going on, Peggy had no time to be nervous or to even be aware of a spotlight.

The celebrant, a somewhat stocky, big-bosomed woman with salt-and-pepper hair, wore a pale blue suit, matching eyeshadow, and red lipstick.

"Peggy, do you declare your love for Denton? Do you promise to honor his life and his love?"

Peggy sighed and smiled. "I do."

Abso-friggin'-lutely! With bells on! Man, just look at him.

"I do," she repeated unnecessarily, and the celebrant took a deep breath, causing her ample bust to swell between the betrothed.

"Denton..."

Peggy forgot to listen to the words. She winked at Bo and heard Denton mimic her reply. "I do." He grinned and repeated those tiny precious words. "I do."

They kissed and laughed and hugged, the three of them. And then they hugged the celebrant, whose breasts threatened to swallow Bo's head.

Before she could catch her own breath, Peggy was engulfed in the arms of her family, Kate smothering her with kisses, a subdued congratulations and pat on the back from Aurora, and a warmer-than-expected hug from Stella, who perhaps recognized herself so easily in the physical reality of the aunt she barely knew.

The heavily pregnant Mariana fought back hormone-enhanced wedding tears, telling everyone in her booming, big-city-girl brashness about how she always knew *these kids belonged together*.

Peggy bent to kiss her mother lightly on the cheek, but the shriveled shell that was Karina Rowling pulled back in horror and dabbed at the spot with her embroidered handkerchief. Peggy could hear her berating Kate all the way across the bridge.

"I want to go back," she cried from her two-wheeled chariot. "I don't like Tokyo. Get me to the airport."

Kate's laughter pealed out like church bells.

Denton and Bo had spent half the morning decking the gallery in streamers of ivory lace and red roses. They'd decorated the one long damask-covered table with pink and red rose petals.

The DJ played old John Lennon hits, with a smattering of Ed Sheeran and Adele. The guests were handed fluted glasses of sparkling apple juice, before dining on mixed entrées of antipasto, fresh oysters, prawns, and rice paper rolls. The festivities were unimpeded by the traditional litany of speeches, and in between courses, they danced on the polished wooden floorboards, admired the local artworks adorning the walls, talked and laughed. By the time they had plowed their way through platters of crispy lemon-crusted chicken, spicy chickpeas, roasted vegetables, and salad, there was barely room for the fresh fruit and cheese, but somehow they managed to fit it all in.

Peggy and Denton were pleased with their decision to forgo a formal dessert, and in keeping with their nontraditional nuptials, there was no wedding cake.

Conversation between Peggy and Aurora was stilted.

"I can't thank you enough for coming," Peggy said.

"It was a lovely service."

Can you forgive me? Peggy's heart cried. "Drink?" was all she could choke out, grabbing a couple of flutes from a passing tray.

"Maybe we'll get around to a big family get-together soon," Aurora said, and Peggy could do nothing but swallow.

"I know I've left it too long," Aurora said. "I understand, finally, that you were not in control of your own self."

"I don't know if you can ever find it in your heart to truly forgive me, Aurora. I am so happy you came."

Kate bounded in between them and flung an arm around each of her sisters with her usual exuberance. "Don't you two go getting all serious now!" She laughed. "This is a time for celebration." She held her glass of juice up. "Cheers!"

When the sisters followed suit and clinked their flutes together, Kate began to sing.

"Oh, my darling, oh, my darling, oh, my daaarling Clementine!"

Aurora joined in easily in her perfectly modulated crystal-clear voice: *"You are lost and gone forever, dear sweet darling Clementine."*

Kate squeezed Peggy's shoulder. "Come on, Peg! Sing along!"

Peggy was nonplussed.

"In a cavern, in a canyon!" her two sisters sang in perfect harmony, without falter. It was as though they sang this crazy song every day.

Kate and Aurora stopped when they realized Peggy was not going to join in their raucous rendition.

"I seem to remember you have a beautiful singing voice," Kate said. "Why didn't you join in?"

"I don't know the song."

"What?" Kate turned to Aurora. "How could she not know that song?"

Aurora peered closely at her little sister. "Surely you remember, Peggy. Daddy used to sing it to us all the time."

Peggy searched her inadequate and faulty memory bank. "I can't remember." Her voice was a whisper.

For Peggy, it was a tiny glitch in an otherwise perfect day. She thought most of her real childhood memories had come back, but she could never remember their father singing that song. Perhaps she had been too young. She'd learned not to let such trifles worry her and shrugged off the confusion on her sisters' faces.

It was a beautiful day. In fact, she had never dared to dream the planets would align and conspire to forgive all her past transgressions. With Denton beside her, she truly believed there was a wonderful life ahead.

But later that night, after she and Denton had made love, gloriously softly and gently, strange fragments of memory crept up on her. In that tiny sliver of candlelit confusion between wakefulness and sleep, she heard the deep, dulcet tones of her father's voice:

Ruby lips above the water...

It was the tune her sisters had sung at the wedding.

Claustrophobia sucked the air from around her. *Where am I?*

In the twilight zone, the eyes of twenty dolls watched her. She was confined. Kate? Was that Kate's face she saw? Aurora? Or was it another doll? She could barely breathe.

Oh, my darling Clementine.

36

SHE stared into the flames of the beachside barbecue. It was around dusk, and she'd gone walking at the less secluded beach, one she avoided in summer due to the raucous families sizzling hot dogs, children squealing and chasing each other over the mossy grass and onto the sand. In these cooler months, it was usually just young die-hard joggers and older couples walking their dogs.

She'd been surprised to see a family, hunched against the wind, eating their lunch. She'd sat on a rock to watch them for a while. The minute they packed their belongings, no doubt berating themselves for their stupidity in bringing children to eat outdoors in such unpleasant weather, she'd gone to stare into the glowing coals they'd left behind.

She didn't often think of that first kill. Considering those that followed, it had been a subdued affair. But that soft, smoky glow brought the memories flooding in.

Fire had always fascinated her.

She was ten years old when she'd broken into the neighbor's house and tipped lawn mower fuel over his carpet. The nasty, dirty old man had been down at the pub where he always was at that time of night. She had often observed him from a ledge behind his property, and she'd been in his house once when he'd taken her there to show her his caged birds. At least that's what he'd told her she was going to see, but the cages were empty.

She loved to play with matches, to watch things burn, that was all. She'd set out to start a fire, maybe even to burn the house down, but she had not originally intended to kill Mr. Briels.

He came home earlier than she'd anticipated, and she had bolted behind the bedroom door.

"What the fuck's tha' smell?" He had a deep booming voice, no less fearful for its drunken slurring. "Fuck! Need to piss."

He swayed his way into the bedroom, and as he navigated a path around the bed to the bathroom, he'd miscalculated both his trajectory and his timing, unzipping his fly way too early. The gray woolen pants started to slide down over his hips.

"Whaz that fuckin' smell?"

Her senses were on high alert, and she was poised to take flight. Half-concealed, she'd be spotted if he turned. Her legs shook with the knowledge, her heart thudding with it.

As she'd stood there, quaking behind the door, as the drunk and lecherous Mr. Briels had turned toward her, perhaps detecting a presence, his pants slipped farther over his thighs and he'd tripped. His drunkenness did not allow for the necessary time between thought and action to break his fall. An awkward stumble, a 360-degree swivel, a muffled panicked cry, then the crack of his skull against the iron railings of the headboard.

"Thank you, God," she whispered with timid reverence.

She struck a match and threw it to the carpet.

Mr. Briels didn't move.

She flung four more matches onto the fuel-soaked bedroom floor, glanced again at the man, who, months before, had pulled her pants down and smacked her and then pushed his penis into her mouth and threatened her with death if she told. She ran from the house and circled around in the early evening semidarkness so she could watch the flames take hold.

"Thanks to my heavenly father," she whispered again, parodying something she'd once heard on television. "Amen."

She didn't get to see him burn, but the big trucks with their wailing sirens arrived too late to save him. She hadn't needed to see it, to know how it would have looked. Ever since she'd disobeyed Mr. Briels and made the mistake of telling someone what he did to her, ever since she had discovered the world was a cruel and evil place and she could count on no one but her made-up version of a God, ever since then, she'd been burning things.

Books. Dolls. Clothes. Teddy bears.

The spasmodic burning had not stopped when she reached adulthood. Not long ago, she'd burned the egg carton and the tea towel she'd incongruously taken from her latest victim's house. She'd retrieved them from the back of her freezer, along with her own T-shirt, and "defrosted" them in the sun. Then she'd dug a scrappy hole in the woods and burned them as much as she could before burying the remains.

It did occur to her, when her efforts at burning the fabric produced an inordinate amount of smoke, to wonder what she would say if anyone sought out the source and questioned what she was doing. She amused herself with the thought that if such an intruder into her private affairs turned out to be a man, she would lure him to her little barbecue and press his face into the flames.

She was unsettled about the way her latest kill had been reported. The evening news, always more sensational than the daily papers, tried to form some connection between it and the murders of the surfer Henry Macinaine and that stupid fat fuck Robbie Aston, but the police spokeswoman discredited the journalists' reporting as sensationalist. The sensationalizing continued online though.

At first she smiled when she read about her heroic efforts. There were no clues. There were only facts. The killer had used a knife from the victim's kitchen. A clean slice across his throat, finished off with a violent thrust to the head. They didn't mention if the murder weapon had been wielded by a right hand or a left. She supposed that was the type of information the police would like to keep up their collective sleeve. No mention of fingerprints. No suspects.

But soon she tired of the ineffectiveness of it all. Sure, she had managed to rid the world of one more piece of scum, but to what end?

When she next read about her latest kill, she smiled, remembering that at least there was no longer a K.R. Carstead writing her drivel about women who kill. The psychologist and her cats were long gone, and good riddance.

See how effective I am?

See how hard I work for you?

Most of the time, she had no recollection of the murders, felt no connection between those men and herself. But then there were days when the memories returned and she felt herself slipping away. She wanted to slide and separate from her daily persona. She wanted to escape from reality. She thought she might wrap a Rambo scarf around her head and a bullet belt around her thigh and sling an automatic weapon over her shoulder. She'd wade into the mountains and lure the men into the valleys, and then she'd fill them with fear and hunt them down.

But then she'd remind herself she could do her best work living and walking among them. It wasn't enough to kill them; she must make them suffer. She must make them afraid. She should make them cower and hide and take tiny fearful steps in the night rather than stride out with confidence and bravado.

Some of her kills were less than satisfactory. She'd had no time to spend with the bodies, to taste blood, caress the slippery entrails. The one in the bushes whose brains she'd bashed in, she hadn't been able to see the fear encroach upon his ratlike features. The man in the kitchen, there was too much blood and not enough time to play. She constantly switched between not knowing and knowing. Those times, in the knowing, she was torn between the waiting, fearing discovery, and the lust for blood, the need to show them what fear was.

Then, she thought of a way to take care of more than one beast at a time.

It was an almost pitch-black moonless night, but she didn't

need the light. She sat on the cool sand at the northern end of her favorite beach and made her plans. In keeping with the exercises detailed in *Visualizing Your Perfect Life*, the self-help book she'd found one day at the beach, she pictured herself at work. She saw herself bending over the prone bodies, attending to the tasks that would make the world a better place.

As she walked home, she forgot it all. She smiled for the quiet joy of peace and sang softly into the cool air.

Oh, my darling...

37

KATE pounded along the bike path, her expensive new ankle-protective, high-impact running shoes making her feel like she was gliding above the concrete path.

It was verdict day for the "Finger in the Pie" case, following a protracted and delayed battle. After a brisk run with no time for a swim, she turned off the path before the south beach and headed around the block, then hit the steep curve that would lead her home. She now thought of number thirty-six as her home, no longer her grandfather's.

She generally dressed for parties in much the same garb as she dressed for everyday work: well-tailored black pants, plain shirt, and Doc Martens. Nevertheless, she did possess blouses with lower necklines in brighter colors, and she had a small box filled with rarely worn jewelry.

She dressed a tad less conservatively for this final day, knowing that, win or lose, she would be roped into cocktails down at the offices of *The Taste*. Most of Lilly and Sandringham's staff had been invited, despite Kate's caution to Adella that they could still lose.

"I know, Kate," the publisher had responded with her customary enthusiasm. "So what can I say? We'll either be drowning our sorrows or whooping it up. You've done a great job, and I just want to say thank you, regardless of the outcome."

"Paying the bill is how you say thanks in this business," Kate reminded her.

"Don't I know it! 'Wounded bulls' are the words that come to mind."

Despite what she'd said to Adella, Kate was quietly confident of victory, but she had learned to deal with the fact that, in cases like this, the law was not clear-cut and the verdict was still up for grabs.

"We must remember that this claim for defamation is against the publisher," Kate reminded the court later that day. "Stephano Corelli is inconsequential." It was a low blow, but she couldn't help herself. She stole a glance at the money-grubbing Stephano and was pleased to see his crushed ego evident in the turned-down lips and the flintiness in his drug-screwed eyes.

Her eyes had flicked to the back of the room. Bloody hell! Detective Nick Timms. She momentarily lost her place, forgot the speech she'd rehearsed. What the hell was Timms doing here?

"We've...we've," she stammered. Took a breath. "We've heard from Adella Banna, and I feel sure you will agree that any malice she may once have felt toward her ex-husband was quelled many years ago. Ms. Banna is far too busy and successful to plot ill will against someone she has absolutely no feelings about."

Another well-timed sisterhood blow. Richard Banna looked at his hands, fidgeting.

Kate glanced beyond him. Relief flooded her veins when there was no sign of the detective.

In that nanosecond, she was pleased to see a different but subtly familiar figure; it was the tall, mildly tanned stranger with the pleasantly lined face she'd first noticed in the lobby two weeks ago. There was something mysterious and fascinating about him, and Kate confessed he might have been partly on her mind when she chose the deep emerald, low-cut silk blouse this morning and teamed it with emerald studs and a gold necklace.

She was pleased to see him giving Adella a congratulatory hug in the foyer after their win and thrilled to notice his attendance at the cocktail party.

"I suppose you're sick of hearing congratulations, but I can't think of a more appropriate word at the moment."

The voice was honey-thick to her ear. He stood just outside the periphery of her personal space as though waiting for an invitation.

"It's not a word I can imagine myself tiring of easily," she replied, turning to face him fully and finally stopping her furtive scanning for the pest that was Detective Timms.

"Then allow me to say you were brilliant in that courtroom."

Up close, he was devastatingly good-looking, with a shock of gray-streaked hair and clear blue eyes fanned with the lines of kindness and surprise and laughter, where many had lines of bitterness.

"I'd like to take credit," she said. "But the law is what it is. The journalist might not have had the purest of motives, and the article no doubt harms Richard's reputation. But the suit was against Adella Banna, and she did everything by the book."

He smiled, all charm. "Ah, but the verdict could just as easily have gone the other way. No doubt there was no shortage of malice and an extreme lack of good faith."

Kate's heart sank. He was sounding suspiciously like a man who knew something about the law. She'd dated a few lawyers in her time—it seemed to be de rigueur in a profession that was slightly incestuous—but had always found them to be hard work, an accusation that had certainly been leveled at Kate herself, she recalled wryly.

A waiter passed, and her flatterer reached for two champagne flutes.

He handed one to her. "Cheers."

She clinked the tip of her glass against his gently.

"Iain Furness." He held out his hand and she shook it firmly, hoping the sudden heat that flared was not apparent.

"Lawyer?" she asked, willing the answer to be no.

He laughed. "Not guilty."

She laughed too and hoped he wasn't another foolish layabout dilettante or an adrenaline addict or married or gay or...

"I'm a teacher."

Not just any old teacher, as it turned out.

Iain Furness was a professor of English literature and faculty of arts dean. He was neither married nor gay and received his "adrenaline" fix via spasmodic trips to visit the far-flung resting places of long-dead poets and the occasional spot of skiing. His interest in the case was mildly academic, but he'd attended court mainly to show his support for his long-standing friend Adella.

Kate was dragged away from his side too quickly, to be lavished with yet more praise from Adella and her many friends.

She was on constant alert, lest Detective Timms return. What on earth did he want?

Contrary to what she'd said to Iain Furness, she did rather get sick of the word *congratulations* toward the end of the evening, coming from so many people she really didn't care about. She scanned the room from time to time, but unless he'd found a comfortable professorial seat somewhere in a bookish corner, Kate knew Iain had left. He was tall enough—well over six foot two, she surmised—so, if he'd been standing in this room, she'd have been able to spot him.

There was no sign of the detective, which flooded her with relief.

When she was able to convince Adella that she really did have to leave—prior family commitments being her fib of choice—Adella had a pleasant surprise.

"I almost forgot," she said digging around in the chic little ruffled Miu Miu purse slung across her shoulder. "Iain asked me to give you this."

Kate examined the card.

Adella Banna, the TASTE.

She frowned.

"Other side, Kate. He's scribbled something on the other side."

Kate turned the card over.

> *Mid-forties, long-divorced, father of two. Dinner?*
> *Iain Furness*

She stared at the phone number and smiled.

"Felicitations," he said when she called him the next day.

"Hotshot English professor," she replied. "You should have been able to come up with that yesterday on the spot."

"Ah, but then you may have thought me pompous and we would not now be having this conversation."

Her laughter bubbled. "True."

As she'd expected, Iain Furness did know something about the law. It had been his original major in college. "Took me two and a half years to figure out it wasn't the field for me," he said.

"I'm glad."

"Why?"

"I'll tell you over dinner."

And so began an easy, steady courtship.

"Why were you so pleased to discover I'm not a lawyer?" he asked later.

"I don't date lawyers."

Kate regaled him with exaggerated tales of the disastrous dates and "micro-relationships" of her past, as they dined on calamari and baked salmon.

Iain confessed to his one and only transgression in his former life as a married man. "But it was a big one," he said. "She was too young, too blond, and too obviously my student."

His wife had not been the forgiving kind.

"What do you fancy for dessert?" he asked as the menus reappeared.

"I'm not much of a sweet tooth," she said.

"I bet I could sway you." His smile was slow and easy, and she wondered if that's how he would play her body. "I make the best affogato outside of Italy."

"I'll let you give it a shot." She wasn't thinking about coffee or dessert.

"I'm too old and grown-up to be coy," she said as they entered his sixth-floor apartment. "I am extremely attracted to you, and I can't bear to say out loud how long it's been since I've had sex."

"Well, let's not waste another second."

She peripherally noted the overflowing bookshelves, supersize modern art canvases, and an ocean view that rivaled her own, but it would be hours before she got around to admiring her surroundings properly.

In the interim, Iain reminded her body what it had been missing, scalding her with the heat of his body, cooling her with his breath. Slowly, he played her. Easy and gentle, building the tension with finesse and expertise.

There was no Nick Timms invading her thoughts. No serial killer. No murderous visions.

Much later, Iain presented her with the affogato he'd boasted about earlier in the evening.

"Ah," she sighed as her tongue distinguished the hazelnut undertones of the Frangelico, beneath the stronger, chocolaty-coffee flavor of the melting ice cream.

"Told you. Is that not the best dessert you've ever had?"

No hesitation. "Oh yeah."

She left at 2 a.m., after they'd made a belated "Let's take it slow" pact and a date for the following weekend.

She was still smiling as she pulled into the garage and switched off the engine.

Pain pierced the side of her head.

She heard a whimper. She couldn't tell where it came from. Inside the car? Inside her head? It sounded like Peggy. Or was it Aurora?

A flash of light beneath her eyelids. A vision.

Dolls' faces.

Peggy's wide eyes. Her sister's mouth opening as if to scream.

Shush, little Peg. Shhh.

Then the pixels of Peggy's face rearranged themselves into a perfect facsimile of Aurora, albeit contorted with anguish.

Kate felt her own panic rising.

It's okay, Aurora. Shhh.

Kate knew it was up to her, as the eldest, to keep them all safe.

She was lost in the dreamscape, willing her sisters to become invisible.

She bit her lip and ducked her head, and as the scream welled in her chest, she mercifully blacked out.

Sunlight crept its fingers through the side window of the garage and stroked her face. She was stunned to still be sitting in the driver's seat of her car, in the red blouse she'd worn for her date.

It was six o'clock on a brand-new day, and Kate had no idea what was wrong with her.

38

NICK relived that little stumble of Kate's in the courtroom. She was such a competent deliberator, and it had been there on show for the judge, the jury, the combatants in that silly "Finger in the Pie" court case. She had all those onlookers enthralled, not to mention the journalists.

Nick had been peeved to see so many senior journalists in that courtroom. You'd have thought they'd be working on stories of a much bigger nature. Like a serial killer in the community. At the same time, he was pleased there was something to distract them. So often, it was overeager reporters who made his job harder, who somehow managed to pry information from police sources and throw it out into the public arena, where it could make life difficult for Nick and his associates. Difficult on two fronts, to be precise. Sometimes, information would be leaked that might cause panic when the police needed calm. More importantly, there'd been times when tightly guarded facts had ended up on the front page, alerting a perpetrator way too early in an investigation.

Which was why he was keeping a lot of his suspicions to himself. No point sharing them with his colleagues anyway, when they were things he couldn't prove.

What he wanted, though, was for these three women to know he hadn't given up on them. He was convinced there was some connection between them and the killer.

He'd made them all uncomfortable, and that was a damned fine start.

39

AURORA shuddered. Her head ached, and there was a ringing in her ears.

"You are thirteen years old, Stella!"

"Well, duh."

Just the sort of response to send Aurora's blood pressure through the roof, but she pursed her full lips and sucked in some air.

Stay calm.

"You should be thinking about study and art and music, and having fun with your girlfriends. Boys can wait. They're not going to disappear off the face of the planet."

"Oh, I can't talk to you!" Stella spun on one childlike heel.

"Don't you walk away from me, young lady!" Aurora was aware of how much she sounded like her own mother.

Stella stopped in defiant mid-stride and turned back to her

mother. "I'm nearly fourteen. And lots of the girls at school have boyfriends and they all have boys at their parties."

And if all the other girls jumped off a bridge, would you follow? It was the first response that came to Aurora's mind, straight from her mother's arsenal, and usually aimed directly at Peggy. She bit her tongue to dam the words threatening to spill from her lips.

"We need to talk about this sensibly," she said softly. "Come and we'll make the batter."

The line of Stella's shoulders loosened as she half smiled. Their Sunday morning ritual as peacemaker: mother and daughter cooking up an enormous batch of pancakes.

But the tacit ceasefire lasted only long enough for Aurora to drag the skillet from the bottom cupboard and reach for the flour.

"I bet you had boyfriends," Stella said.

Perhaps it was the expression on her daughter's face when Aurora turned back from the pantry that set her teeth on edge anew. With her lanky, dull-blond hair falling across one eye and her lips in a half sneer, Stella could easily have been Peggy.

"I was much older," Aurora said through gritted jaw. "And there was a certain type of boy I wouldn't have been caught dead with."

Stella slammed the drawer shut and threw the whisk on the countertop with such force it bounced onto the floor and rolled under the table.

"You don't even know anything about Benny!"

"I know he plays football. I know that crowd." Peggy's first boyfriend had been a football player too. "Honey, you only have to listen to what's been on the news these past few days to know what they're like."

"Come on, Mom. He plays for the school team, not the NFL."

"Nevertheless, I know the type."

"I suppose all boys who play football end up being rapists like those two guys who've been arrested?"

"Don't be silly, Stella. I'm just trying to say there are particular cliques that attract a certain type of person. You don't want to be mixing in that crowd."

"But you haven't even met him."

"I am older and wiser than you, and I know a thing or two."

"That's right. You're a dried-up old witch!"

Stella spun and stormed from the kitchen, ignoring her mother's outstretched hand and anguished expression.

Aurora folded her arms onto the counter and slumped forward in an uncharacteristically awkward pose. She knew enough psychology to realize she was projecting Peggy's unfortunate life onto her daughter. She knew her problem wasn't so much Stella's age as it was the choice of boy. It was Aurora's fear that her daughter might get a taste for the bad-boy jock, the type of boy Peggy had chosen when she was young. Aurora wanted for her daughter friends who enjoyed concerts and art galleries, boys from good families who had a sense of right and wrong. She didn't want Stella mixing with all that flagrant testosterone. Fifteen-year-old football players were, Aurora thought, just a hop, skip, and a touchdown away from being one of those men in their twenties who'd been arrested last week for the horrific rape of a young girl.

Jason unexpectedly sided with Stella.

"It's only puppy love," he said. "How could you think anything else? She's thirteen, for God's sake."

"Jason, the boy she is talking about is fifteen, almost sixteen."

"Yes, but for all we know he's a good kid who comes from a good family."

"He plays football." Sometimes Jason could be so naive, and his arched, questioning eyebrows caused her exasperation to segue to anger. "Football," she repeated.

He stared at her strangely for a moment. "So what does that mean? He's probably fit and disciplined. When other teenagers are drinking beer behind the shed and smoking dope, this young kid is probably training."

"For heaven's sakes. Football players were always Peggy's redneck of choice."

"And there's the problem. You're projecting your old Peggy fears onto Stella again. Just because she bears some physical resemblance to your sister doesn't give you the right to assume she has similar psychological characteristics."

"How dare you say that to me!" Her voice had grown shrill and desperate. She knew Stella would be listening to this argument, and Aurora had so wanted to present a united front: mother and father steadfast in unison against almost-fourteen-year-old girls having boys at their parties.

"How dare you insinuate I have anything but my daughter's best interests at heart?"

"Come on, darling. That's not what I said, and you know it."

"Leave it alone, Jason. You have no idea what's really going on here, and you are not helping in the slightest."

He raised his hands from the kitchen countertop as a form of protest. "Let's calm down now."

"Believe me, I'm calm." Her voice was low now, almost a whisper. "I'm telling you, don't fight me on this."

She walked away.

"Where are you going now?"

"For a walk."

"Again?"

"Yes." She looked at her husband challengingly. "Again. In case you haven't noticed, women seem to be immune from this serial killer."

"Not immune to police surveillance though, it seems."

"What on earth do you mean?"

"After Kate was questioned and we had police around here asking all sorts of things, I saw a detective lurking around."

"What?"

"He was sitting outside in his unmarked car. I saw him again recently too."

"How do you know he's a detective?"

"I've seen him interviewed on TV. Timms, I think it is, the one who's always trying to say it's not a serial killer, always trying to tone things down."

Aurora snorted, showing a bravado she didn't feel. "What a load of rubbish." She wondered if Jason was just making it all up to cover up the real reason he didn't want her out alone. "I don't care about any of that. I'm going for a walk, like it or not."

For a moment it seemed he might take on the challenge, drag up her old lies. Those days were just under the surface like some festering subterranean quake: the tales of going for walks and playing sport and visiting girlfriends, the lies that had allowed her to frolic like a teenager in the car with Arnaud or strip naked so he could paint her and then tease her to heights of ecstasy.

Aurora's memories were still there.

And Jason's hurt and suspicions were never far away.

She walked for more than a mile before her head began to clear. Maybe that detective really was keeping an eye on them. Kate's strange behavior, Peggy's sordid history.

Shit! Peggy, again.

She knew Jason was right in a way. Visions of Peggy sometimes crowded her mind, clouded her thinking. But it was also true that she wanted nothing but the best for her daughter. Aurora was well aware of the devastating effects of mixing with the wrong crowd. You only needed to look at the Rowling sisters for proof. Same upbringing, same parents, same childhood. And yet one of them had gone bad. Peggy had run around with the wrong crowd and become sucked into the underbelly of society, while her sisters had gone on to live normal, straightforward lives.

Peggy: trying to kill herself with alcohol and drugs, living in squalor. Sure, she had her act together now, but Aurora looked back at the cost and was terrified her daughter might pay a similar price.

Perhaps if that morning's headlines had not highlighted the harsh realities of football players on the loose, Aurora might not have snapped so quickly at her daughter.

FOOTBALL PLAYERS CHARGED WITH RAPE

"Yes Aurora, but don't forget," Kate had warned when Aurora called her earlier. "The law maintains they are still innocent until proven guilty."

She'd been horrified at what appeared to be Kate's cavalier attitude. "Don't tell me you don't remember how it was that Peggy first went off the rails?"

"Of course I remember. And for all we know, it was probably wild little Peg who led those young men astray."

The girls knew scant details of those early forays of Peggy's onto the wrong side of the tracks. They knew Peggy got drunk and had sex with boys, and they had discovered through friends she'd been at an all-out orgy. They'd tried to help their parents bring Peggy back into the fold, but it had proved to be a lost cause.

"Oh, come on," Aurora said. "I can't imagine it was Peggy who introduced them to alcohol and drugs and wild orgies."

Kate's groan was loud in Aurora's ear. "It wasn't that long ago, Aurora, when you acted as though Peggy was the devil incarnate and you'd have accused her of anything. Anyway, I'm trying to make the point that it was a different era; they were different men. We don't know anything about the accused men in this article or about the woman who has accused them."

"Girl," Aurora interrupted. "The girl who was raped is sixteen years old. You can't refer to her as a woman."

"Okay, okay, point taken. Anyway, why are you getting so upset about it?"

It had haunted Aurora all morning. When Stella had come to her with plans for a beach party with boys involved and then confessed she had a boyfriend and his name was Benny and he was a football player, the newspaper article had flashed before Aurora's eyes like a warning beacon and she'd hit the roof.

Overreaction, Jason had accused.

Dried-up old witch, Stella had called her.

But the alcohol-fueled binges of these testosterone-charged men, and the damage they could inflict on the young, were well documented and more than a little frightening.

As Aurora walked back along the shore, she began to calm. Yes, she was a mother bear, and it was her innate duty to protect her offspring. But she knew she'd overreacted.

She would need to remain cool and calm if she was to get her point across to Stella and Jason. She rehearsed her spiel in time with her steps. A bunch of girls for a sleepover was a perfect party for a fourteen-year-old. Boys could wait; sixteen was a suitable age to go out with boys.

She slipped her shoes off in the laundry room and walked through the hallway to the kitchen, calmer and more in control than when she'd left.

"I'm back," she called to Jason, who was sitting on the deck eating his customary Sunday lunch of a pastrami and avocado sandwich with a glass of low-carb beer.

"I see that," he called back, his face made more handsome with a half smile.

She poured a glass of wine from the opened bottle in the fridge and joined him on the balcony. "I'm sorry I lost my temper."

"Most unlike you," he said.

She brushed her hand along his shoulder as she passed to take a seat opposite him.

"Where is she?"

"She went out."

Her heart stuttered. "What? Alone?"

"No."

"Well, who with?" She tried to stop her voice from quavering. "Where did she go?"

Jason took a hefty swig of his beer. "She's gone to see a movie."

"Who with?"

"Benny." Jason reached for her hand. "Don't worry, honey. You know I wouldn't let anything happen to our precious girl."

"Then how could you have let her go?"

Breathe, she told herself. Just breathe.

Jason caressed her fingers. "I wish you'd seen him. He's a nice boy who likes Stella and wants to spend some time with her."

Aurora stared at her fingers. Her hands were the body parts she was most proud of. The long, harp-plucking fingers; the smooth, soft skin; the well-manicured nails. She pulled her hands away from her husband, slowly and calmly.

"Okay, you win," she whispered.

"There's nothing to win, honey. It wasn't a contest."

He reached for her again, but she clasped her wineglass tightly with both hands.

"We both want what's best for Stella," Jason continued.

"Agreed." Her voice was less than a whisper now as she stood from the table.

"Now don't go off in a huff."

"I'm not in a huff. I just want to be alone." She went to her music room, to the comfort of her special seat, to straddle the smooth curve of the harp, to caress its strings. In times of stress, the harp was her child and her lover; it was both masterful and subservient. With gentle coaxing, she could mold the harp's sounds into whatever she wanted them to be. She could create her own universe by redirecting the air around the strings.

She meditated as she played, forced a smile to her lips. Jason was right.

40

PEGGY sat on a rock watching the swell of the sea as tears traced narrow rivers down her face. She barely noticed until the saltiness at one corner of her mouth startled her.

She swiped at the tears and tried to pull herself together.

Get a grip.

How could these awful cravings start attacking her now? It had been years, for fuck's sake!

She wasn't a fool. She understood completely what the professionals had been telling her. She would always have to be vigilant. She got that. But she had simply never imagined that the yearning for alcohol would come back as strongly as it had returned today.

Why? What was different about today?

She'd struggled with some minor psychological problems since the wedding or even before that, since Denton had moved in. She'd inwardly debated the notion that it was time to destroy her secret log—the one she kept hidden in the wardrobe—mainly because she would be forever terrified Denton would find it but also because she wanted to prove to herself that she was moving on.

She was a happily married woman and a joyful and competent mother. She was studying for an accounting degree, she had a driver's license and a secondhand car, and she and Denton were considering a new home.

And yet, throughout the past week, familiar dreams had resurfaced.

She was usually trapped in a box with Aurora or Kate. It was dark. Something terrible was happening. She wasn't sure how she could see through the darkness, through the walls of the great big box. But she did see, and what she saw made her want to scream.

She gasped. The air became stifling. She couldn't breathe. She squirmed, trying to get air into her nose. It was impossible to breathe through her mouth because something was blocking it.

What was it?

Oh, it was a hand.

The hand pressed harder and harder, and Peggy's terror escalated. She willed the owner of the hand to hear her silent plea.

I can't breathe. Help me. I can't breathe.

But the hand pressed harder.

The little girl Peggy stared in silent horror at the images flashing before her until, mercifully, she blacked out.

Peggy would have variations of the same dream, just like she used to. The difference was that, when she'd had those visions before, she used to drag herself out of bed and drink or drug herself into a stupor so total it would sometimes keep the nightmares at bay for months.

Now, as she swayed back and forth on the rock, remembering last night's version of the dream, Peggy knew she'd answered her own question. She knew why her alcoholism had chosen to rear its ugly head again and make her pray for someone to funnel vodka down her throat or mainline something sweet into her veins. The cravings came now because the dreams were back. What she had to figure out was why the nightmares had resurfaced.

"You've always known recurrence of the cravings is part of life," Dr. Leichardt said later that afternoon, his dulcet voice failing to evoke the familiar sense of calm in his patient.

Thankfully, Peggy had been allowed to ditch the judgmental Dr. Chamberling. She'd served her time with the appointed psychiatrist, and the courts no longer had any jurisdiction over Mrs. Peggy Price.

She so wanted to feel calm and confident, as she usually did in Dr. Leichardt's presence.

"But why now?" she persisted. "Why now?"

"It could be hormonal," Dr. Leichardt suggested.

"What? Like PMS?" Peggy could detect the brittleness in her voice.

"Possibly." The doctor didn't seem phased by her uncharacteristic abruptness. "Any changes in your cycle?"

"I suppose it could be that." Peggy was vague as she mentally calculated days and dates.

"Holy shit!"

Why hadn't she thought about it?

"B-but I'm on the Pill," she stammered. "Surely, I couldn't be."

"Stranger things have happened, Peggy. How would you feel if you were pregnant?"

Peggy's immediate reaction was that she'd be happy, thrilled, ecstatic. She and Denton had discussed trying for a baby in a year or so. What was twelve months when you were talking about a new life?

But as she made her way home after the appointment, she carried a great sense of unease. If altered hormone levels could make her yearn for alcohol so terribly, what was the point of being pregnant? She didn't think she'd be able to get through months of this. Thinking about it made her subconsciously picture the precise location of the nearest hotel, four blocks away.

She imagined walking in there, saying hello to the bartender. Just one glass of beer. She could feel the soft froth on her upper lip, taste the cold, bubbly amber fluid. Her knees weakened, and she leaned against a redbrick fence. Fern fronds from a stranger's garden caressed her shoulder, providing a momentary comfort, and she continued homeward.

"Fuck," she whispered.

The pregnancy stick confirmed what she knew.

"Fuck."

That same word was uttered with various nuances and intonations throughout the afternoon and night.

"Oh, fuck" was Denton's soft utterance, knowing she had been taking the Pill. "But will the baby be okay?"

"Dr. Leichardt thinks so, but I guess we won't know for sure until later."

Earlier in the day, the psychiatrist had urged her back to the previous months, until she'd remembered the fierce stomach bug that was probably responsible for providing a brief window of opportunity for her unpredictable body to jump up and grasp.

"Jesus, Peg! Fuck!" Kate said, later in the evening. "How do you feel?"

"Happy, I think."

"You think?" Kate's voice softened.

Peggy didn't say what she wanted to say. *Help me, Kate. The dreams are coming back.*

Thankfully, *fuck* was not Bo's choice of word. In fact, for quite a few seconds he was speechless.

And then he hugged her.

"I'm so happy, Mom."

"For me or for you?"

"For both of us. And for Denton too, of course."

"Fuck," Denton whispered again into the darkness, in the early hours of the morning. "I can barely believe it."

"Me either," Peggy whispered.

Denton pulled her closer, snuggling her head into his chest. "I detect a note of trepidation."

She took a deep breath. She needed to tell him of her fears.

I have the most chronic craving for booze, she wanted to tell him.

"I'll be happy once I know the baby is all right" is what came out instead.

She wanted to jump out of bed and fling open the wardrobe door, unlock the bottom drawer of the cupboard, lift out the false bottom, and lay the fearsome tome that was her secret diary upon him.

Here, she would say. *Here's the woman you are married to, the woman who's carrying your child. Here is the monster within. Help me.*

But she didn't of course.

She would have to fight these demons all over again, and she would have to do it alone.

Kate visited the next day with a bunch of mixed flowers.

"You should see the garden, Peg. Almost as good as it was when Grandpa lived there. Now you can drive yourself, you can go down anytime, even when I'm not there."

"The dreams are back." Just like that, Peggy blurted it out.

"What?"

"The dreams are back."

"Oh, Peg. Maybe you need to continue with the doctor."

"I'm not going back to that Chamberling bitch. I'm still seeing Dr. Leichardt though."

"And what does he say?"

"He says it might be hormonal."

"You'll get through this, Peg. All that police questioning wouldn't have helped. All that stress."

Peggy was pulled into the comfort of her sister's arms.

The cravings are back, she wanted to say, but she knew Kate's sympathy would extend only so far.

"Are you having any trouble distinguishing between your nightmares and reality?"

Peggy shook her head. "Don't worry. Grandpa's not in my dreams now."

"Because I've got to tell you, Peggy, I know it's an illness, I know it is out of your control, but I won't be able to help you if you start making up those frightful stories again."

"Kate, I know our grandfather was a good man. I would never say or do anything to hurt his memory. Isn't it you who always tells me it wasn't me? It was the liquor and the drugs, you always say."

She was relieved to see Kate's changing expression ultimately settle upon reassurance.

I need a fix. "I'll be fine," Peggy said. *Oh fuck, I need a fix.*

"Jesus, would you check out these bloody headlines," Kate said, grabbing the paper from the table.

FOOTBALL PLAYERS: A LAW UNTO THEMSELVES

"Bastards," Peggy muttered.

"That's the modern media for you, Peg."

"I was talking about those football players. Not the journalists."

"Oh, not you too. I would have thought you of all people would be prepared to keep an open mind."

"But they raped that young girl," Peggy said.

"There!" Kate slammed the paper back onto the table. "That's exactly what I'm talking about. How do you know they raped her? Those men have not been convicted of anything."

"I know the type."

Kate huffed, and Peggy knew she was in for the stern "innocent until proven guilty" speech she'd heard a hundred times before. But Kate seemed to sense she was not up to the sermon this time.

"At least the football players have knocked the serial killer off the front page for a second," Peggy said. She was sick of being on edge about it, of Denton constantly talking about it.

"Speaking of which," Kate said, "has that detective been back? The one who came asking about me buying the house?"

"No. Why would he?" Peggy felt queasy.

"I don't know; I just thought he might be making a nuisance of himself."

As Kate hopped into the car, she asked, "Are you sure you're going to be okay?"

"I'll be fine."

But Peggy wasn't fine. She tried to lie down, thinking if she could drift off to sleep, the cravings would go away. After tossing and turning in a pool of sweat for ten minutes, she jumped out of bed and scrambled around in her wardrobe, emerging with her horror diary. She sat on the bed and with a great thick pencil gripped awkwardly, scrawled F-U-C-K across both pages, the oversize capital letters filling the white space.

It made her feel better for a moment. Her heart rate steadied and she stopped perspiring and shaking. But then, she began to turn the pages backward, reading what was written there as though she were a stranger stumbling upon this horrific book of dark poetry and mad meanderings.

She retrieved the older books from the drawer. Pages and pages of profanity. Sketches of evil horned creatures. Vengeful bile splashed across the pages.

She tried to imagine seeing it through Denton's eyes, and she knew without a doubt she would lose him. If he ever stumbled across these diaries, he would probably walk straight out the door and never look back. He might call the authorities and have Bo taken away from her too. She would lose everything.

Before she had a chance to think of it any further, she raced to the kitchen and rummaged around in the bottom drawer for a box of matches. She ran to the backyard, holding the pile of books out in front of her as though it was some moldy, disease-infected lump.

The flame caught easily. Part of her wanted to stamp out the fire immediately and retrieve what she could of the diaries, but she fought off the urge and sank to the ground, her arms wrapped around her torso like a comforting blanket, and she rocked backward and forward as she watched the words burn.

When she eventually unfolded her arms, it was to discover she'd crushed the last of the diaries to her chest, saving it, for what she didn't know.

Inside, she tucked it into a new hiding place, determined to forget about it.

I can do this.

She cleaned the bathroom for the second time that day and scrubbed all the taps and basins in the house.

She wished Bo still wanted her to meet him after school, but he'd decided he was old enough to travel to and from on his own.

She started to sweat again and went to rest.

As she pictured all her words reduced to ash, she felt herself sinking. So tired. So terribly exhausted.

The dream was so lifelike; she could smell the jonquils in the front yard of the big house on the corner and then the oranges as she walked past the fruit and vegetable store. And oh, the euphoria when she entered the bar. Some of her old football friends were playing pool, and she waved to them, recognizing the familiar lustful expressions. They knew she'd be good for a lay if they gave her enough alcohol.

Just a beer, she told the bartender. She'd start off light and work her way to the top shelf. The glass was so well chilled it was burning her hands as she lifted it to her lips. But before she got to taste it, she was sucked out of that bar as though by some enormous vacuum cleaner into yet another, far less welcome dream.

Little Peg was peering through a slot, a long, narrow window.

Something covered her mouth and one nostril. It was almost impossible to breathe.

She swiveled her eyes to the left. Aurora. It was Aurora's hand covering her mouth.

She'd been here before.

She reached out in the opposite direction from Aurora and touched the familiar cherub cheeks of one of her grandmother's dolls.

Now she knew where she was. It wasn't a cardboard box as she'd always imagined before. She and Aurora were in the fireplace. Surrounded by dolls. The long window was actually the space between the top of the solid fire screen and the overhanging bricks of the hearth.

She forced her eyes sideways to plead with Aurora once more, but Aurora had been replaced by Kate.

She turned her head away, and when she looked back, she was alone. But, still, she could not breathe.

Holy shit. Oh my God! What is happening?

Peggy woke with a maniacal scream.

41

NICK spent hours going back over that old Rowling case trying to find anything, anything at all that would give credence to his suspicions, often shooting the breeze with Tony Walsh, who'd worked on that case.

"I assume this Niles Hemingway is the senator?" he asked Tony, flicking through the pages.

"One and the same," Tony said.

Nick's pen rested at the top of the page containing the senator's statement.

"What was his place in this case?"

"He was interviewed about his relationship to the family. He was a close friend of Andy Rowling. Was well known to the girls. And to their grandfather."

"And, in your professional opinion, there was nothing in those allegations against the grandfather that would stick?"

"Definitely in the clear. All alibis covered. Every ounce of evidence examined. I can categorically state that it was all disproved beyond any doubt. And I reiterate that's not beyond reasonable doubt. Beyond. Any. Doubt. Whatsoever."

"So, the grandfather was squeaky-clean."

"Ah, come on, Nick. When is anyone squeaky-clean?"

"Fair point. What was your take on him overall?"

"If I'm perfectly honest, he struck me as a man with plenty to hide. His son—the girl's father—was, as you know, already dead, but I've got to say, if he'd been alive, there'd have been quite a bit of mud sticking to him."

"What sort of thing?"

"For starters, there was an investigation within the organization over swaths of donation money unaccounted for."

"Did anything stick?"

"No. We suspected an internal cover-up but nothing was provable."

"Anything else?"

"Well, there was a lot of innuendo around Rowling and his wife spreading their good deeds around the world. You know how those do-gooders are."

"I don't really. Enlighten me."

"All just rumors, Nick. They were constantly in areas where there were vulnerable underprivileged people. Those places are rife with corruption—trafficking, pedophile rings and things like that."

Nick raised his eyebrows.

"Believe me, there were a few people who had an extremely low regard for Andy Rowling. He was known to take advantage of the underprivileged, underpaying staff or not paying them at all. More than one witness used the term 'slavery.' But as I say, nothing stuck. And there was nothing to stick to the grandfather either, apart from the fact he seemed somewhat evasive when it came to his son."

Andy Rowling was something of a sleaze, no doubt about that, but there'd never been any charges laid against him. And, of course, he was long dead before Peggy Rowling brought allegations against her grandfather.

"And what did you make of Hemingway?"

"As greasy as they come. But untouchable. Well known in church circles, arts benefactor, best friend to the mayor. And now, as you know, the conquering hero, returning from his worldwide escapades as a senator of some standing."

Nick reread the old statement from Niles Hemingway. It seemed reasonably straightforward. He'd been a long-term friend of Andy Rowling's. The men had worked together on a number of church initiatives, had been regular visitors to each other's homes.

Hemingway had lost touch with the family after the death of Andy Rowling, but he recalled Andy's father was a good man, a hard-working ex-serviceman. He understood that Andy's youngest daughter had strayed from the path, but he'd had no further contact with the girls.

Nick read it and reread it, trying to put a finger on what it was that seemed to ooze from the words on the page, but there was nothing. Just Nick's hunches.

42

SHE took the memory of a week's worth of inflammatory headlines with her.

TWO FOOTBALL PLAYERS
QUESTIONED IN RAPE CASE

and

CLUB SUSPENDS ACCUSED
FOOTBALL PLAYERS

She'd changed in the hotel bathroom, emerging dressed to thrill in fishnet stockings and a leather miniskirt, with a wig of tight curls and dark makeup. Her push-up bra provided something for any half-drunk man who came near her to focus on.

RAPE ACCUSATIONS STUN FOOTBALL COMMUNITY

After everything in the news, she had expected it might be harder to pick them up. They were football players, after all. Not A-grade, to be sure, not so young, not such highly promising athletes as those who were so recently charged with rape. No, these guys were older, a little less toned.

Hadn't anyone told them to keep a low profile?

She stayed in the shadows, in the corner of the back bar, watching them. She soaked up their arrogance, listened to their laughter and their lewdness, watched them pawing at a couple of fillies silly enough to join in with them.

Some girls would never learn.

She had no choice. It was up to her alone to weed out these creatures, to destroy them before they choked the whole world with their beastly wants and their disrespect.

TWO FOOTBALL PLAYERS ARRESTED

She had her eye on a few favorites and positioned herself on the bench by the back parking lot as they said goodbye to their equally drunk mates.

She hunched over, making pathetic sobbing noises.

"Hey, sweetheart," drawled Sleaze Number One, so confident in this world that was his for the taking. "Watsamatter?"

She looked straight up and noticed he was unable to make eye contact, being immediately diverted by the pale skin of her upper breasts.

"I'm just so lonely."

She'd booked a luxury room at a nearby five-star hotel, she told him. Stocked it with Blue Label, baby oil, and porn. She was a stranger in town, and she was supposed to meet with a guy she'd hooked up with on the internet that afternoon, but he hadn't shown.

"Or maybe he did," she sobbed. "Maybe he saw me from a distance and thought I was ugly."

"Impossible," said Sleaze Number Two, sidling in, seizing the perfect opportunity. "I mean, look at you! Check her out, Stan!"

Stan—a.k.a. Sleaze Number Three—dumped any vestige of shyness he may have had and took the bait.

"Impossible," he echoed.

"Come on. We'll walk you to your hotel," said Number One, caressing her knee.

FOOTBALL PLAYERS FORMALLY CHARGED WITH RAPE

She kept thinking about the headlines. Well, those two rapists might be safely behind bars, but she had three potentials right here in the palm of her hand.

Their progress was slowed by the occasional hand cupping of one tit and a squeeze of her nipple, sending her slightly off-balance. When they reached the park, Number Two dragged her behind a bush and pushed up her skirt, discovering she wore nothing underneath.

"Oh man, that guy really doesn't know what he's missing out

on." He pushed his fingers inside her crudely, and she moaned. It wasn't an act. She was highly aroused but for different reasons than Number Two imagined.

Before they reached the street, she handed the spare room card to Number One.

"I need to get a bag out of my car," she told them. "I'll meet you there."

Before they could protest, she took off at an awkward stiletto-heeled run. She realized it was a gamble—they might get jittery and decide to take off—but it was a gamble she had to take. She'd telephoned as Marlene Trimbole to book the suite, and when she'd dropped by dressed in tracksuit and dark glasses to collect the key, the clerk had barely given her a second glance as he swiped the stolen credit card.

Now, she ran down the side alley and entered the hotel through the security parking lot. She made it to the room in plenty of time to have three very stiff and highly laced scotches and one weak scotch-and-water poured.

"Nice digs," said Number Two, flinging a drunken arm around her shoulders in a proprietary fashion.

She guessed shoving a couple of fingers into someone's vagina in a park equated to first fucking dibs. She wanted to laugh aloud at the thought.

"Drink up," she whispered. "I'm feeling lucky now."

"I'm the lucky one," he drawled.

She sang softly as she waited for him to guzzle his drink. "*You are lost and gone forever, Dreadful sorry, Clementine.*" She continued to sing as she led him to the bedroom.

"Make yourselves comfortable, boys," she called over her shoulder.

She removed her clothes deftly, leaving the suspenders, fishnets, and high heels for his viewing pleasure. He moaned as she undressed him, and she was surprised to see a substantial erection. Obviously not quite enough drugs.

She sat on the floor and patted the carpet beside her. "Lie down here and relax," she said.

"Why not the bed?"

"Oh, we need nice solid carpet under us for what I've got planned."

He was docile as a contented cat as she laid him on the floor and tied his wrists to the built-in granite and chrome legs of the bed.

"Just relax while I get us another drink," she whispered as she reached for the regulation hotel-issue white robe.

"Aw, don't cover that beautiful body," he said. "Let 'em get a good look."

She smiled enigmatically and dropped the robe to the floor.

Sleazes One and Three certainly did get a good look. Number One actually sauntered across, meandering crookedly to where she was pouring the drinks, to cop a feel.

"Isn't he looking after you in there?"

She glanced over at Sleaze Three, the quieter and more slightly built of the trio. His cocktail seemed to be having a far greater effect. She smiled playfully at Number One and handed him another spiked scotch. "Perhaps you'd like to join us in the bedroom?"

"I won't be much good to you if I drink that," he slurred.

"Come on, your pal in there is going to have another one, and believe me, he's well and truly up for it, if you know what I mean."

She left him sipping his drink and went over to Number Three. With her back to Number One blocking his view, she pushed a little white pill between Number Three's lips and helped him swallow it with another hefty slug of scotch. He'd be completely out in a couple of minutes.

Back in the bedroom, Numbers One and Two smiled at each other conspiringly as she quietly latched the door.

Just look at them, she thought. *Their beefy muscles, their privilege and arrogance.*

She supported Number Two's neck, parted his lips and helped him drink another glass of laced scotch. She checked his constraints, then deftly pressed a strip of tape across his mouth. He was too drugged to be shocked, and his eyes continued to smile.

She took Number One to the corner and pressed on his shoulders until he was kneeling before her. It had not been part of her plan to have two in this room at once. The sense of power had overtaken her, acting like a drug, making her think she was invincible.

She pulled off her wig as she writhed against her victim and moaned and stared over at the smiling eyes of Number Two, his lids getting heavier by the second. She could tell he was fighting the sleepiness, loath to give in, so good was the show. Eventually, he could hold out no longer and his eyes closed.

Seconds later, as she reached for the shelf behind her, visualizing the mess she was about to make, she orgasmed in a rush of fluid and a barely contained squeal.

Then she pulled Number One's head back fiercely by the hair and dragged a blade straight across his throat. He gasped. Gurgled. He had no chance to wonder what hit him as she drove the knife into his chest, and when he collapsed in a pile of filth at her feet, she repeatedly stabbed him in the back, biting back the screams of hatred threatening to spill from her lips like lava.

Suddenly anxious that Number Two might wake from his stupor and somehow manage to writhe free of his constraints, she jumped on him and plowed the knife into his chest and then his belly, ripping the blade clear to thrust it back in again.

What a beautiful knife it was.

When she examined them both, she was disappointed they were so obviously dead. Her panic was annoying. Her ego had gotten the better of her when she'd put them both in the room together, and then she'd forgotten about taking her time and savoring the moment.

But she consoled herself with a mental picture of Number Three, fast asleep in a drug-induced stupor in the other room. He even had a name. "Stan," they'd called him. She would take Stan slowly.

But first things first: there was much to do.

As she set to work, her mind was a blur. She bent to the task of cutting these evil beings and exposing their innards to the air while older demons played in her mind. Dark shadows came at her, demented eyes leered at her, terror froze her, pinned her, abused her poor tiny body.

Well, I'm not frozen now.

She giggled as she sliced and fondled.

She was far from frozen now.

"*Oh my darling,*" she sang as she worked.

She didn't spend as long with the bodies as she might otherwise have done. In the back of her mind was the thought of her third victim, Stan, sleeping like a baby in the other room.

But fifteen minutes later, panic hit her like a sledgehammer. Stan—sleaze Number Three—was not asleep in the chair where she'd left him.

She had two bodies in the bedroom: one almost decapitated, the other partially eviscerated, and her third prospective corpse was nowhere to be found.

What time was it? How long did she have before the cops turned up?

She couldn't just run. She'd have to calm down and clean up before returning to the real world again.

She took the knife into the shower with her, still singing—more in an effort to calm herself now.

"*You are lost and gone forever...*"

She soaped vigorously, smiling and laughing when she thought of those emasculated, gutted, disgusting animals on the floor of the bedroom, then grimacing with the effort of stilling the panicked frenetic beating of her heart.

"God, keep me safe," she prayed. "Let me get home on time."

She wiped all the surfaces, handles, and countertops. She was proud of her efforts, even as she chided herself for their ineffectuality. She knew there would be evidence all over the place but, provided she got out of there fast and got home in record time, there would never be any reason to suspect her.

She dressed and donned the wig again, smiling wryly as she surveyed her battlefield one last time.

She took the elevator straight to the basement and left via the emergency exit.

"You are lost and gone forever, oh, my darling Clementine."

43

NICK Timms found himself staring into the depths of a bottomless black pit as he surveyed the carnage in that hotel room.

He was, yet again, the first senior officer to arrive, and if he'd hoped he had already seen the worst imaginable when he'd spied the horror at the scene of Robbie Aston's murder, he had another thing coming.

The bodies—carcasses, he instantly thought of them—were almost secondary to the butchery displayed around the room. The incongruity of the five-star accommodations intensified the magnitude of the whole bloody mess.

Nick, who'd been told where the bodies were, had headed straight for the front bedroom in what was a three-bedroom corner suite, indicating on his way that the suitably gloved Officers Argents and Wisper should guard the other rooms.

In the few moments of solitude available to him before Crime

Scene and Pathology arrived, he stood inside the doorway of the main bedroom and surveyed the mess.

The abdomen walls of the first body were open from the navel to the chest. One eye stared in a kind of cold, milky horror at Nick. A gaping hole, evidence of what was once another eye on the opposite side of the head. Blood rivulets made random patterns around the body, as if someone had let off a little plastic bottle of streamers, like the ones partygoers popped on New Year's Eve. Bloody ropes of intestines trailed from the cavity and ended wrapped around the wrists: macabre shining bracelets.

Body number two had been propped against the wall, wedged between the wardrobe and a side table. For one second, the face seemed to be grinning, and Nick almost laughed through his haze of quiet shock. But then he realized the grotesque smile had been slashed into the man's face with a knife.

"Fuck," he whispered through clenched teeth. "Fuck."

A loud heavy thud and a cry dragged him from his horror and from the room. "Argents?" He walked briskly back through the archway into the living area of the suite. "Wisper?"

At the kitchen counter he spied one of the young officers. She was rooted to the spot, staring at something Nick couldn't see. To Argent's left, Nick saw Samuel Wisper, flat on his back, out cold.

"He fainted," said Denni Argents as she turned.

Nick relaxed and reclipped his gun, at the same time registering the female officer's gray pallor.

"You look like you'd better sit," he said, indicating the open door.

Argents reached the door in two strides and almost crumpled over the threshold.

Nick's eyes followed her and lingered on her pitched-forward form for a moment. He didn't want to drag his gaze from her because once he did, he would have no option but to see what had drained the color from her face and caused her fellow officer to black out.

Eventually, he could put it off no longer. Despite having a damned good idea of what he would be met with, his every fiber experienced a fierce shock. He stared at the dining table for a long time, his gaze becoming distracted by incidentals, like the intricate patterns the blood had stained into the back of one of the chairs, the way the glass table reflected the blue of the sky from the windows beyond it, the bloodred color of the empty vase on the table, placed there by some evil interior designer with a nasty sense of humor.

At the same time, he was seeing the strange arrangement on the table. His brain took inventory, even as he tried to comprehend the enormity of it all: one eyeball, cold and dead; one kidney; one penis, small, insignificant, sad; one ear; two toes; and what may or may not have been part of a liver.

He dragged his gaze from the grotesque still life and peered through the huge bank of windows to the almost cloudless sky, the blue-green ocean with distant whitecaps and bobbing buoys, the nearby yachts—expensive toys for rich boys—pedestrians rushing to cross the road at the lights, getting ready to start their workday. Everything outside this room was normal. Everything was just the same, Nick told himself.

The world might be normal, but Detective Nick Timms felt he was anything but. He wondered if he would ever be normal again.

He turned to Denni Argents slumped at the door. "You okay to give me a hand here? Let's see if we can rouse your buddy."

Nick stayed in her line of sight, blocking any view of the anatomy displayed on the table, clocking Denni's determination to keep her face averted anyway. She crouched over Samuel Wisper, who, as he came to and sat up, automatically craned his neck to re-view the astonishing sculpture on the table. Nick imagined the inexperienced officer was still in denial. He probably wanted to look at the surface of the table, to see it bare, to wipe the images from his brain.

Nick stood his ground, successfully blocking the view. "Get out of here. Both of you."

The moment Officer Wisper stood on shaking legs, Nick had him turned around. He eased them both toward the door, relieved to see the pathology team had arrived.

He couldn't bear to think about the housekeeping staff who had stumbled on this scene less than an hour ago. Given the state it had reduced the two officers to, he hated to think of the effect it must have had on the cleaners.

He left the forensics team to do their stuff. He had no desire to stay in those rooms.

The carcasses had names. He had their driver's license details from the wallets, and it was time to work out what the hell these guys had been doing, how they'd ended up in this chamber of horrors.

It took only half an hour to confirm Marlene Trimbole was

indeed missing her Visa card, a fact she'd been unaware of until detectives came knocking. In one hour, her alibi was confirmed.

It took less than three hours for Nick and his team to find the families of the victims, talk to some friends of the deceased, and hear about the football players' drinking binge at a nearby bar.

One more hour and Nick had a stunned Stan Dozzini sitting at an interview table, trying unsuccessfully to sip from a plastic cup. Every time he got the cup halfway to his mouth, the shaking would become so uncontrollable, he'd have to lower the cup again.

"Let's go through it one more time, Mr. Dozzini."

Stan had not been fully asleep in the chair in the five-star hotel room. He hadn't been quite drunk enough or foolish enough. In a lucid moment, he'd wondered what they had all been thinking. With football-player rape headlines fresh in their memories, how had they managed to find themselves in a high-class hotel with a woman who was quite obviously mentally unstable?

He was very drunk and feeling the effects of whatever she'd put in the scotch by the time she'd forced that white tablet between his lips, but there was a fragment of his brain that cried out some sense. Something was out of kilter. His father once said: *If something doesn't feel right, doesn't look right, doesn't sound right, then it's probably not right.*

Stan had managed to lodge the tablet between his back teeth and hold it there with great effort while swallowing the healthy slug of scotch she'd forced on him.

Then, after he'd heard the door to the bedroom close and when the moans of his mates indicated the action had begun in earnest, he'd slipped out the door as silently as his drunken and drugged state would allow. Bouncing off walls, he made it to the elevator and was relieved he'd had the foresight to take the spare key card, which allowed him to ride straight down to the dark anonymity of the parking lot and through the side exit. The minute the fresh air hit him, vertigo had buckled and twisted the footpath. He'd tried to walk and then he'd crawled but only as far as the side hedge, where he vomited and passed out in the garden.

He would never know how close he'd been to the tip of the murderer's boot as she'd run from the scene.

"What time did you wake up?"

"I don't know," Stan said for the third time. "It was dark. I didn't look at my watch."

"And what time did you arrive back at your house?"

"Five."

"Five o'clock this morning?" At least Stan's story coincided with his wife's. She said she'd been worried sick about him.

"So what were you doing between the time you woke up in the night and five o'clock this morning?"

"I was tired and confused. We'd all had way too much to drink. I went to the beach. I guess I fell asleep again."

"You didn't think you owed it to your friends to see if they were all right?"

"I heard them before I left. I could tell they were having a good time. They would have roasted me for not joining in the fun."

Stan had been more concerned about his wife than he'd been about his fellow teammates. Truth was, he wasn't overly close to them. If it weren't for the fact that they played for the same club, Stan didn't imagine they'd be friends. Most of the time, he thought of them as being childish, always playing stupid pranks, laughing too loudly, partying too hard. Yesterday had been different, he admitted. He'd had so much to drink that, for a brief period, he'd thought of himself as one of them. He had liked being included in their games, he'd thought he would enjoy screwing that chick they'd picked up. Despite all the beer he'd had, he had been as horny as hell thinking about the things he could do to her.

He tried to be as truthful with the detective as he could. He hadn't left for any altruistic reason. He hadn't been worried about cheating on his wife; he hadn't felt any sense of obligation to protect the woman involved. He still wasn't sure what had made him come to his senses. One of last week's online stories had flashed before his eyes about football players being a law unto themselves, about two guys who'd been charged with rape.

"I thought the girl was a bit of a fruitcake," he told Detective Timms. "I dunno. Maybe I thought she might decide to turn around and say we raped her."

Nick didn't doubt Stanley Dozzini was telling the truth, but he wasn't about to let the smart-ass little bastard know it, preferring to let him suffer for a while, let him believe he was a suspect, leave him to sit in a room and stew in his own perspiration and fear. He only kept the football player for an extra two hours, but Nick could see from the quiet spots in the young man's eyes, it had been long enough.

The detective spent the afternoon going over his notes, in particular focusing on the vague description Stan had provided of the woman they'd picked up outside the pub.

Slim. Curly brown hair, cut fairly short.

"Actually, I think it was a wig," Stan said.

Heavily made-up. Dressed in a short black skirt, fishnet stockings, high-heeled boots, low-cut shirt; blue or green, he thought. No distinguishing features.

Due to the amount of beer Stan had consumed, he couldn't remember much about the woman or about the events just prior to his leaving the hotel suite.

"She was humming and singing. It was the same song all the time."

When pressed, he didn't think he recognized the song and couldn't remember any of the words.

Nick thought it might come back to him. When the shock wore off. When he knew he had his wife's forgiveness. When it sank in just how lucky he was. Maybe he'd remember the song, and maybe he'd remember a whole lot of other stuff. In Nick's experience, it was often the way.

In the meantime, he wondered what could have happened to a woman to enable her to kill so easily, to butcher and mutilate. What sort of hatred was that? What sort of psychopath could be capable of this?

44

SHE remembered some things so easily; others came to her in strange motion-picture-like flashes. It had happened that way all her life, or for at least as long as she was aware.

"Show me where he touched you," her father had said when she told him what Mr. Briels had done.

"I need to see exactly," he said when she pointed. "Take your clothes off." And because she trusted her father, she took her clothes off and stood before him, her body shivering with a mixture of cold and humiliation.

"And did he show you his penis?"

She had lowered her stinging eyes to the floor.

Like a long-drawn-out accordion of horror, her father's zipper had been lowered. He'd touched a gentle finger to her chin and turned her face so she could see his stiff offering.

"Did it look like this?"

She wondered if she'd fainted then, because she remembered nothing else. She didn't remember eating dinner that night or going to bed. She remembered nothing of the school term that followed or of games played. Whole months fell into the dark void.

When she'd told him how Mr. Briels took her into his house and touched her in private places and showed himself to her, she had expected her father to go on a killing rampage or, at least, to go to the police and have the nasty man locked up. Instead, he'd seemed quiet and withdrawn. He'd told her that the behavior of Mr. Briels was natural, and as the months and years unfolded, she had come to accept that such was her lot in life. Some little girls were born to a duty to serve men, to touch and be touched. The chosen girls were far more special than all the others, and they couldn't tell other girls because there would be too much jealousy, and they couldn't tell adults because adults may accidentally tell other girls and everything would go horribly wrong.

Mr. Briels still came to visit. He was good friends with the others; they went to the same church, the same clubs as her father. Despite the warnings, she did try to tell her mother but was shushed out of the way. When she found some words for her grandfather, he seemed not to hear.

She had no one to talk to, so she stole a canary from its cage on her friend's porch and took it to the park at the end of the street, right next to Mr. Briels's house. She told the bird what Mr. Briels had done to her, and by the time she'd finished talking, the canary was dead, so tight was her grip on its fragile neck. She sobbed for hours. She was sure she didn't mean to kill it.

Less than a year later, she'd set fire to Mr. Briels's house, and he'd been reduced to a bloated, charred mess.

Years later, when she tried to recall all the men who came to visit her father, it proved difficult, as they had all become versions of one man in her mind. They were of a similar age and stature; they wore the same expression of lust: eyelids heavy, full lips jutting out with need, flies open. Some would pant; some groaned. What she remembered most was the pride clear in her father's eyes and his gentle smile as he looked at her nakedness and watched the men enjoying the spectacle.

The men came to her father's studio downstairs in the basement beside the wine cellar. The studio was lined with scholarly books: biographies of great men (and a few women), tomes containing sketches and schematics, world travel guides, glossy picture books of famous landmarks, books of history, anthropology, archaeology, psychology, ancient religions and medical practices. At the end of the bookcases was a screen depicting petite Japanese women with straight black hair and tiny bandaged feet. The women carried trays and towels toward a naked reclining man, a slip of white sheet protecting his modesty. Behind the screen was a bed where her father napped from time to time when he broke from whatever scholarly mission he was currently undertaking.

At the other end of the studio, past his study desk and computer, was a spacious lounge area that contained half a dozen leather chairs for lecherous men to sit in so they could ogle her.

People came to the studio only if they were invited. Not even his family was allowed unless formally requested. It was an unwritten rule.

The inevitable had come to pass. She imagined it was preordained. Behind the screen in her father's basement office, she had lost what was left of herself, lost all hope.

"You will always belong to me now," he'd whispered after she had screamed her muffled protest against the palm clasped tight across her mouth. "Whatever happens, you will always be mine."

And later when he helped her to wash and dress, he reminded her of how special she was. "Don't forget. You must not tell another living soul."

She'd nodded solemnly.

He kissed her forehead in such a gentle, fatherly manner that she briefly wondered if she had dreamed the whole encounter. Perhaps everything had been a dream.

Oh, Papa.

45

AURORA, PEGGY, AND KATE sat perfectly still.

"Say cheese!" Stella said.

The three sisters responded in unison. "Yoga!" It was a long-ago tip from their mother, stretching the mouth more naturally.

And there they were. Three sisters who shared so much, who each had traits in common but who were, in many ways, poles apart.

The grandfather clock chimed midday as Stella raced off to the back room to print out this latest and best picture of the sisters.

An observer stumbling across the photograph might notice how the smile on the thinnest of the sisters did not reach her eyes.

Aurora was trying to appear upbeat, but in her heart she was angry with Jason, fearful for Stella, and wary of Stella's companion.

It had taken a long time for Kate to talk Aurora into this

family gathering in Grandpa's house, and when she'd eventually embraced the idea, it was Jason who'd made a fuss about inviting Stella's "friend" Benny.

In Aurora's mind, everything about "Benny" belonged in quotation marks: his "friendship" status, his "good looks," his "athleticism," his so-called "likability." To Aurora, he was a young man who was capable of corrupting her daughter.

Just before the photo pose, Aurora had tried to keep a smile plastered on her face as Benny dangled a bunch of cherries just out of the reach of her fourteen-year-old daughter's innocent lips.

That's why Aurora's smile didn't reach her wary eyes. She was frightened. Most everyone was frightened of the idea of a serial killer in their midst, but Aurora's fears were much closer to home.

The photograph showed her soft and sexy in a plain white linen shift worn with a simple strand of pearls, her chestnut locks falling in gentle waves around her face and neck and cascading over her narrow shoulders. Just visible over her right shoulder, the smooth wooden arch of her harp; she'd promised Kate she'd play later in the afternoon.

She longed for a glass of wine. The familiar uncharitable thoughts about Peggy lurked at the edges of her brain.

Why did Peggy's litany of illnesses overtake their whole lives? Why should Aurora have to forgo that comforting glass of wine?

She chided herself for being mean-spirited.

Really, it wasn't too much to ask for a few hours of family time with her sisters, in the house that harbored so many memories for them all.

She almost had to pinch herself. She never imagined that she would ever be in the same room as her little sister, let alone feeling good about it.

But here she was. The last conscious thought she'd had the night before was about Peggy. She'd thought about Peggy's suffering, deeply, for the first time and without the old anger, without the traumatic thoughts about their grandfather. She'd tried to slip into Peggy's skin, to imagine living daily with the guilt of what she'd done. Aurora's first thought upon waking that morning had also been about Peggy. She'd thought about how grown-up her little sister was: married, a mother, pregnant again.

Aurora's second thought had been for her daughter, and she mouthed a silent prayer that Stella would be spared a life like Peggy's.

Anyone eyeing the photograph would no doubt be drawn to the image of Kate, not just for her central position but for her jaunty boyishness and frank expression, the way she filled her allotted space with her wide smile and easy posture.

Kate sensed Aurora's tension, and she understood her fear for a daughter on the brink of womanhood. Despite the lawyerly hat she wore that saw the headlined football players as quite possibly innocent, she sometimes thought she could wrap her hands around their nasty necks. She knew the type, knew their capabilities.

Benny, however, had nothing to do with those men, and he seemed like a fine young individual.

Kate imagined some of Aurora's tension also sprung from playing happy families with a group of people who, in recent history, had been anything but happy.

It was a part of life Kate accepted, but she refused to let it dampen her sense of joie de vivre. She had dreamed of this day for years: the three girls together again in Grandpa's house, old hatchets buried, past sins forgiven.

Kate's eyes took on an added sparkle every time they came to rest on the professor, as she'd affectionately dubbed her robust and attentive lover.

After years of flighty all-or-nothing flings, of lusty sex and wild adventure, of jobs she'd abandoned on a whim for some tantalizing ideal of love, she had finally found it. There was no doubt in Kate's mind that she was in love with Iain, but this time it wasn't that wild rose-colored idea of passion; this was the real deal. He knew her body like it was part of his own DNA, and he held the distinct position of being the only man she'd dated who was both fantastic in bed and anything but boring out of it. In her past relationships, there would invariably come the day when she'd glance across a breakfast bar and wonder what on earth she had to talk about with the man who'd screwed her senseless the night before. She and the professor always found things to talk about.

As the photo was taken, Iain sat in a tapestry-covered wing chair in the corner of the living room, listening earnestly to Bo's synopsis and opinions about the continuing craze for vampire fiction. Kate smiled delightedly when she saw one of Iain's scholarly eyebrows shoot up in unguarded surprise as little Bo spoke of *unrequited love*.

Bo was the child Kate would have hoped for, had she ever been of a mind to procreate. Not that she wasn't fond of Grant and

Stella, but there was something about Bo's fiery resilience and mature intelligence that fascinated Kate.

Iain had broached the subject of children on their fourth date.

"I've had my time, contributed all I'm willing to contribute to the human race," he said, referring to his two semi-estranged children. "You've got to know right now, it's not negotiable."

Kate ruffled his gray-streaked mop of hair. "Don't look so serious, Prof. I must have a faulty clock. I vaguely heard it tick once, but it was for a metaphorical moment."

She had no desire to clutter the world with yet more children. The earth's resources were stretched enough without her adding to it.

"Besides," she said, "my ego is way too big to accommodate any mini-me's."

In a strange role reversal, she was constantly warning Iain not to go out alone at night. The more that was reported about the killings, the more he agreed with her.

Kate's happiness would have been complete, were it not for the continuing blackouts. Just last week, she'd woken to the chill of the cold laundry tiles against her cheek, her back spasming where it was jammed against the corner of the freezer.

Nevertheless, her exuberance and joy were evident in the photo. Short brown curls lapped at her forehead and caressed her tiny ears. One arm was flung around Aurora's slight shoulder, the fingers of the opposite hand twined around her little sister's straight blond hair.

The youngest sister, it had to be said, was not blossoming in pregnancy. True, it was early; she was just starting to move from semi-zipped uncomfortable pants to actual elasticized waistbands.

Peggy had long ago given up thinking this day would materialize. Aurora had come to the wedding and she'd managed a few catchups with both sisters, but they were awkward affairs, marred by talk of serial killers and a detective who seemed intent on driving them all insane.

Still, here they were, the three of them, squeezed onto the sofa with Aurora's harp behind them and the grandfather clock standing sentinel to one side.

Peggy briefly looked down at her clothes before Stella took the photo, smiling ruefully at her lack of style. There was Kate beside her, fit and trendy in capri pants and a designer T-shirt, and, further along, Aurora, who was her usual study in understated elegance.

Peggy had dressed with care that morning and had arrived in her own inimitable style in a vibrant red-and-purple blouse, oversize ceramic earrings, and the silver heart necklace Bo and Denton had given her on her birthday. Her smile was gemlike in its sincerity, but she also wore a gray pallor, and her hair was even lankier than usual, her face drawn.

Peggy was fighting a war. Every day, she strategized and positioned and fought and retreated and attacked and, so far—knock on wood—she had won every battle.

She relied heavily on Dr. Leichardt, and she'd finally admitted to Denton it wasn't so much the morning sickness that was slapping her around and wringing her out as it was the nightmares, the hauntings and the old lusts and longings.

"Would you like to talk some more about the dreams?" Dr. Leichardt had asked on her recent visit.

She'd told him about being confined in the fireplace.

"Not a box this time?"

"I think it always was the fireplace," Peggy said. "It just seemed like a box."

She described the sense of reality of someone's hand over her face and nose, her sheer terror, her inability to breathe, the strange smoothness of the doll's cheek, the terrible pain in her head.

"What do you see from your vantage point in the fireplace?" Dr. Leichardt's deep, calming voice almost drew forth the visions she could not face when awake, but they quickly slipped away again.

"I don't know."

"Tell me about the dreams," Denton said two days ago. "Maybe they'll frighten you less if you get them out in the open."

"I can't."

Despite her illness and her lack of sleep, Peggy's smile for the camera was a sincere one: wide and natural.

46

DENTON stumbled upon Peggy's remaining diary of horrors, and it shocked him to stillness. He was unable to marry these fierce scribblings with the woman he loved, and now he was second-guessing the statement he'd given to Nick Timms two weeks ago, the interview he'd kept secret from Peggy.

Soulmates, they'd called each other. Both had suffered severely for their addictions, Peggy more so because of the heightened vulnerability of femininity and her exposure to hard drugs. Denton had only the demon drink to deal with, but it had nearly killed him, and he'd always doubted he had enough strength left in him to love someone the way he'd fallen for Peggy.

He had told it all to Nick Timms. Said he knew about her past, knew about the demons she battled, but he was convinced she was well. He was certain she was in no way connected to a mass murderer.

He certainly had thought they were made for each other. Now he was far from sure.

He had known about her hidden diaries, having once inadvertently glimpsed her through the window retrieving one of the books from her hiding spot. From his vantage point atop the ladder where he was clearing out the gutters, he'd turned his face away but not fast enough to miss her furtiveness. He'd never tried to snoop then, despite having ample opportunity.

When he'd begun to worry about her state of mind, he'd sought out that hiding place, only to find the diaries were gone, so he'd put them out of his mind.

But then, he'd been up in the attic checking the insulation when he found it, full of scribblings that indicated there was something evil lurking within his wife.

The other concern he had was the way she sometimes cried out in her dreams, things that astonished him, terrified him.

And why had her cravings returned?

Why now?

The question started to haunt him. Had he made a mistake by marrying her? Did she feel claustrophobic? Was it really just the hormones released through pregnancy? And if it was, how on earth would she cope with a new baby?

He placed the photograph back on the table, slowly, methodically, and then slid it away from him as though moving it away from the newspaper he'd been reading would distance his wife from the frightening snippet of information reported there.

In the continued hunt for the murderer of

two local football players, police have taken the unusual step of releasing new information in relation to the alleged killer.

Detective Nick Timms, who has headed the task force on this and other recent gruesome murders, said the detail was being released in the hope it would trigger some recollections from others known to the killer.

Detective Timms last week admitted his fears that the murder of the two football players was possibly linked to the deaths of Henry Macinaine and Robbie Aston, and could be connected to others, but he refused to elaborate.

One of the three football players in the company of the mystery woman managed to escape and has remembered further details about the night.

By his own admission, the football player—who cannot be named at this stage for legal reasons—had consumed a large quantity of alcohol, and his recollections are hazy.

The witness does, however, recall the woman singing the same lines of a song, on repeat, an obscure Western folk ballad.

Denton had tried three times to continue reading the article to its conclusion, but each time he reached the song title, his eyes glazed in shock.

How unusual was that song? He asked himself the question over and over.

Just because he'd never heard it before he met Peggy didn't mean it was that rare, surely.

Yet, when he recalled Peggy singing the lines in her sleep, his blood ran cold.

"Oh, my darling," she sang in a croaky distant voice as she tangled in the sheets and sweated and panted and cried, before hurtling upright.

"It's okay, sweetheart," Denton would soothe. "Just another dream." Then he'd rub her back and stroke her hair until she fell asleep again.

Just another dream, he told himself. An ordinary old song. Ludicrous to imagine that dear sweet Peggy could be in any way involved. But in light of the horrific diary, was it really such a stretch of the imagination?

He held his breath when he showed her the article. She'd just come in from her beach walk, her hair had been whisked by the wind, and she was glassy-eyed, fresh, and happy.

"Oh God," she said. "I hate reading about this." She'd barely read the first paragraph before pushing the paper away.

"You really should read it," Denton urged as he went to the counter to refill his coffee. His hand shook as he poured. "Do you want a piece of toast?"

"Mmm, okay, thanks."

Denton cast his mind back to the date of the latest murders.

Had Peggy gone walking? Had Denton still been at work? How long had she been gone? She'd attended a few extra courses to accelerate her studies. Was she at a night class then? Had he and Bo been watching a movie? Or was that the evening Denton had taken heavy-duty painkillers to ward off a rare migraine?

His mind continued to dart from one possibility to another.

Peggy picked up *The Daily* and continued to read while Denton watched surreptitiously from the kitchen nook.

He thought he detected a slight squaring of the shoulders as she reached the last few paragraphs.

"That song," she whispered.

IAIN found Kate picking beans in the garden, bathed by the late-afternoon sun. It was day three of his one-week sleepover at Kate's.

"Isn't this the song you and your sister were singing on the family day?"

She skewed her lips and marked her face with dirt as she pushed a few stray locks of hair behind her ears.

"'Clementine,'" he said. "Is that what your father used to sing?"

She held the basket of beans out to him. "Here, grab this."

She swapped the basket for the newspaper and stood to her full height, arching her strained back.

She started to read from the top of the page, but Iain reached across impatiently and pointed to the last paragraph. "Here."

"'Oh, My Darling Clementine,'" Kate read aloud. "Yes, that's the song all right." She glanced at him abruptly. "What? Do you think I could be the devil's handmaiden?"

Iain roared with laughter, and Kate grinned.

"You'd better be on your best behavior tonight," she said. "Or I'll chop off your toes and sing to you."

"Oh no!" Iain put down the basket and covered his ears. "Take my toes if you must, but I'm begging you, please don't sing!"

And then he ran, at top speed, which, for a professor of literature, wasn't too shabby.

But he was no match for Kate. Despite tripping over the rake handle, she caught him in fewer than ten strides.

"You are such a pathetic runner," she said, clutching him into a bear hug.

"And might I say in return that, as a singer, you make a mighty fine lawyer."

At the kitchen table, Kate read the whole article as they threw the tops and ends of the beans onto the other side of the paper.

Iain was enjoying this holiday time together. Neither of them had voiced it, but he thought of these sleepovers at Kate's house as a sort of trial for...what? Living together? Marriage? He wasn't sure, but he knew he wanted to be with her all the time. He hated the coldness that crept in whenever she left his apartment in the middle of the night. He loved waking with her in the mornings, although it hadn't taken him long to realize he had to wake up ahead of the sun peeping over the horizon if he was to get any good-morning presents before she hauled her gorgeous body into her bathing suit and sweatpants.

Kate suddenly stopped reading.

"My God," she said. "You don't think Peggy could be capable of..."

Iain stared at her, bean in one hand, paring knife in the other. "Peggy?"

Kate shook her head and continued to snap the tops off the beans. "I'm just being silly. There must be heaps of people who know that song. And anyway, Peggy didn't even remember how Father used to sing it to us.

"Aurora," Kate mumbled.

"That's another weird thing I've noticed," Iain said.

"What thing?"

"You always refer to him as your father."

"Hmm." Kate seemed distracted. "That's who he was."

"I know, but Peggy says 'Dad,' and Aurora calls him 'Daddy.'"

It struck Iain as odd that all three sisters referred to their father by a different term.

When Kate said nothing, he persisted. "Why do you think that is?"

"What are you now? My shrink?" she snapped.

They ate their dinner of saltimbocca, Sorrento-style, with their freshly picked green beans, on trays in front of the television like an old married couple and, later, kept the theme going by forego-ing any form of lovemaking, opting instead to perch themselves against a pile of pillows on the king-size bed and tackle the jumbo crossword. All the while, Iain tried to silence the questions that roiled like an ominous ocean within him.

Without the sex, he didn't fall into his customary deep sleep, so he was aware of her restlessness long before she flung back the covers and sat bolt upright in bed.

"Oh my God!"

"It's okay, honey. You must have been having a bad dream."

He tried to caress her shoulders and pull her gently back to the mattress, but she shook away from him and flung herself out of bed.

"Oh shit, Iain. That song. I'm terrified."

"Come on—don't be silly." Iain flicked on the bedside lamp. "Even if you thought for one moment your little sister was capable of murder, surely you don't think Peg would have had the strength to overpower those two men, let alone the demonic nature to disembowel and Christ only knows whatever else was done to them."

"I'm not talking about Peggy now!" Kate's face was white, a thin film of sweat had broken out over her cheeks, and her hair was matted and stuck to her forehead.

Iain scrambled out of bed, untangling himself from the sheet in a frenzy, and grasped her by the shoulders.

"Kate, you're delirious. What are you talking about?"

"It's not Peg I'm suspecting now."

"Oh, so now Aurora is mentally deranged as well?"

"No. Me! I know we laughed about it before, but what about the blackouts?"

"Don't be ridiculous." He kept searching her face, wondering if some part of her was still asleep. Perhaps this is what happened when she had the blackouts.

She'd told him about them last Sunday. Said she'd had at least a half dozen. "And that's just the ones I know about," she'd told him.

"What did the doctor say?"

Kate had confessed that, after first discussing it with the doctor and finding no apparent cause, she was loath to bring it up again.

She'd thought if she wasn't sick, she didn't want to have a whole barrage of tests when there was still a chance the blackouts would go away of their own accord.

"Calm down now." He grabbed her a little more roughly than intended, but it had the desired effect. She snapped out of her terror and allowed his arms to encircle her, but no sooner did he think she was coming to her senses than she started to shake.

"I really am frightened."

"Stop it. This is ridiculous. Fuck, it's just a song."

"I need to call Aurora."

"Not now. In the morning."

Just a song that many people would know. Just a song. Iain repeated the three words silently as he held Kate tightly in his arms as if his thoughts would keep her fears—and his own—at bay.

JASON cleared his throat. "She's not here, Kate."

He'd never quite worked out his feelings about Kate. He wasn't sure if he liked her or loathed her. Perhaps it was both.

"What do you mean, she's not there? Isn't this her cell phone?"

"Yes, but she doesn't take it with her."

"It's six in the morning."

Right there, Jason thought. That's why he didn't like her sometimes. She was too strident and demanding. Too confident. Maybe too boyish.

He ran a hand through his thinning hair.

"You know what she's like. She's probably been out walking since five a.m."

"Damn. I'm sorry, Jason. I didn't mean to snap."

Now her voice was low and sultry. Right there, Jason thought. That's what he liked about her. The way her voice could claw at some sexual yearning from deep within him. Sometimes he tried to imagine what she'd be like in bed. Where Aurora would often just lie there with her exquisite fine-boned body, Jason imagined Kate throwing those muscular legs around him.

Right there, Jason thought, as his erection throbbed. Now he was back to loathing her for making him feel that way when—really—she was such a tomboy.

"Do you remember how we were talking about that song at our big lunch?" Kate asked. "'Oh, My Darling Clementine'?"

"Yeah. Sure."

It wasn't the first time he'd heard about Andy Rowling singing. But it was the first time he'd heard the sisters singing it themselves: Aurora with her fine soprano-like voice, which matched the angelic string sounds she could coerce from the harp, Kate with a boisterous, butchering voice that couldn't truthfully be classified as singing.

"It's been mentioned in the paper. In connection with those murders," Kate said.

"What? Our family get-together?"

"No. That song. The murderer, the one they keep referring to as 'Satan's Handmaiden,' was singing it the night she killed them."

Jason thought having the conversation was like pulling teeth. "And?"

"Well, don't you think it's odd? I mean, it's such an old song. Who even sings it? Who would know that song?"

"Plenty of people, I imagine. Have you lost your senses? What are you saying? Because it's an unusual song your father used to sing to you, then one of you girls must be a murderer?"

"No, I'm not saying that. I…I just wanted to see what Aurora thought, I guess."

Jason couldn't keep his mind from straying to Peggy. Now that was one sister who would never succeed in rousing an erection. She was a totally screwed-up piece of work. "Do you think Peggy would be capable of…?"

"No," Kate said. "No, I don't. Really, I never should have brought it up."

Jason shook his head. Peggy might have a few screws loose, but even she couldn't be that evil. "Aurora then?" The idea was ludicrous. He had a sudden irreverent thought. "Ha! Maybe it's your mother." He immediately latched on to a visual of Karina Rowling lurching out of her wheelchair with a bloody cleaver in her hand, singing "Daaaaaarling Clementine" before hacking her victims to pieces and racing back to the dementia ward.

Kate laughed raucously.

There, right there, Jason thought. That wicked sexy laughter. Another reason for liking her.

"Ah, here she is now," he said as Aurora came through the side door.

"Your sister," he said, holding the phone toward her. He detected a slight hesitation. "Kate," he added, and Aurora seemed to relax. Obviously, a couple of hours at a family lunch did not yet translate to little inter-sister confidences with Peg on the phone.

Aurora took the phone. "Kate? What's up?"

Jason turned away quickly, embarrassed by his thoughts and

his body's reaction to Kate. He listened to his wife's side of the conversation, half interested in her reaction to Kate's hysteria, but all he heard was "Uh-huh, hmm, yes, no, of course not, okay, uh-huh," as Aurora wandered up the hallway.

"What was that about?" he called after she hung up.

"Oh nothing," she said as she headed to the kitchen. "Kate being Kate. Going on about the professor as though she's the only one who's ever..." Aurora's voice disappeared with her body.

Not a word about the song? Strange, Jason thought.

He tried again later, over coffee and the morning paper. "What else did Kate have to say?"

"She was just waffling about that old Clementine song. Nonsense, really." Aurora glanced at him. "Since when have you been interested in what Kate has to say anyway?"

Jason stood and took his cup to the sink before his wife had time to register the flush creeping from his neck to his face.

Perhaps it was the guilt over his thoughts that made him project his angst onto Aurora late the next day.

"Tell me, did you and that lover of yours have nicknames for each other?"

Her face instantly flushed crimson. "What a ridiculous question. No, we did not have nicknames."

"Then maybe you could explain to me who you were calling for in the middle of the night? Who the hell is Papa?"

47

KATE glanced at the wall behind Anna Winslett, then at the desk, the window. She couldn't bear to look the young doctor in the eye as she blurted out the sordid details of Peggy's experiences with psychiatrists and psychologists.

Kate had been spurred back to the doctor after seeing Detective Timms again. Twice. Once at the top of her street, another time at a park bench with a female police officer. Part of her had wanted to confront him, to find out what he thought he was doing, but something stopped her. Instead, she'd jogged in a circle and high-tailed it home.

She needed to find a way to get Timms off her damn case. And why had Peggy said she'd never seen him again, when Denton admitted he'd been around?

By the time she got around to giving Anna a brief overview of her latest sleeping problems and continued blackouts, it seemed clear that psychological help was the way forward.

"I'm sure you know, Kate, that one bad psychiatrist does not damn a whole profession."

"I know, but I can't help but be wary."

"This man I was telling you about is a friend of my father's. You couldn't find anyone more highly respected in the profession."

Anna pushed a card across the desk, navigating it around the paperweight.

Kate stared at it for a moment, her perfect vision allowing her to read it from a distance. She burst out laughing. "You have got to be kidding me!"

Anna grinned.

Kate picked up the card, raised her eyebrows, and tried to stifle the laughter. "Seriously? Dr. Freud?"

"Seriously."

Alessandro Freud was, as Anna Winslett had indicated, a highly respected member of the psychiatric community. Kate's standard form of research—Google—unearthed a plethora of accolades, awards, speeches, articles, and breakthrough associated with him. His published papers included an essay on the link between depression and cardiovascular disease, and the weirdly titled *Gentle Waves: The Neurophysiology of Emotion*. In his younger years he had completed some important drug studies, and his work on the links between marijuana use and psychosis was often cited in specialist journals. He was in demand on the after-dinner circuit, and Kate laughed loudly when she came across a picture of him, a comedic interpretation of Albert Einstein with his shock of thick gray hair and devilish expression.

In the flesh, he came across as warm and sexy, with a high forehead and a humorous twinkle in his eye.

"I did once think of adopting a pseudonym," he said when Kate told him she found his name to be quite hilarious. "But then I thought, what is life without a sense of humor?"

The doctor's office was atypical, surprising in its modern aesthetic. Not a high-backed maroon leather chair in sight, no antique hardwood desk, no safe traditional paintings in expensive frames. The only neutral thing in the consulting room was the champagne-colored wall paint. The rest of the room screamed personality. The leather of the modern club chairs, in which patient and doctor sat opposite each other, was yellow; the top of the occasional table between them, a prop from the show *Wheel of Fortune* set beneath a circle of glass.

"My producer daughter nabbed it for me," the doctor said.

On the far wall, a thick impasto oil by prominent local artist Simone Azire depicted a red vase bursting with yellow daisies, with two crushed daisy heads and a squashed bee offsetting the gaiety of the rest of the painting. Opposite was a photographic display of a much-loved golden retriever and a pair of weathered slippers in a box frame.

Kate's gaze lingered on the photographs of the dog, recalling an article she'd read online the day before about a dog trained to imitate Hitler. Her easily distracted mind combined with a photographic memory conjured the headlines she'd seen merging with the sidebar to that story: *Mother is paralyzed in a freak pole dancing accident.*

She tried to dispel an image of her own stroke-affected mother pole dancing. Stared at the framed slippers. Admitted she was trying to focus on anything but her own problems.

It was easy to warm to Dr. Freud, who showed not the slightest surprise at or annoyance over Kate's distrust of the psychiatric profession.

"I'm feeling some urgency creeping in," Kate admitted, giving the doctor a little background on the song and its connection to a serial killer. Dr. Freud agreed it would be best to fast-track her appointments.

"Unlike my namesake," he said, "I'm not a skilled dream interpreter. In fact, the heavy reliance on sexual or aggressive desire being used to read the latent content of dreams is somewhat outdated." He glanced at the ceiling, then back to her, before adding: "In my humble opinion.

"I can prescribe something for you," he said. "With drugs, we can alter your sleeping patterns to deal with your nightmares and rewire your brain so blackouts would be highly unlikely to occur. However," he said, pausing to take a sip of water, "that would not lead to any understanding of what may or may not have happened to you."

Every time Kate started to discuss hypnosis, she became short of breath. "Just being here talking to you makes me think of Peggy and her fake memories."

"I can certainly understand that. How would you feel if we

got another professional to assist? Another psychiatrist of your choosing, not an associate of mine. That way, you will have two people caring for your well-being.

"In addition, I'm going to suggest we don't use age regression, at least not initially. We'll try some free association in the hypnotic state. What do you think?"

As a supplement to the hypnosis sessions with Dr. Freud and Dr. Conway—the softly spoken therapist who'd been *delighted and honored* to work alongside the famous Alessandro Freud—Kate and Freud attempted to dissect what the doctor referred to as Kate's flashbulb memories—the flashes that came to her in full, clear Technicolor, small vignettes from the past. They were usually harmless movies: little Peggy falling over and scraping her knee on the gravel, Nan pushing a stray curl behind Kate's ear before setting to work on creaming the butter and sugar, Kate looking down from the henhouse at Aurora and Grandpa sipping from mugs on the front portico. Those memories were clear and detailed right down to the shade of the red of Aurora's cup or the order of the utensils Nan had lined up on the kitchen table.

"What you need to keep in mind," Dr. Freud told her, "is that just because these recollections are clear and vivid does not mean they are infallible. Despite the name, there is strong evidence to suggest those types of memories are not of a snapshot clarity or accuracy and, can, in fact, be entirely incorrect."

"Do you mean they are the types of false memories Peggy had?"

"Not exactly, no. From what you've told me, your sister's were induced. Those flashbulb ones of yours are spontaneous. Nevertheless, they could be one hundred percent true, one hundred percent false, or any number of shades in between. I am merely warning you against accepting anything totally at face value."

That was perhaps the best piece of advice Dr. Freud offered, because three days later, it was what Kate held on to when, under hypnosis, she "recalled" a terribly suffocating experience of being pushed down on a bed and sexually abused. The recollection did not come about through regression but through word association. Dr. Freud had taken words from one of Kate's nightmares: *bed, breathe, pillow, Grandpa's house.*

"Is it possible you have appropriated the sensations you describe from a movie or a book?" Dr. Conway asked after the session.

Kate nodded, still shocked, ready to grasp at any straw, relieved she had two doctors to discuss these latest developments with.

"How could we explain her ability to see the man if she had been asleep on her stomach?" This from Alessandro Freud.

"I suppose there could be a number of possibilities," said Dr. Conway.

Dr. Freud jumped up and retrieved his whiteboard on wheels from the far corner. As he started to write energetically, he reminded Kate of a wild professor she'd seen on a retro ad for Cadbury chocolate. *Why is it so?* the ad professor had asked in a distinctive Latvian-accented drawl.

"Possibility number one," Dr. Freud said as the marker squeaked its way across the board. "Kate only *thinks* she was asleep before the event. Maybe she has simply not yet recalled the events leading to it.

"Two," he said. "It was not her on the bed. She may have seen the event through a window or a hiding place."

"But it certainly seemed like I could feel it."

"Empathy, Kate," Dr. Conway said.

Dr. Freud continued to write. "Yes, empathy is a powerful emotion. Three. She has projected that image onto the perpetrator, perhaps because of some perceived wrongdoing."

He stopped writing, marker poised in the air, and addressed Kate directly. "What I mean is, you may have felt he had wronged you in some way before, and so, when this happened to you, you simply projected his image onto another person."

"Another option," Dr. Conway said. "It had happened before, so Kate assumed she knew the perpetrator."

Dr. Freud scribbled option four onto the board.

"I think it was option two," Kate said, her voice barely above a whisper.

The two doctors studied her intently, and Dr. Freud spoke. "Can you explain why you think that?"

"In the nightmares, I'm always watching something like this. I didn't tell you before, but I sometimes thought the man in those dreams was my grandfather. When I was awake, though, I always knew it wasn't him. Now I know why I imagined him there."

She glanced at each of the doctors and then fixed her eyes on the whiteboard. "It was his house, so I assumed it was him."

It was someone else.

One word hovered in her brain.

Papa.

48

PEGGY screamed with rage and pain.

"Get it out!"

Someone was stroking her brow.

"Just breathe, Peg."

She swiveled her head frantically so she could face him squarely with her sweat-soaked pain and anger.

"Fuck off, Denton."

She saw him blanch and glance over at the midwife, and it pleased her pain-addled mind. "Don't tell me when to breathe."

This whole scenario was the icing on some devilish joke of a cake. She wasn't supposed to be in this position yet.

It had been shock that sent her here. First, Detective Timms turning up to interview her again. He asked a few questions about Kate and the house, about Aurora, but it was clear that, this time, he had his sights fixed on Peggy.

He dragged up some of Peggy's history. His questions were

relentless. Then, out of the blue: "What can you tell me about Niles Hemingway?"

Peggy's eyes had narrowed. "The senator? I don't know much about him at all."

"Oh?" The detective seemed to exaggerate his surprise. "I was led to believe he was a friend of your father."

Peggy wasn't sure why she'd pretended not to be familiar with Mr. Hemingway; something about him had always caused her heart to beat an irregular rhythm.

"Oh yes, I'd forgotten that" was all she said to Nick.

The bigger shock was the detective asking if she had any diaries. That's what made her blood really run cold.

After he left, she'd dragged the ladder to the bedroom so she could retrieve that last diary and get rid of it. But it was gone. She'd practically pulled the room apart, but it was nowhere. She couldn't shake the idea that Denton had taken it. Bad enough if he'd seen it, but the idea that he might have told the detective about it was horrifying.

The contractions had started with a vengeance then, as though the new life she carried had decided it couldn't bear to be held by such a monstrous host.

In the hospital, Peggy's brain softened between the contractions and she stole a look at Denton. "I can't do this," she whispered.

"You have no choice, Peg. We are here. This is happening. If there was any way I could do it for you, you know I would. But I can't. That means you have to do it."

A nurse came into the room to speak in hushed tones to the midwife.

"I need drugs," Peggy said loudly to the newcomer.

"No, you don't," Denton said.

The nurse made tsking noises at Denton and, turning away from the midwife, addressed Peggy.

"We'll see what we can do, Mrs...."

The midwife grabbed the nurse's arm. "I shouldn't have to tell you to read the notes. Mrs. Price is a recovering addict."

"I'm not an addict!" Peggy screamed as the pressure bore down on her again. "For Christ's sake, you have to give me drugs if I tell you to!"

She turned her head to glare at Denton again, and in a low menacing voice, she told him: "If you say 'breathe' one more time, I will kill you."

She caught his look of horror and—What was it? Fear?—just before she straightened up, arched her back and let out another bloodcurdling scream.

In an earlier lucid moment, she'd recalled their family discussion about names.

Bo had suggested Barney.

"What, like Barney Rubble?" Denton asked. "I can't imagine your Mom being happy with a name from *The Flintstones*."

Bo had backed down on that one.

"Let's try one more push," the midwife said, and Peggy knew they'd insist on a cesarean if something didn't happen now.

Another scream erupted from her as she pushed fiercely.

She stopped. Took a deep breath. With one last, almost anticlimactic grunt, she pushed her son out into the world.

The mewling sounds and a mucilaginous cry before her son was whisked away at least told her he was alive.

They'd decided on the name Cosmo at that family meeting. But not before Denton had suggested Andy, referencing her dead father.

The very idea of it had caused her to feel violently ill. Disgust and anger filled her senses as she'd tried to swipe the image of his name and face from her mind.

"Are you okay, Peg?"

"Fine," she'd managed to mumble. "But Andy? No. That's a hard no."

Her father's face swam before her now in her exhausted state. His name was stuck in her thoughts, his face and the faces of the others. It made her cold to her bones.

As she drifted to sleep, she thought about her newborn son. Cosmo. This time she'd do everything right. She knew that once her hormones regulated themselves, the cravings would be gone.

Suddenly, she was wide-awake. It came to her again, as it had during the previous months: this might be how God would punish her for being such a poor mother to Bo and for all her past sins. Her newborn, dear Cosmo...perhaps he was dead already.

"Is the baby all right?" she croaked.

Denton looked to the nurse, who insisted the baby was doing well. "He'll have a little more to get through, minor respiratory issues and the like. And there will be some special-care needs to protect against infection." She smiled. "He's looking strong, Mrs. Price, very strong."

She drifted again, the specter of her father receding.

But soon, she heard singing.

Darling Clementine. A song she didn't even remember, and yet that tune, those words flashing on her inner eye, held a spine-chilling horror.

Papa.

49

NICK's Persons of Interest list had, over the past few weeks, been refined, before stalling at nine, and most of the names didn't set his heart pounding. But there were three that did: Peggy Price, along with Kate Rowling and Aurora Dwyer.

Those three women, they were the names that caused his hackles to rise. And yet, they were not all high on the official list.

One of the prime suspects was Saoul Wakefeldt, a known druggie with a penchant for bondage who lived with three women in a trailer on the other side of town. At various times, the women had shoplifted for their de facto, and they'd stolen cars for him. One of the women had recently been caught trying to coerce two young girls into her car with the intention, she confessed, of *taking them home to Saoul*. But the real reason they were on the police radar and high on the Persons of Interest list was that one of Saoul's concubines had been reportedly singing "Oh, My

Darling Clementine" outside the trailer two days after the murder of the football players.

The randomly generated operational name was cause for some grim humor around the station, but Operation Daisy Chain was time-consuming, laborious, and extremely frustrating. For Nick, the operational name inadvertently conjured an image of entrails draped around wrists like bracelets.

In a corner of his brain was the constant ticking of an unforgiving clock. A serial killer of this nature—and they were now sure that's what they had on their hands—didn't inexplicably stop the carnage.

When he sat listening to tapes of conversations between the drug dealer—Person of Interest Number Two—and the undercover detective who was endeavoring to purchase drugs and porn, he heard that clock. *Tick. Tick.* When he questioned P1, P3, and P5, it was there again. *Tick. Tick.* When he reviewed the evidence in the previous murders, he was often frustrated at the chugging pace of the machinations of the law. Limited surveillance budget. Unmatched DNA evidence. Lives were at stake, but past lawmakers had deemed citizens' civil liberties more important. *Tick. Tick.*

Operation Daisy Chain covered a number of different territories and areas of interest, and just like a necklace of flowers, the litter of clues overlapped and connected in a deceptive linear manner. Another small-time drug dealer's every move was documented as he flew interstate up to three times a week and then crisscrossed his way around his sales area, but he'd recently been removed as a person of interest. A snuff porn supplier became well known to the officers working the case, as did the whereabouts of a variety of women with tenuous connections to the old ballad that had now started a live concert in Nick's head as he tried to speed up the process.

Time accelerated to match all his efforts.

Tick. Tick.

50

KATE knew she was no murderer. But it had seemed clear from Detective Timms's line of questioning that he thought either she or one of her sisters was.

"I'm getting sick of your fishing expeditions," Kate had said the last time she'd encountered Timms. "If you think you have something to connect my family to this evil, then you'd better put your cards out on the table."

After the sessions of hard work by Alessandro Freud, it had become clear Kate's blackouts were a direct result of a traumatic event in her teenage years.

But that wasn't something she was prepared to share with Nick Timms yet. "And if you have any more questions for me, I'll address them only with my lawyer present."

She had stewed on the results of her sessions with the psychiatrists. If she'd ever been sexually abused—which she highly doubted—and somehow blocked it out of her mind, she at least knew categorically she had not been raped.

She'd lost her virginity to Peter Bruxton, a boy who was two days younger than her. It had been at Kate's sixteenth birthday party, and as she recalled, Peter's birthday was the following week.

It was awkward and embarrassing, messy and fast. Kate had always regretted that it had not been someone more dashing and substantial than Peter. But there you had it. She had been a virgin, clear as the bloodstains on the back of Peter's jacket upon which they had lain and which Peter had subsequently thrown into the dumpster in back of the YMCA hall where she'd held her party.

It was time to face facts. She had some momentous decisions to make. She knew that the girl on the bed who she saw in her dreams had been raped, and while it was feasible Kate may have witnessed the rape of a stranger, she strongly believed the victim was one of her sisters.

Timms was not going to be put off anymore and had agreed it was a good time to think about a lawyer.

Now, here she sat with Blake Lilly at her side, suitably briefed. The two detectives were perched opposite: Nick Timms and Tony Walsh, their arms on the table, leaning forward a little too eagerly, it seemed to Kate, the recorder whirring softly between them.

The thought of Peggy being questioned like this was horrendous. Who knew what accusations could surface?

"I want to ask you about an old folk ballad: 'Oh, My Darling Clementine.'"

Blake put a hand to Kate's forearm and raised an eyebrow in her direction.

"It's all right," she said. She knew she was cornered. "Yes, my father used to sing it."

"You don't seem surprised that I asked you about it."

Despite the fact it had been reported, Kate couldn't help but wonder if Iain hadn't tipped Timms off. Iain had been hounding her to go to the station voluntarily to tell them about her family's connection to the song.

She had steadfastly refused. "What, and have them question Peggy? What a disaster!" Iain couldn't properly comprehend her reluctance; he was not privy to all that had transpired with Peggy and their grandfather in the courts.

Now Kate was left with no choice but to address it. "I read the papers, Detective."

"And you didn't think this was something you should come down to the station and mention to us?"

"I don't think that tone is necessary," Blake said.

Kate thought she'd get a dig in anyway. "I would have come in eventually. Probably once you stopped harassing me and my sisters."

She and Blake were in and out of that interview room within fifteen minutes.

But the detective had one more question, thrown at her nonchalantly as she was about to cross the threshold.

"Does the name Niles Hemingway mean anything to you?"

Kate stilled. Breathed. "Senator Hemingway? What could he possibly have to do with any of this?"

"Probably nothing," Nick said. "I just noted he was close to you and your family."

"Then why bring his name up?"

Nick shrugged.

"I get the impression," she said, "that you are trying to trip me up in some way. What I cannot understand is why."

On the drive back to the office, Blake asked why she thought the detective had mentioned Senator Niles Hemingway, but she had no answer.

"Can you pull over, Blake?"

With one foot on the grass curb strip and one foot still inside the car, Kate vomited.

51

SHE could control herself no longer.

The song refused to budge. Even in her normal life, as she went about her day-to-day tasks, the words pulled at the corners of her brain.

Oh, my darling Clementine.

It was a call to arms, some unseen mystical message from God that there was more killing to be done.

Lost and gone forever.

All these years, she had lived her double life, managing to sneak away to let out her Mr. Hyde. She'd even managed to keep it from herself so that consciously she remained blissfully unaware of the carnage her unconscious mind was capable of. But recently, the lines had begun to blur, and from one moment to the next, she forgot if she was Dr. Jekyll or his monster. Was she a victim or a perpetrator? A woman or a monstrosity?

Her shoes were number nine.

In the early evening of a hot, sultry day, the song won.

Sandals were for Clementine.

It overtook her mind so completely she could think of nothing but the powerful aphrodisiac that was murder: the sight of a throat pulsing its surrender, moments before she streaked a blade across it; the acrid smell of male fear when one of her subjects realized he was down to his last few breaths; the slinky, almost elusive touch of entrails sliding over her skin.

Oh, my darling Clementine.

52

NICK's daisy chain seemed to be unraveling. Despite often sensing they were on the verge of a breakthrough, the team was stuck on a dead stem going nowhere.

Then they got lucky.

Years later, in a courtroom, Nick would have loved to be able to say it was his perseverance and tireless work ethic that led to the solving of the riddle and the arrest of the serial killer. He would have liked nothing more than to be lauded for the finely honed detective skills that led to more men being saved from certain death and mutilation. But then, as now, he knew it mostly came down to luck.

Information relayed via radio at six thirty on a Wednesday evening put Nick on alert. "P6 has entered the Stratt Street Club through the rear parking lot."

Nick jammed on the brakes, threw a U-turn, and sped to the

sports club, calling for backup. "No sirens," he ordered. "But get there now."

It wasn't unusual for a woman to be visiting the Stratt Street Club on pretty much any other night of the week, but he couldn't think of a reason for P6 to be there. In addition, Nick knew that Wednesday was the one night when the club rooms were closed. On a Wednesday night, you'd be lucky to see a few sweaty athletes working out in the gym. The thought made him plant his foot harder on the accelerator.

53

SHE was humming just before she let herself into the gym via the back door of the Stratt Street Club, having scored the key over a week ago from a club member's bag. Another moment of serendipity, she'd thought at the time, in a world full of them. Men were so utterly stupid and predictable that all one had to do was ask directions in a simpering helpless voice and they would totally lose focus. Slipping a hand into a bag was nothing.

Yes, men were stupid, but also evil.

Once the key was in the door, she remained silent, but the song continued its merry tune in her head.

You are lost and gone forever, Dreadful sorry, Clementine.

The song was her only company as she stole into the shower stall and silenced his protest with her mouth over his.

She rammed the blade to the hilt into the soft flesh of his torso right beneath the rib cage. For a moment he went limp and almost sighed into her mouth, but then he began to struggle, grabbing her other arm tightly, lifting his knee, lashing out at her.

She buckled, the breath knocked from her. She felt her strength wane.

Her heart pumped frantically.

"God help me," she whispered.

The man stilled for a second, the fight between adrenaline and shock playing across his face. His hand inched toward the knife blade lodged in his chest, giving her the leverage to push against his arm with her own, slanting the knife farther upward.

His mouth formed a silent *O*, and she knew his life now belonged to her.

She pulled the knife down and out and thrust it in again, over and over, until his strength faded completely.

He slid down into a pink lake. Clear water continued to shower upon him, collecting the thick red blood on its way, turning the shower base into a swirling modern artwork.

Ruby lips above the water, blowing bubbles soft and fine.

As she sang, she cut around his lips, deftly removing his grimace, the agent of his petty lies.

But alas I was no swimmer, so I lost my Clementine.

She wanted to play with him some more but reminded herself there were other men in the complex. They'd arrived later, so she imagined they'd still be sweating over their manly machines in the main gym. But she was no fool. She knew her chances of barging in there and killing two men without one of them turning the tables were almost negligible. She would need to lure one out of the way first, get him locked up, then come back to him later.

She knew how to jam the equipment cupboard from the outside; she'd tested it. All she had to do was get him in there. Then she would seduce the other one. Once they had their cock in her, they were too easy to kill; no strength was required, just finesse.

She waited for her heartbeat to become regular.

She bent to whisper into the dead man's ear. "I'll come back for you."

Even without lips, he appeared to be laughing at her, his big teeth mocking her. She straightened and kicked her shoe into his face.

Then she had to wait a little longer until she was cool again.

She opened the door and calmly walked the steps, counting as she went until she reached the landing.

She placed the knife by the door. Wouldn't do to show her hand to the next one too early. If only she had looked down at her soggy clothes and bloody hands, she might have thought to leave the other men alive. But she was lost in that slimy evil netherworld.

Oh, my darling Clementine.

She was ready.

Poised for the next hapless victim.

Prepared.

She pushed against the double doors and confidently stepped over the threshold.

She was not prepared for Nick Timms.

54

NICK and the team stood, rooted, with guns raised.

Officer Samuel Wisper, who had fainted in a five-star hotel room when he last witnessed her handiwork, willed the killer to twitch. He hoped she had a gun, or something like a gun. He wanted her to reach for it, give him an excuse to blow her away. Officer Denni Argents also hoped the woman would reach for a weapon.

Detective Tony Walsh, who was now convinced he was looking at the person responsible for a couple of long-ago unsolved murders, felt calm, his double-handed grip on his revolver steady.

Officer Rose Selford, who'd been working long days and nights at Nick's side, knew she wouldn't hesitate to shoot the specter of evil in front of her.

Nick's adrenaline thumped, but he retained a cool head.

"Hands up where I can see them. It's over," he said. "Where's your weapon?"

She indicated the door behind her.

"Get down on the ground," Detective Walsh yelled.

Nick swallowed hard as he fought off the images of body parts displayed on a glass tabletop and tried to reconcile the woman before him as the face of evil. "Hands behind your head."

All of a sudden, they were mobile. As Tony Walsh supervised the cuffing of the suspect, Nick followed a junior detective and one of the officers to the back locker rooms, praying they would find nothing. Or maybe they'd find some hapless man gagged and bound but otherwise unharmed.

What they found instead was a dead, lipless man in a shower stall, and Nick was filled with a deep despair when he registered that he was not as surprised or repulsed by the sight as he should have been. Because of that, there would always be a heavy rock of sadness in the pit of his stomach.

55

NICK had expected to feel more. They had her. He should be elated, at least relieved. But somehow, his senses had dimmed.

Back at the station, they failed to get anything concrete from her. She jabbered constantly, nothing that Nick could get a handle on. That is, until one word: *Papa.*

Finally, that name nestled itself with another in his brain. Could it be?

He left the murderer in the hands of Tony Walsh, while he went to question first one sister, then the other, who'd been brought in and held in separate interview rooms.

Now that they knew their sister was guilty, their memories seemed to come a little easier: the abuse they saw and failed to comprehend, the lies and secrets that surrounded their father and his friends, the denials of their mother, the silence of their grandfather. It didn't take long for Nick's suspicions to be confirmed.

Every killer has their reason, Tony had said to Nick some weeks back and, since then, Nick had been working nonstop to uncover it.

There could never be anything to excuse the horror and the trauma that the murderer had wreaked, but at least Nick believed he'd revealed what her demented mind would call a reason.

"Why that name?" Officer Selford asked.

"Because of the writer, I assume," Nick said. "It's what they called Ernest Hemingway."

It was too late to bring Andy Rowling and his father to justice, but there was still time to make one man pay for his sins.

PROBABLE CAUSE ARREST WARRANT

ARRESTEE NAME: Niles Hemingway

A.K.A.: Senator Hemingway; Papa

CRIME(s): Aggravated Sexual Assault of a Child; Rape

56

PEGGY proved to be far stronger than anyone had anticipated.

It was no longer just a dream of being stuck in a box. Under the supervision of Dr. Leichardt, she was able to face what she never could before.

She had been so young when Papa had come to visit that day. Kate had been showing her which dolls she should leave because their clothes were so old and brittle that the buttons were liable to break and it would be a shame to damage the beautiful outfits.

The door to the sewing room had crashed open, and the two sisters instinctively pushed themselves farther back into the fireplace when they heard moaning and groaning and slippery kissing noises.

They had stared at one another in the semidarkness behind the protection of the screen.

There was a groan, then: "Oh, Papa."

Papa?

As Aurora was forced onto the bed, Kate clamped her hand over Peggy's mouth. At first, Peggy thought Aurora must have done something really naughty for which she was being punished.

By the time it was over and Papa had carried Aurora from the room, the pictures in Peggy's head had already become jumbled.

"Why was Papa here?" Peggy had asked Kate later.

"I don't know what you're talking about" was Kate's response. "You do babble on sometimes, little Peg."

After that, Peggy forgot the incident.

Except in her dreams.

In her dreams, she recalled the event and she recalled the room. And years later, with the dubious help of an unscrupulous psychiatrist and a poor mix of drugs—illegal and prescription—the dreams mingled with reality and turned into an alternative scenario that caused so much heartache to Grandpa and, in the end, to Peggy as well.

Now, Peggy's sorrow over the treatment of Grandpa disappeared. There could be no doubt their grandfather, at the very least, knew the evil that lurked in his son's soul. He had to have known his granddaughters were constantly in danger. It was also highly likely, given that the event happened in his house, he knew their father's friend Papa and knew what he'd done.

KATE was bereft.

"What is my excuse, Iain? As the oldest, I should have done something."

"You blocked it out. It's what people do when something is too horrendous to face."

"You were a victim too," Alessandro Freud told her. "Don't lessen his guilt by turning this inward."

It would take some time to comprehend that her grandfather was not the innocent beloved man she'd wanted him to be, that her father was not the inconsequential and benign human she'd painted him as, that the evil sludge that was Senator Niles Hemingway was about to cop what should have come for him many years ago.

"Fucking Papa," Kate mumbled.

She had to be strong for Peggy and her tiny newborn. And for Grant and Stella. The children would need their auntie Kate.

Iain was her rock. "Can I stay with you until the house is sold?"

"I thought you'd never ask."

Her beautiful dream home—Grandpa's house—held no allure now.

AURORA rocked in the straight-back chair, alternating between babbling nonsense and singing.

It wasn't always the same song. Sometimes, she sang old Beatles tunes or hummed complicated symphonic pieces.

When they asked her questions, her answers were obscure.

"Daddy loved me the most," she said when they asked about her childhood. "Papa loved me even more." Sometimes she'd laugh, sometimes cry.

"Fall is the forgotten season," she replied when they wanted to know why she felt compelled to kill.

Days later, when Nick Timms asked her how many people she had killed, Aurora ran a perfectly manicured hand through her matted chestnut hair and lowered her lids coquettishly.

She smiled at him with the gentle eyes of a soft woman, her full lips curved, and once again, he was astounded that evil could package itself so seductively.

Her eyes turned flinty. "You want to know how many?"

Nick nodded, needing an answer but dreading it at the same time.

"Not enough. That's how many."

He pushed the heel of his hand into an aching temple.

"Papa's singing was better than Daddy's. *Oh, my darling Clementine.*"

When Nick looked at her again, he fancied he saw a thick gray sludge surrounding her body, seeping down and over the floor.

"Thirty-one," she whispered.

He was instantly alert, hoping like hell he'd misheard.

"You've killed thirty-one people?"

"No silly." She giggled. "Thirty-one million. I just remembered. That's how many times the pendulum in a grandfather clock swings from side to side every year. Thirty-one million times."

How I missed her! How I missed her,
How I missed my Clementine,
But I kissed her little sister,
I forgot my Clementine.

Acknowledgments

It takes a village, the saying goes, to raise a child.

The same goes for books. Every book I write is like a precious baby. I hold it close, protect it, nurture it. But, at a certain point, it must set off into the world where other people contribute to its growth.

For that reason, I have a few people I'd like to acknowledge:

My agent, Michael Cybulski, and his team, in particular, Lisa Heidke, Dennis Fisher, Ros Harvey, and Laura Fulton.

Whilst ultimate responsibility for the writing rests with me, I give my heartfelt thanks to the team at Sourcebooks, USA, but, in particular, senior editor MJ Johnston, whose enthusiasm for my work and expert editorial guidance is greatly appreciated, as well as copy editors Jessica Thelander and Sara Walker, and sensitivity reader Dee Hudson. To the designer of *Sister, Butcher, Sister*'s cover, Erin Fitzsimmons, my effusive gratitude for capturing the essence of the book so well. And thanks to Mandy Chahal and Emily Engwall for all the marketing and publicity support.

Gary Thompson, my sidekick in life, was one of the early readers of this manuscript and had some terrific suggestions to go along with the endless cups of tea and coffee. Thanks, ol' mate.

But wait, there's more:

Cass Moriarty, for writerly chats, advice, and uplifting conversations and for always making this awkward author feel like part of the cool crowd. My "go-to" writer friends: Jessica Andreatta and Janelle Gayler, for unconditional support, and my editing buddy "She Who Shall Remain Nameless." Australian literary champion Lisa Hill (for intellectual stimulation and for being in my corner, even when I stray from my usual path). Debbie Perkins (for unconditional love and laughter). Vince and Maria Catanzaro (for always making time for this wandering soul). Tina Thomsen: cheers for all the acting and scriptwriting shenanigans. Thanks, Briar Jay, for makeup and photo fun.

My son (Dylan) and daughter-in-law (Joanne), who give me a home base when I need one, as well as love and hugs. They are also parents to the best "grand-puppies" in the world: Jax, Sammy, and Sarge.

Tammy Tabor, my darling *skin and blister* (sister). Despite being younger than me, she is much wiser.

Let me add:

Thanks to the many pets who have kept me company as I roam the world and their owners who entrust them to me. There are too many to name!

To all the extraordinary booksellers, librarians, and passionate readers: thank you.

Are there more?

Absolutely. But there's only so much space available. In my heart though? There's always room.

About the Author

KD Aldyn is an Australian-born nomadic writer who almost always wears black, sometimes red. When she is feeling optimistic, she dances like Elaine from *Seinfeld*. *Sister, Butcher, Sister* is her first crime thriller.